animal envy

animal envy

a fable

RALPH NADER

Seven Stories Press
New York • Oakland • London

A SEVEN STORIES PRESS FIRST EDITION

Seven Stories Press
140 Watts Street
New York, NY 10013
sevenstories.com

Library of Congress Cataloging-in-Publication Data

Names: Nader, Ralph, author.
Title: Animal envy / Ralph Nader.
Description: Seven Stories Press first edition. | New York : Seven Stories Press, [2016]
Identifiers: LCCN 2016017520| ISBN 9781609807528 (hardcover) | ISBN 9781609807535 (ebook)
Subjects: LCSH: Human-animal communication--Fiction. | Human-animal relationships--Fiction. | Political fiction. | BISAC: FICTION / Political.
Classification: LCC PS3614.A38 A85 2016 | DDC 813/.6--dc23
LC record available at https://lccn.loc.gov/2016017520

Printed in the USA.

9 8 7 6 5 4 3 2 1

Once upon a near-future time, a linguistic software developer, who is simply known as Human Genius, provided a digital translation application between mammals, fish, reptiles, birds, and simpler organisms to permit them to communicate with one another simply by using their own language signals, which would be automatically converted into understandable signals across species to their respective receivers. The lone Genius, operating without any external authority, also provided another application, which, after a set interval during which subhuman species got to speak to one another, allowed them to communicate through a hyper-advanced converter to human animals.

As can be imagined, for animals the learning process really took off. Wisdom and illuminations immediately began expanding. One day an Elephant—a majestic matriarch—proposed to a Crocodile and a Dolphin that, using a remote, they convene (with dozens of species) a global assembly whose purpose would be to talk to human animals. Having carefully observed human actions and suffered pain and anguish at the hands of humanity, the animal kingdom could see that human animals were themselves depressed, self-doubting, and shrinking in self-esteem, though this inner unease was partly covered up by their aggressive behavior, which reflects a violent outward arrogance that has no equal on earth.

Within a week, the response to the Elephant's invitation became overwhelming. Shortly a virtual assembly gathered to discuss the best ways to approach the human animals and how best to organize the different animals' numerous requests to tell these human animals what is uppermost on their minds. Soon one hundred hours were reserved for the great TALKOUT, as they called it, in which mammals, reptiles, fish, and birds from all over the planet would concisely speak to human animals of what they've wanted to tell them forever but could not, until the Human Genius came along.

They knew that to make their core message palatable, it would have to be framed in a way that was ingratiating and flattering to humans' self-interest. The approach was worthy of Gandhi or Mandela. Animal strategy was to lift up the spirits of their human masters, flatter them, then show that both sides had mutual interests in protecting wild habitats, and that this involved reducing arbitrary violence and other genocides inflicted upon the animals, sometimes to the point of extinction, such as happened to the passenger pigeon.

They were not going to rely on appeals to justice or fairness, but on showing human animals how useful the animal kingdom can be to humans the more humans understand them. After all, about three quarters of viral and bacterial infections in humans come from the animals and insects, so an understanding between the different species would help with disease control. Animal scientists and ecologists already know this, but it will have more effect coming straight from the source, the animals felt.

As the animals hammered out their strategies, important suggestions came from a blue whale, joined by a shark and a walrus. They urged that, given the explosively temperamental nature of human animals, the better part of discretion would be to have one subhuman after another particularize their praise of specific attributes of humans—physical and mental—that subhumans had never attained during their lengthy period of evolution. Emphasize in our discussion that other animals are biologically unable to perform the way humans do, the walrus underlined. The shark especially stressed the need to use the word "subhuman" for themselves. The very word would emphasize their inferiority, and, the shark explained, this would massage humans' spectacular egos and open their minds to listen. The shark chuckled, adding that given his species' remarkable adaption to their ocean environment, many millions of years before humans arrived on the scene, it would be advisable to be humble, and play down the spectacular achievements of animals, especially fish.

The virtual animal assembly concurred with the strategy and commenced formulating concise messages of praiseworthy envy and laudatory expressions followed by pleas for humans to take the longer view, discover the many secrets of the animal world, and diminish the violence against them and their habitats.

The animal strategists decided that first to the "mike" would be two domesticated animals since such animals are better regarded than wild animals. Some domesticated animals, such as horses, are lovingly described as "magnificent beasts," and all of these animals are widely viewed as worthy of protection, useful as mascots and often photographed and videoed. Next at the mike would be animals that are in emergency situations needing help or in predicaments that offer a ripe teaching moment to the human animals, concerning how urgent the situation is for some animals. Also, through the hours, there would be a stress on providing a diversity of animal viewpoints, both to provide a multidimensional picture to human viewers and to maintain morale and fairness within the animal kingdom. At least that was the hope for the line-up. Commencement of the hundred-hour TALKOUT to the human world was transmitted through the Human Genius.

The TALKOUT Begins

Up first, by design, were the domesticates, themselves objects of both pity and envy by their feral cousins, some of whom were already grumbling that domesticates got first place.

The horse began, keeping to the envy strategy, in a light-hearted way. "Oh, humans, carried by we the horse corps for so many centuries into work, battle, markets, visits, processions, and varieties of entertainments, how we envy your ability to wipe your asses after defecation. We horses are unable to eliminate these residues, which discomfort us in so many ways, including during lovemaking. Sure we can sleep on our four feet, but we'd trade that gladly for your ability to flush."

Ripples of delighted laughter coursed through the mass of mankind, eyes affixed to their screens. This intensified their attentiveness for what was about to follow.

Next up, the dog mixed envy with modesty. "Wuff, humans, for many millennia we have been your loyal guards, lickers, companions, and, being partly descended from the wolf, your hunting hounds. Our sense of smell, your scientists say, is over two hundred times more sensitive than your sniffs. That is why you use us to track lost persons, fleeing criminals, explosives, drugs, and now—woof, woof—even to detect human cancer.

"Yet you seem not to understand how blessed you are for not being able to smell so much. We dogs are overwhelmed by your smells; in your homes from the cooking, smoking, fresheners, oils, toilets, sweat, and dust mixtures. Imagine smelling all this two hundred times more than you do, every day! You should no longer wonder why, when you walk us each day to get our and your exercise, we immediately try to sniff anything natural, whether from the soil, leaves, bark, bushes, or other passing dogs and cats.

"You're so fortunate that your noses are more decorative, apart from breathing, and that you're developing separate artificial sniffers for use when needed.

"And you big city folk who get irritated when you hear police, fire, and other sirens passing by your neighborhood, note that we hear them constantly from distances all over the city."

Believe it or not, this early in the TALKOUT, there was already an unscheduled appearance, a Kenyan-based hyena, who felt canines were not properly represented by a mere dog, and pushed to the front of the queue to unburden herself of a thinly veiled gripe: "Humans, let me be clear, hyenas do not laugh. What you describe as laughing is not laughing. Would that we had that capacity for expressing joy and delight as your voices do. Our cry is just that, a form of communication often under stressful conditions. You, humans, on the other hand, are capable of almost endless vocal nuances reflecting many of your moods and intents. We have almost none of these wonderful ways to express ourselves."

The Elephant nodded in satisfaction as, after a minor complaint, the hyena got with the program and offered some broad flattery to humans.

The finch hopped up next to continue the comments on the skills of human vocalizing. "I, like any songbird, like music even when it doesn't communicate anything about danger or territoriality. But we songbirds are very limited and very repetitious. In the early morning, you humans like our singing but seem content with hearing the 'same old song.' But humans have a singing voice with enormous variety and tone and, even without your voice, you make beautiful music with your many instruments. Also, you rhapsodize about it, make poetry and films about it, and you're always making new kinds of music that reflect your culture and feelings. Can you help us diversify our sounds? Can we learn to do so or are we too limited by nature? We songbirds find some of your music almost hypnotically soothing, such as 'Clair de Lune.'"

The finch spoke these words with such emotion and gentleness that tears came to the eyes of many human viewers. Repetition works sometimes. The Oberlin Conservatory sent messages to other conservatories for a conference devoted to what the finch had discussed. A singing band in Sao Paulo began composing a song to honor the finch and other songbirds. Views from the insect world were not so positive; mosquitoes and earthworms were distinctly unimpressed, seeing the finch as going on a frolic, but not discussing its consumptive mercilessness when it came to swallowing insects.

The wolf began with a prolonged howl as if speaking to the moon. "I, a much misunderstood animal, wish to second the finch's request. The howls of the wolves scare humans as they echo through canyons or bounce off mountain walls. We wolves cannot help our limitations when it comes to vocalizing sounds. But we would like to learn to howl or bark in a more varied manner, not from your domesticated dogs, who seemed to have learned nothing in this regard for centuries, but from your millions of super-dedicated dog lovers and protectors of wolves from extermination.

Unfortunately, the wolf's plea was met with "howls" of derisive laughter from humans. The wolf's stereotyped image was still in their minds. Some saw it as a ruse by the wolf to develop different sounds by which to communicate to one another so as to elude hunters or the hated collar-around-the-neck naturalists. Others suspected that the wolves had some hidden agenda. A girl named Olivia, who had read gobs of pages about wolves, seen videos about wolves, and traveled with her father to Wyoming to view the wolves in the wilds, said in a brief text message to all wolves, "Don't make too much of this negative human response. There is room to just live and let live."

The chimpanzee wanted to amplify the hyena's earlier point about humans' ability to express their emotions. "You know, humans, although our DNA is almost the same, we can only look with wonder at the variety of facial expressions—both deliberate and instinctual—that you can generate many times an hour. Sure, chimps can express fear, anger, pain, and, with a little child, compassion. Through your experimentation with us, soon to be phased out we hope, you know we are very limited in such facial signals. Your two percent difference in DNA from us makes a big difference. P.S. We don't envy your arm strength though. You get us angry and with one solid smack we can tear your head off. So, in zoos, for your protection, please, adults and children, keep your distance. It is not easy staying calm under a sentence of life imprisonment."

"Taking off from my friend, the chimpanzee," said the Australian kangaroo, "even though we are marsupials and can hold our front paws in a vertical position, how we would love to have the seemingly limitless gestures that you humans can generate with your limbs. Some of you can hardly speak without automatic-type gestures of your fingers, hands, and arms—sometimes your feet and legs too—that conform precisely to what you are saying, effortlessly. Roos stand in awe of that ability to better convey your words with visuals. Were we to have that capability, it would have saved many of us from your relentless hunters."

By this time, millions of viewing humans were feeling pretty proud of themselves as many children were making faces and gestures—exaggerated—to each other.

The great birds perched high in the air were observing all these testimonials with skepticism. They chirped to one another through the software app. They had formed a caucus that felt that some balance to the uplifting presentation was needed. Too much of an avalanche of envy and praise can nourish more human hubris, adding more perils to subhumans. The caucus agreed that it was time to get humans thinking about the value of subhumans as advisors. They chose one of their wisest members as a spokes-bird.

The guiding TRIAD recognized the justice of their ideas and allowed an owl to break the admiration spell. "Oh, humans, although your solid wastes have increased the number of mice for my diet, and I heartily thank you for that, I feel impelled to convey some words of caution, words that, viewed from another direction, may reduce your fears about the future of our planet.

"Let me put it plainly. I and my fellow owls *do give a hoot* about how you live, for you are destroying our forest habitats, which eliminates our future. Remember the spotted owl in the U.S. Northwest, which was protected by your own Endangered Species Act. That act also protected your forest from clear-cutting, preserving the wilderness for your children.

"But other owls are not protected. We cannot be left just with barns in which to raise our young. I can't get my mind around this contradiction. Never have you humans known more about the natural world of creatures and vegetation, of water, soil, and air. And never have you destroyed more of the natural world in so many avoidable ways. While your scientists are producing piles of knowledge daily, your other activities are polluting, poisoning, clear-cutting, eroding, melting, and extinguishing the natural world at an accelerating rate. So smart, yet so not, you humans lunging toward omnicide. Anyway, just a thought. The mice are nice, though the frogs are disappearing."

The soaring eagle and the hawk were listening intently to the Owl, and nodding their feathered heads in agreement. With their sweeping aerial range, they had a broader perspective on the world and its decay than land- or ocean-based mammals, they felt. Their eyesight was remarkable, an evolutionary reality necessary for the survival of these raptors, these exquisitely developed predators.

"Oh, humans," said the eagle, pushing to the stage behind his owl friend so he could keep up the drumbeat of criticism, but, at the same time, seeing the need to begin with a little more (assumed) envy in order to sweeten the message, "your most powerful nation, the United States, has elevated me as your national bird and symbol. But I am merely an exalted vulture bird with only about the biggest lift capacity for the prey I clutch in my talons. How I envy your agile planes: their grace, speed, height, and maneuverability. Even your balloons display great steadiness and stamina in the air.

"Yet these same planes and their bombs and missiles have

been used toward ever greater destruction of everything in their path. Sometimes the explosions are just the beginning, followed by radioactivity and other forms of silent violence that remain for an eternity. Yes, I agree with my nocturnal comrade, the owl. For the smarter you become, the more self-destructive can be your results, a paradox you have heard from your more environmentally sensitive people. But just as the United States reversed course and protected us eagles from extinction, we hope you humans can reverse course on the larger matters of life on earth."

Just as suspected by the mother elephant, *with humans, truth was not the way to go*. For, as their audience studies were showing, once some of the faults of humans were mentioned, in the vast human audience, fascination began to be interrupted with skepticism. Brilliant software specialists and futurists suspected a ruse unfolding of human origin and loudly spread their suspicions around the globe. News outlets carried their doubts to their mass audiences. The masses began to murmur; some returned to their daily work. The animal kingdom absorbed this emerging loss of credibility and spotted the culprit, the deep feeling among humans, with their blurred grasp, that the animal kingdom could not possibly have enough intelligence to understand the world's problems and dilemmas. It was all, humans suspected, a clever stratagem of culture jamming from that Vancouver-based magazine or somewhere, said one talk show host in New York, the notorious Rush Limburger.

We Interrupt This TALKOUT

The TRIAD of Elephant, Crocodile, and Dolphin who launched this TALKOUT exerted their privilege and called a recess to discuss and adjust to this rising disbelief among the humans. All this was too much for the Crocodile, who bowed out with a splashy apology. Immediately, the Elephant recruited the Owl, who had spoken so eloquently earlier. The Elephant knew this appointment would mollify the bothersome bird caucus. The three went into executive session with the help of another special app.

They all knew the problem under which their ancestors have been smarting and hurting from forever: Humans think we animals are terminally dull, stupid, and only survive through instinct programmed by our DNA. They ignore our brains, sensory perceptions, and reliance on feedback to guide our actions, not to mention our complex social organizations. How could such facts be brought up without offending humans? The challenge was what to do about the animal transmission's waning credibility.

The Owl suggested simply citing the latest research by humans about the intelligence of dogs, dolphins, octopi, spiders, and others. They could quote the human scientists who have made these "discoveries."

"What would be most valuable is if our messages prompted scientists and the ecologists to go on their mass media and spread the word," declared the Elephant. "We must carefully choose this lineup," she went on. "It's a make or break decision for our entire TALKOUT and the beneficial follow-ups we envision."

The Owl was chosen to make this reorientation to humans immediately following the recess.

The TALKOUT Turns Scientific

"Oh, humans, we have learned that some of you are expressing doubts as to the authenticity of our observations, which do not fit with your image of us as being restricted to vocal outcries such as roars, chirps, cackles, hisses, and other subhuman sounds. Those among you who have studied us know that such images are inaccurate. The more you know about us, the more you discover that we have multiple intelligences and special attractants defined by our need to survive and reproduce that are quite astonishing. To us, intelligence, which includes the ability to size up situations, receive a combination of sensory signals, and react accordingly, is something that you have not recognized because it is beyond your multiple-choice standardized test measures.

"Modesty prevents me from recounting your findings about the owl species: its eyesight, sonar, accuracy in rapting, and the like. But consider your own scientists' reports: elephants remember, magpies grieve for their dead, crows train their offspring to make tools, and otters teach their little ones how to dive for fish. Here are the words of one of your science writers.

> Scientific research shows that many animals are very intelligent and have sensory and motor abilities that dwarf ours. Dogs are able to detect diseases such as cancer and diabetes and warn humans of impending heart attacks and strokes. Elephants, whales, hippopotamuses, giraffes, and alligators use low-frequency sounds to communicate over long distances, often miles; and bats, dolphins, whales, frogs, and various rodents use high-frequency sounds to find food, communicate with others, and navigate.
>
> Many animals also display wide-ranging emotions, including joy, happiness, empathy, compassion, grief, and even resentment and embarrassment. It's not surprising that animals—especially, but not only, mammals—share many emotions with us because we also share brain structures—located in the limbic system—that are the seat of our emotions. In many ways, human emotions are the gifts of our animal ancestors.

Finishing the quote, the Owl returned to her own point. "We are not inclined to simply cite your secondary sources, however empirically precise they are. There are many in the animal kingdom who want to tell you their own stories to illustrate that their intelligence is not some DNA-imprinted 'instinct' producing automatic conditioned responses. Admittedly, before we heard the murmurs of doubt, we did not expect to assume this burden. There are so many other reasons for understanding us that would be to your own benefit. But I cannot avoid quoting your eminent philosopher, Jeremy Bentham, for another dimension in our opening pleas for understanding. In 1789 he wrote:

> The day *may* come, when the rest of the animal creation may acquire those rights which never could have been withholden from them but by the hand of tyranny . . . [T]he question is not, Can they *reason*? nor, Can they *talk*? but, Can they *suffer*?

"Sentiments like this led to the early animal protection laws in Europe during the next century, at least for the domesticates.

"Now let us start with the testimony of our friend, the brown squirrel."

"Thank you, Owl, and good day to you humans. I cohabitate around with you, sometimes, to your irritation, even inside the walls and attics of your homes.

"You probably think of me as an impulsive, jumpy animal flitting from one tree to another and across lawns and sidewalks and roads with no seeming purpose. Oh, how I wish that were so. Instead, we squirrels live lives of nonstop fear and want. At any time cats can dart out of nowhere to mangle us or our young ones. Cars can squash us. Disease can claim us. Hunters, including teenagers, can shoot us. For weeks at a time we are near starvation, in a weakened state that hawks seem to sense from on high. Our nests must be carefully selected, not just to protect our little ones from predators, and secure them from falling out, but to protect them from storms, winds, and humans chopping down branches and trees.

"And that's not the only threat. The other day a man scooped up precious fallen acorns. He does this every day before we can get at them for our meal and storage for the winter months.

"We live in terror of our surroundings; yet we survive because more often than not we make the right little and big decisions. We can detect which acorns will last to winter and which ones have to be eaten soon. That is not 'instinct,' that is squirrel intelligence.

"I challenge you to swing from tree to tree, sometimes on thin branches, and have our record of perfect leaps many feet above the ground or road. We can judge space, weight on the branch or twig, timing, moisture, and many other what you call variables. Have you ever seen us miss and fall? We see you fall often with your feet on the ground. And nobody wishes to eat you. We watch you all the time. We have to.

"Sometimes we start building our nest high in a hollow of a dead tree with its tall trunk still standing. Halfway done, we see that this was not a safe or convenient choice. We stop and select another site. That is not instinct. That is intelligence, which, as you study us, you'll be able to explain better than I can now because you have another kind of intelligence. Raising our families is no small matter of impulses. We have to process an enormous amount of information quickly and react quickly, apart from escaping immediate pursuit of predators such as rattlesnakes whose own scented, shedded skins we lick and absorb to evade them. My time is up. Thanks for listening."

Next up was the Elephant carrying on her massive shoulders the long burden of her species as beasts of burden, circus performers, and victims of poachers for their ivory tusks, leaving thousands of dead elephants rotting under the tropical sun, with others facing extinction unless park rangers can protect them. The Elephant knew she had to leave such strong and painful feelings aside since she was there to lance the boil of human ignorance regarding animal intelligence. She had to tell stories.

"The story of Babyl has been confirmed by elephant researcher Iain Douglas-Hamilton. Deep in the Samburu National Reserve in northern Kenya was this young female, Babyl, who had a partially disabled walking gait that slowed her down, a condition she had for years. The elephants in the herd never abandoned her. They would stop and look around to see where she was lagging behind. Often the herd matriarch would feed Babyl. The herd made sure Babyl would not become dinner for the lions. What did the herd have to gain from always waiting for Babyl? Nothing but a sense of empathy and inclusiveness.

"Then there was the meeting of two female elephants, Shirley and Jenny, who were reunited after being separated for twenty-two years and suffering abuse in the entertainment industry. Arriving at an elephant sanctuary in Hohenwald, Tennessee, they remembered when they were together long ago and roared at each other and pressed to remain next to one another. Shirley was over twenty years older than Jenny, a calf at the circus when they met."

Touched by these stories, millions of humans Googled for other elephant stories by their handlers and researchers, and were rewarded with pages of how intelligent these animals have been.

It should be clarified that the Human Genius had helpfully provided the animals with apps that allowed them to access the vast knowledge acquired by humans over the millennia concerning the animal kingdom. A huge rate of absorption across the entire range of human information crossed species after species, going even to the insect level. This "epistemological windfall" was immediately reflected in the ensuing callouts.

Prime Primate Time

Now the first primate stepped up. It was a bonobo. These monkeys belong to a separate and distinct species that genetically is as closely related to humans as chimpanzees. A buzz of anticipation skittered through the animal kingdom. If anyone can persuade humans of animal intelligence, it has to be the primates, some were saying. But others were asking, why the bonobo when it could be the chimp, baboon, the orangutan, a rhesus monkey, the majestic gorilla, or the great ape, all of whom have been studied by the likes of Jane Goodall and many of her colleagues?

The Owl and the Elephant knew why they wanted the bonobo first. It was good public relations because the bonobos are more peaceful than most other apes, are female dominated, share food and resolve conflicts peaceably, and let off steam with an intense sex life that makes their primate cousins seem prudish. By contrast, Goodall's work with chimps shows that among them there is a constant occurrence of murders, cannibalism, and organized group wars.

The bonobo spoke: "Humans, when you see us in nature films, you make much fun of us. But, if you really studied us, we could teach you how to make peace, how we practice community, equality, and are cooperative in raising our progeny.

"We primates are very different from one another and that is so even within a species or subspecies. Take savanna baboons in Africa. They are not pacifists like us. Their male rankings come from who kills who in matches. Moody males often strike out at innocent, weaker members of the troop. But under stresses such as deadly epidemics, these baboons have been known to change their aggressive ways, moderating and becoming more cooperative and congenial with each other.

"That shows we are not controlled by instinct but shift behavior depending on circumstances. Your own eminent behavioral scientist Robert Sapolsky writes that we apes have a 'culture' consisting of 'local behavioral variations, occurring for nongenetic and nonecological reasons, that last beyond the time of their originators . . . [they are] multigenerational.' Chimpanzees do special dances during thunderstorms and strong gusts of wind. Gorillas hold wakes for their dead.

"In connection to this last point, recent research has astonished humans when they discovered that primates respond with protective mourning in relation to the corpse of a band member or an infant, even against their own safety interests.

"An article in *Eureka* made the telling point: Among a group of bonobos, Mimi, the group's alpha female, stood guard over the dead Lipopo's body. When the caretakers tried to push the corpse out of the enclosure with long poles, Mimi fought them, viciously. She grabbed the poles with both hands, wrenching them away from Lipopo. She called to other bonobos, who helped her fend off the humans from both sides. Even when the vet arrived with a tranquilizer gun, Mimi stood her ground, her mouth open wide in a scream that's inaudible in the silent film that records this behavior. Mimi was willing to risk an encounter with a gun to protect the body of a mere acquaintance. 'That's why I started to cry,' Hare, the author of the article, said. 'I don't know why she did it.'

"'The results of primate-behavior studies can be humbling for humans because they often call into question our anthropocentric view of the world,' the writer concluded."

"We never knew that," said, in essence, millions of human viewers to one another, not a few of them moist in the eyes. The TRIAD felt the message was getting through.

The bonobo continued, "In the equatorial jungles, we have so many decisions to make day in and day out that if made wrongly would mean our end. Still, we have our limits. Our larger primates have never learned to adjust to being turned into bush meat by human carnivores. Because you didn't know enough about us, our cousins transmitted to you the deadly AIDS virus. Is there any greater evidence as to how our fate and your fate are tied together?

"Remember the essence of your discoveries about the animal kingdom, whether by animal scientists, anthropologists, or caretakers: the more you learn about us, the more intelligent we become to you. There is humility in that expanding observation, is there not?"

Millions of humans began to murmur in agreement, reflecting their own experience. At Harvard University, Howard Gardner was smiling. His groundbreaking book *Multiple Intelligences* tore apart the arrogance behind the standardized, multiple-choice tests given students. Now he heard the bonobo talk about the "multiple intelligences" of the primate animal kingdom. His tweet affirming this reality assured many thousands of his Twitter followers around the world.

A whale had more to say on the cultural system of animals. "Humans, according to your own research on us and on monkeys, you have come to the conclusion that many mammals, at least, learn from one another. The journal *Science* reports that wild South African monkeys changed foods because of peer pressure in a controlled study. While we whales, facing a reduction in the amount of small fishes, learned by the actions of an innovator whale who smacked the ocean loudly with its tail, to make a big noise and a great splash before blowing bubbles to corral small fish such as herring that we whales savor. The thump brings the fish closer to the surface. So we whales, like monkeys, learn by imitating, just like you humans have done for a long time."

Underwater Examples of Intelligence

Not to use his position on the TRIAD for his own advantage, but the Dolphin couldn't help but notice that this talk about the cultures of apes and whales made him think of the culture of his own species.

The bottlenose dolphin decided to seize the moment and

reveal the latest findings made in Shark Bay, Australia, by Georgetown University marine scientists, which was that the traits of "inclusive inheritability" and culture are not exclusive to humans. They found that these dolphins bond over their use of tools and share their knowledge only with a small circle, which humans would call cliques, and pass it on to their progeny. This is learned behavior, not innate instinct. It all started with the scientists noticing "sponging Eve," a dolphin that scraped her nose while searching for food in rough sand. She did not like this, so she broke off a piece of sea sponge to protect her beak, a skill she only taught her children. Twenty years later, knowledge of this sea sponge tool did not spread among the whole dolphin population in the area. There were thirty-six spongers and sixty-nine non-spongers over a twenty-two-year period. The spongers were more cliquish and had stronger bonds with each other than with non-spongers.

"So, just as you have human subcultures, we do as well, and I can attest to this personally as one of the spongers," said the Dolphin proudly. "Just like you humans, we tend to associate with dolphins most like ourselves. We even have cliques for social reasons, since sponging is a solitary behavior and not needed for collaborative foraging."

Further information about dolphin intelligence was conveyed by science writer Meeri Kim: "Dolphins have long impressed people with their sharp minds and humanlike traits, such as calling each other by name, goofing off and even understanding numbers. Now a scientist has found that [they] can recognize an old friend's whistle, even after they have been apart for 20 years—the longest social memory ever recorded for a non-human."

Kim continued: "This recorded feat of long-term memory puts dolphins in the same field as other highly intelligent creatures, including some monkeys and elephants, both of which have been known to recognize unrelated members of their species after time apart."

More jaw-dropping by millions of human watchers. Many

had long known that dolphins are unusually smart for a subhuman animal, but this was something else again.

The Dolphin felt his message was getting through and decided to tap into this rising respect, by inviting a special compassion action. Since he was a member of the TRIAD, he had more leeway than the other species to present his point of view.

"Humans, a terrible situation has developed with Mexican and other nations' boats that are fishing for tuna with huge ground nets. We feel deep sympathy with our tuna friends and find ourselves fortunate that humans have not developed such a taste for our flesh. However, these nets are catching many of us along with the tuna. The fishermen haul in the tuna, which the Japanese pay hundreds of dollars per pound for, and let us dolphins go drown in the nets. Many thousands of us have drowned entangled in this way. Dolphins, unless seriously injured, never drown; we know how to swim. Since you Americans have a law prohibiting such wanton destruction and protect our species, can't you do something with these other nations? Connect your intelligence with ours for the sake of animaltarian values and ecological balance in the oceans.

"A last observation. Humans are talking a lot about BIG DATA these days with massive exponential data flowing from computer technology. Your NSA (National Security Agency) admits it can hardly process one percent of the data, so they are working on pattern detections. Maybe you should look to animals as you try to fathom how to establish this form of recognition.

"We animals have remarkable ways to ignore and filter through nature's messages. Elephants can communicate with each other miles away with high-frequency language humans cannot hear with their ears. Elephants can even distinguish whether a human voice is that of a man or woman or child while moths can sense one another's presence from long distances. The members of the animal kingdom filter in just what they need in a welter of 'BIG DATA' called nature. You would be wise to find ways to use only information you need in a welter of BIG DATA, compiled by your sensors and computers. Otherwise you will be flooded with so much data as to be suffocated and rendered inert, much as a paramecium is gagged by its own exudations. Watch the big cats or the sharks or the whales or the dolphins process just the information needed for their purposes. They teach all a lesson that less is more."

Parrot Talk

Earlier, in the envy section, animals had lamented their inability to communicate as fully as humans. Now, as the TRIAD concentrated on presenting animal abilities, they realized this thought needed a little tweaking, so they brought on an animal who actually could say a lot more *in human speech* than humans gave him credit for.

Along came a green-rumped parrotlet, not the most exciting plumage, but adorable nevertheless. This one was the size of a parakeet and lived on a parrot ranch in Venezuela. These parrotlets are pleased to be studied by scientists there who have arranged over a hundred artificial boxes in which they can nest and raise their fledglings just off the ground. As the parrotlet prepared to speak, owners of captive parrots displayed special fascination. Since the days of ancient Greece, humans have captured and bred parrots that are smart, with exceptional memories, and who, of course, have this unique ability to mimic human words and phrases. Some, like Alex, the famous African gray parrot, who was studied for three decades, have shown that in captivity, they can use words in the correct context.

"I know how you teach our captive siblings in your cages a few words, some bad words, to repeat all the time as if we, free or captive, do not have a mind and voice of our own. You are mistaken. Our calls, vocal mimicry you call it, are intricate. They serve many purposes such as negotiating flock separations and mergers. We learn these calls; they are not genetically programmed. We have complex societies, imitate each other, even have dialects. Our contact calls are so fast, your ears can't hear the variations. We give our chicks contact calls, just as you humans give your children names. The person who knows most about us is Karl Berg of Cornell University. He says that we can be the best animal model for understanding how you humans acquire speech. 'Like human infants, parrots are born dumb and utterly helpless, and have extended dependent childhoods and relatively large brains. Also like humans, parrots hit a key developmental milestone when they begin to learn their "names." There's a moderate convergence between parrots and humans.'

"Far away in a large San Diego home, the owner had built an intricate aerial home for two large Amazonian macaw parrots—one of the largest open-air domestic cages in the country. I was lucky to be able to talk to them with our new technology. I was ashamed by what I found. Living with humans had dumbed them down. I told these macaws about all the words I can say.

"'Who cares,' said one to the other. 'I'm just waiting for our master to upgrade this place. All he has taught us are twenty words and we greet him every day with . . . "You're the boss, you're the boss." He likes that a lot, especially after he's lost a case in court. As long as we lay an egg every two years, he's happy.'"

That segment had gotten a good laugh and the Owl sensed that the grumbling doubts about the TALKOUT's authenticity were receding. She advised the Elephant and the Dolphin to continue the planned program.

The Wolf's Words

Having established the intelligence of some animals as far as their abilities and societies, it was time to link these skills to the bigger ecological picture.

The Owl chose to resume dramatically. She introduced the wolf. Thousands of Western ranchers pricked up their ears.

"I am the wolf, probably the most misunderstood and hated big mammal in North America. That is why our numbers are down drastically. Mama wolves are losing interest in raising their cubs. Our wolf packs face elimination. We have become more aware of our plight and our dwindling habitat. There are only a few thousand of us left. Without our natural habitats where our customary prey lives, we sometimes hunt your cows and sheep but not very often. The ranchers then want your lawmakers to allow them open season with high-powered rifles and even helicopters. We are helpless. Let me make the case for wolves taken right out of your own ecological knowledge of our ways and impact. I am not going talk about our many skills but about our significant place in any natural system we inhabit.

"Your greatest environmentalist, Dr. Barry Commoner, wrote that the first rule of ecology is 'everything is connected to everything else.' Look how we wolves are connected to so much that you hold dear.

"Each creature plays a role in creating and maintaining the complex ecosystems we all live in. But carnivores are most often the head engineers that keep systems in balance. Without carnivores, ecosystems have a tendency to collapse.

"The gray wolves of Yellowstone, for example, helped regulate elk populations, which in turn protected young plants like cottonwood saplings from overgrazing. But wolves were systematically hunted down in Yellowstone and disappeared from the park in 1926. Seventy years later, the ecosystem was collapsing: the elk population had exploded; young trees rarely made it to adulthood; birds, bugs, and other small animals had to compete for space; and soil was rapidly eroding, clouding streams and damaging fish habitat.

"In 1995, biologists from the U.S. Fish and Wildlife Service began reintroducing wolves to the park. About ten years later, Oregon State University conducted studies to measure the health of the ecosystem. They found a direct correlation between the reintroduction of wolves and the recovery of Yellowstone's nearly extinct cottonwoods. With wolves back, elk were less likely to forage in the open streamside areas, giving seedlings time to grow. With more cottonwoods and willows surviving, fewer areas suffered soil erosion, and birds, insects, fish, and other creatures benefitted from a larger variety of habitats for nesting and foraging. Park managers used wolves to help them restore habitats essential for the survival of hundreds of species."

The wolf added: "It's not just about us. The same could be said about the buffalo and the ecosystem of the sprawling grasslands in the upper Midwest or how critical beavers are for watersheds.

"One added plea if I can indulge in some myth busting. We do not attack humans. You can count on the fingers of your hands the number of humans killed by our wolves over the past century. Yet we are used as a symbol for the most violent of your thoughts and folklore, though there are some exceptions in your stories, such as intimate tales of wolf families raising a lost boy infant.

"Please take us for what we are and can do for you, being natural environmentalists who may cost you a few cattle due to loss of our habitat yet bring you far more employment in the tourist industry by attracting happy city children and their parents to 'watch the wolves.'"

By now the Dolphin was feeling uneasy. The wolf had expanded the argument to point to the need for different species to keep the ecosystem in balance, that was the topic he said he would be focusing on, but then—you know how impetuous a wolf can be—he got into special pleading, even, implicitly, impugning fairy tales like "Red Riding Hood." Certainly, he was telling hard truths, but the Dolphin didn't think humans were ready for that yet. The Dolphin's magnificent sensitivity and empathy let him realize and convey to the Owl and the Elephant that humans were starting to think they were being lectured to by self-serving animals using human knowledge to make their case.

"What's this," said one human watcher, "the Discovery Channel in reverse?"

The Dolphin advised they get off the "hard stuff"—that is, reportage of scientific facts about the intelligence and ecological importance of animals—and get a bit touchy-feely, telling humans what their lives are like, where they live, how they fight for survival and raise the next generation. Being a subtle inhabitant of the ocean depths, the Dolphin believed that the best points can be made indirectly. After all, they were speaking to the human race and its big brains! Enough of them would get the point of the need for restoration or what the most alert of them call "re-wilding." Seeing how animals interact in their environment would show both the need for keeping these natural habitats intact and the danger of tampering with them. To counteract the negative impressions created by the wolf, the Elephant thought about starting off big. She realized that humans loved disaster movies and stories about calamities, so bring on the Chernobyl beaver!

The TALKOUT Gets Touchy-feely

Humans remember the Chernobyl nuclear power plant disaster in Ukraine in 1986. Then they forgot that 110 square miles are now an exclusion zone, completely depopulated of human beings, with empty houses and other buildings hauntingly disintegrating. The famous talk show host Phil Donahue took his crew there, at some risk, to show millions of his viewers what the blown-open reactor could do to human habitation. The Chernobyl beaver brought the situation up to date.

"I am a radioactive Chernobyl beaver, and there are plenty of us now that human predators cannot come around to destroy us. With several hundred thousand people evacuated—not counting those who have died the slow death from radiation poisoning—we beavers have had a paradise of freedom. The deadly engineering of Soviet-style collective agriculture we have now undone. We have restored one of Europe's great marshlands, according to your film *Radioactive Wolves*. Yes, there are radioactive wolves, eagles who build nests in abandoned fire towers, dormice that pick their way through trapless ruins. Yes, the animals of Chernobyl are thriving when they aren't dying. Radioactive levels in the bones of animal carcasses are so hot they shouldn't be touched with bare human hands, say your naturalists who visit once in a while.

"You may say that our animal life, not being bothered by the radioactivity, demonstrates how much lower an order of sentient life we embody. You would be having cancer epidemics, nervous breakdowns, and panic if you had been living here since 1986. OK, what we don't know—until the apps came—can't bother us. We take each day one at a time and now we know that we are a rare laboratory for your study of living organisms existing in a nuclear-toxic zone. The larger lesson may be what we can do for you if you just let us alone. Enjoy the marshlands!"

The beaver didn't simply exit the stage. He waved on his cousin, a beaver from a U.S. forest, who wanted to say a few words for his un-radiated fellows. "In the past you humans have completely misunderstood us. Your early colonists viewed our dams as major nuisances, impeding river traffic. Moreover, in North America we were slaughtered as ruthlessly as the buffalo to make fur coats and charming hats. Our numbers were depleted so they fell from in the tens of millions to a recovering six million at present.

"Now, when scientists have finally begun to appreciate us, beaver experts are seeing how beneficial our free services are to the ecosystem. One academic report notes that we beavers are a major defender against 'the withering effects of a warmer and drier climate.' You humans have further discovered that we 'raise the water table alongside a stream, aiding the growth of trees and plants that stabilize the banks and prevent erosion. They improve fish and wildlife habitat and promote new, rich soil.'

"Furthermore, it's being recognized that in the dry western United States, we are 'hold[ing] back water that would otherwise drain away.' Seeing all these good things we provide, you humans should want to attract us to various locations. As our admirer, scientist Jeff Burrell, has written, 'We can spend a lot of money doing this work, or we can use beavers for almost nothing.' This is just the point the TRIAD has been making to you humans."

Those two beavers left humans plenty to chew on.

Sex and the Single Sow

The pig got the next call. That last sensational topic had been rather depressing, so the pig was going to talk about the next favorite topic of the human public, right after disasters: sex. This would be much less threatening. She would build up to it slowly, and would remember to watch her words, having been cautioned by the Dolphin to stay away from the topic of pork chops, that is, factory-farmed pigs, which she might mention in passing but not dwell on.

"I am a pig. I know you humans have given that word many meanings to describe some of your worst attributes: gluttony, greed, filthy habits, cruelty to the weak and powerless. I know that if I really had those attributes, I couldn't control myself, and I would be giving you graphic descriptions of how we feel so cramped when we are fattened for slaughter that we can scarcely turn around in some industrial farms. We wonder sometimes why we were born other than to be chopped up and eaten. Just imagine how a young pet pig feels walking with its master past a butcher shop featuring ham hocks on sale.

"But I'm not going to talk about that. I want to mention some other connections we have to human animals. Recently, your animal scientists have made discoveries about us. We are deemed quite intelligent. Our biology is good enough to be used to repair your bodies. And now you are starting to clone us for medical restoration of your bodies, so-called zootic transfers of entire organs such as pig kidney transplants.

"Even so, you might be a little more careful about your exuberance here, changing the nature of nature has what you call 'unintended consequences.' Presently millions of our piglets are dying from a mysterious deadly virus and the carcasses are sometimes buried near shallow groundwater used for drinking by humans.

"But I digress. I am here to speak of bestiality. I am a female pig in Germany. Humans have made advances to me and other sows. It has gotten so out of hand that the Bundesrat has voted to criminalize 'using an animal for personal sexual activities' with fines as high as thirty-four thousand dollars, as was reported in the *New York Times*. There is a big debate with zoophiles arguing that 'as pair partners,' we 'are perfectly capable of expressing whether or not [we] desire sex.' The law says that they are forcing us to 'behave in ways that are inappropriate to [our] species.' So, it's not just pigs with whom the zoophiles want to copulate; it is any number of different animals that catch their fancy, including great danes. I may be speaking for more than the pigs when I say that we are not free to express our desires.

"First we are under total coercion, sensing what might happen if we persist to resist. After all, what are they raising us for anyhow? Second, there is no attraction there, no matter what the aggressor looks like. And they dare to call themselves zoophiles. Zoos to us are prisons. Please listen to the animal kingdom. There are signs among you humans toward normalizing animal contacts, buggery, sodomy. Where are your veterinarians?

"The way I see it, this sexual fascination some humans feel for animals is no more than a perverted version of real, *platonic* affection that naturally appears when humans and subhuman animals live in close contact.

"This purer love was brought to my attention by recent articles by two accomplished writers, who went into emotionally intimate details about singles who lived for many years with animals, one a riveting, possessive owl named Mumble and the other an intuitively alert, jealous, self-regarding cat. Shall we say that those two animals occupied a major part of the humans' life at home?

"Here is what the Marie cat lover wrote in the *New York Times*: 'I lived with the same cat for 19 years—by far the longest relationship of my adult life.' He admitted to several casual affairs with women, in front of his cat. 'Under common law, this cat was my wife. I fell asleep at night with the warm, pleasant weight of the cat on my chest. The first thing I saw on most mornings was the foreshortened paw of the cat retreating slowly from my face and her baleful crescent glare informing me that it was Cat Food Time. As I often told her, in a mellow, resonant, Barry White voice: 'There is no *luuve* . . . like the *luuve* that exists . . . between a man . . . and his cat.'

"Mr. Kreider fed our imaginations when he described how 'I loved to bury my nose in her fur when she came in from a winter day and inhale deeply of the Coldcat Smell.' There are many ways to make love without penetration, you should know.

"Wait and see. Your legal scholars are making great headway in arguing that animals—at least mammals—should have legal personhood, which would give them legal rights. The first cases are entering the courts with primates as plaintiffs. The animal care and protection business will, of course, be very supportive of any prospects of profits when siding with the mammals. Already states are considering allowing pets to be buried with their owners. Mark my word, multispecies weddings are on the way, regardless of our own preferences to stay with our kin. I, the pig, rest my case."

A collective gasp rose from a viewing mass of humans who had not heard of these developments.

A horse, who also believed in platonic feelings between humans and subhumans, but didn't take it to the extreme that the pig did, pranced forward. She gained immediate attention due to her noble bearing and glossy coat. Some viewers thought they recognized her.

"I am Rachel Alexandra, the first filly in eighty-five years to win the Preakness Stakes. My racing days are over—too soon I think—but that is not my decision. I am now what my masters call 'a foundation mare,' or what to me is a foal factory. There has to be more to life than just making babies.

"Please allow me to speak about a very sensitive subject, which the pig introduced. Look how far those humans have progressed in the hearts of their fellow human beings with normal man/woman instincts. The advance of tolerance and understanding of formerly condemned and attacked relationships brings me to my subject, now entering open controversy in Germany. As the pig has already mentioned, following months of debate, the German Parliament has passed an amendment criminalizing 'using an animal for personal sexual activities or making them available to third parties for sexual activities and thereby forcing them to behave in ways that are inappropriate to their species.'

"Zoophiles object, saying that their relationships with their pets or 'partners' are fully mutual. The group Zoophilic Engagement for Tolerance and Enlightenment argues that animals are perfectly capable of indicating whether they like this kind of sex. Zoophilia is seen as the final stage of the sexual liberation movement.

"You see I love Brent. When I was very sick after giving birth to my filly, Brent sat outside my Stall 13 for fifteen hours a day. He groomed me, walked me, fed me, gave me my medication, and even checked my Facebook page. My affection for Brent was noticed by the *New York Times* whose reporter, Melissa Hoppert, wrote that I 'had a bit of a big crush on Brent,' according to Dr. Bonnie Barr, a physician at the Rood and Riddle Equine Hospital. Brent Comer finds her 'totally inspiring,' with a great will to live. My last foal was so complicated with my illness that it probably ended my ability to produce another offspring at the famous Stone Street Farm. When I saw Brent, he 'was in tears.' When I returned from the hospital, my heart went out to him. If it is totally a matter of both of us being in love, what's wrong with making love to one another if that should happen? What's wrong with, dare I say it, being married? Who does it hurt? Can we at least discuss multispecies relationships?

"After all, you slaughter cows, goats, pigs, mules, even horses. You eat us. You boast about sleeping with your pets, dogs, cats and others. You spend more time with your pets by far than you spend on your 'democracy.' You shower you favorite animals with luxuries beyond description. You train war dogs to fight your enemies and detect explosives and drugs. You work us to the bone. We consider it crossing over into torture. Yet you see zoophilia as a taboo and criminal, calling it bestiality. The times are changing."

Another animal pushed forward, since he had something important to say about animals' sexuality as it applied to house dogs.

"I'm supposed to be the star Maltese at the fifteenth annual Broadway Barks cat and dog adoption event, a benefit for animal shelters and adoption agencies in New York City. OK, I don't mind being showcased and I hope I get adopted by a good family. But the hostess, Bernadette Peters, with all her good intentions, seemed insensitive when she said: 'It's important for people to see how beautiful these animals are, how adoptable they are. They're all healthy, they're all spayed and neutered, they all have their shots.'

"May I say in reply: You've taken away our dreams of ever having children, of ever having sexual love with a purpose. How would you like it if we were on top and we began showcasing you, Ms. Peters and Ms. Mary Tyler Moore and Mr. Harvey Fierstein, and said how healthy you are, having taken out your reproductive organs or castrated you? I'll bet a hundred sweet barks that you'd be more than upset.

"Where are the animal welfare agencies when we need *our* animal reproductive rights?"

All this talk about sex, even this last complaint, didn't hurt the ratings one bit, but even so, the TRIAD felt the questions of interspecies love and the evils of neutering should not be allowed to get any more attention. As they had originally conceived this touchy-feely approach, it was not only about making humans feel all soft inside. It could be turned to advantage by showing how lovely animals were under threat of extinction. (It was a strategy well known to charity fundraisers.) So, going back to that strategy, they called a visually arresting animal to the mike.

A Zebra Speaks Out

"I am Grévy's zebra. Your nature magazines and tourists have taken many pictures of my kind with what you've called our 'dazzling striped hide,' our large, round conical ears that can rotate in any direction without moving our bodies, and our set-back eyes. You might say we have evolved in ways to ward off lions and other attackers. But we are in hard times, having lost two-thirds of our grasslands near the horn of Africa, very little of it protected. We're only two thousand left in the wilds, mostly in a sixty-two-thousand-acre buffer zone near Mount

Kenya. We are very much endangered," said the Grévy's zebra with visible, deep sadness.

"Just imagine what millennia of evolution have done to us to survive animal predators. One of your Nature Conservancy magazines described us as 'hidden in plain sight,' with our black-and-white stripes forming a type of camouflage known as 'disruptive coloration. The stripes break up the outline of the zebra's body, making it difficult to spot—especially when viewed through grasses and scrub in the African bush.' But we can't evolve fast enough to deal with habitat loss, hunting equipment, and crowding on fewer and fewer grasslands. And we never will. *Please help us!*"

Humans by the millions dabbed their eyes, seeing for the first time in the TALKOUT a desperate appeal to ward off extinction. The animal rights organizations worldwide took notice and prepared for appeals to save the Grévy's zebra.

We're Endangered Too

However, the TRIAD, who had not been monitoring animals' reactions as closely as they had been those of humans, were blindsided by hundreds of species who believe themselves to be endangered, calling the TRIAD and asking to be recognized for a similar appeal. Those species that are not on the endangered species list formulated by humans were keen to take this rare opportunity to make the case for protection from extinction. The petitioners for human compassion included the polar bear, the Oregon spotted frog, the Canadian lynx, the elfin woods warbler, the wolverine, the Eastern Massasauga rattlesnake, the Pacific walrus, the lesser prairie chicken, and the Dakota skipper butterfly, their danger having been underlined in *New York Times* articles.

There was no way all these animals could get on the mike

so the TRIAD set up a special news desk at which a finch, a gnat, and a sea turtle would evaluate danger levels. If they came across a case where the animal group petitioning was in real, present danger, they would ring an emergency bell, signaling that a spokes-animal could take the stage to plead for that group, and the bell did ring often.

Animals That Humans Think They Know

Meanwhile, they saw the humans were longing for more stories, more touchy-feely ones, but ones, like those about the pig and cat, that dealt with animals they were familiar with; that is, domesticates of some type. To comply with this and also massage human egos by pointing to a positive program humans had established, they brought forth a heifer from Heifer International, one week away from leaving the facility to join a poor African family in Malawi.

"I'm a heifer," she said, "a special kind of heifer raised by Heifer International, a group that has helped fourteen million families in the last seventy years. You're asked to gift me to a family who raises me for my milk and breeds me to produce a calf every year. The protein in my milk, I'm told, will transform sick, malnourished children into healthy boys and girls. My surplus milk will earn money for the family for clothing, school fees, medicine, and improvements at the home. You can gift me for only five hundred dollars.

"I'll admit, humans, that Heifer International, which also invites gifts for sheep, goats, and water buffalos, represents a higher order of intelligence than we heifers will ever have. But we should get credit for having the skills of making your predictions accurate after we land at our destination. No small performance. A Thai farmer was heard to say, 'If I die, my family will weep for me. If my buffalo dies, my family will starve.' A water buffalo increases crop yields with its manure and is able to carry far more bananas to market than a human, among other benefits it offers host families.

"So why, oh why, if Heifer International is so successful, aren't there hundreds of such groups increasing the number of all domesticated animals in the developing world? A good hen can lay up to two hundred eggs a year and can eat food scraps, help control insects, and fertilize gardens. A flock of chicks goes for a twenty-dollar gift. As former president Jimmy Carter, himself a farmer, said, the gift of one animal can bring health, prosperity, and peace. Instead you give or discharge weapons of mass destruction in many areas of the developing world, which brings war, death, and poverty. Tell me what is so smart about your human intelligence?"

That last note was a bit sour, but then captive beasts have a certain license with humans so long as they obey and do what they're told. The TRIAD decided to make a calculated risk. If humans wanted to hear about animals they were familiar with or thought they were familiar with, then, the Dolphin proposed, what about having some zoo animals testify?

They had recruited a trio from a large modern zoo to step up. The gorilla and the giraffe came forth with a watery guest, the intelligent, scrappy giant Pacific octopus, the camouflage specialist.

The gorilla started off upbeat, wanting humans to know that modern zoos are different than the old zoos where animals were often displayed in small cages. Most of the animals are now born into captivity and given more natural room to roam, though the zoo designs must be such that the animals are visible and able to be close to visitors separated by glass (as with the octopus) or bridges. The idea is not just to protect the animals' physical and mental health but to, in the words of zookeeper Satch Krantz, assure 'that they are moving about during the day, they are foraging, they are doing the things they do in nature, to provide that experience for the guest.'

"Visitors want an emotional bond with the animal. 'Connecting kids to nature, connecting people to nature,' said Tony Vecchio, director of the Jacksonville Zoo in Florida.

The really wild animals watched this unveiling of what they have long viewed as prisons with amazement. They were muttering among themselves. To them there was no such thing as "wild" animals in prison zoos. More recently, they came to realize that perfecting animal reproduction in the prison zoos lessened the urgency of protecting these species in the wild. And with sperm and egg banks proliferating, they wonder whether humans will care at all about their survival in the wilderness. Luckily, the humans were not privy to these disturbing musings.

They were watching the next spokes-animal, the giraffe. "I do not harbor the illusion," said the giraffe, "that my keepers care about my species' desire to roam far and wide. They think protecting me from predator lions should make me happy. Because of the new apps I can now tell them that their own founder, Benjamin Franklin, once said that 'those who prefer security over liberty deserve neither.' That's the way I feel. Give me the freedom of the grasslands of my forebears and I'll take my chances with the lions."

Now the feral animals were nodding their heads in agreement.

Meanwhile, the Pacific octopus came forward. Of all the speakers, she felt most cramped in the zoo, regardless of the little cave given to her. "Sure I'm safe from predators but confess to being bored out of my mind from incarceration. That's why I nervously change my colors and textures so often and why I slam into the tank wall in frustration. I also have no companionship, no one to love or be loved by," said this beautiful specimen so brilliantly adapted to the ocean depths' known 250,000 aquatic species. "I know that our brothers and sisters in the wilds cannot liberate us, but at least do not deride us, for we are at the manipulative mercy of our human wardens."

Reading the e-mail feedback from humans, it was noted that many were interested in a controversy at SeaWorld, which was not a zoo, but still a place where animals were kept in captivity so they could be displayed to the public.

It seems that a documentary about an orca whale in captivity killing its trainer and implicated in two other fatal attacks earlier is outraging the accused company SeaWorld, which is fighting back. The film producer, related the Dolphin, asserts that "killer whales are 100 percent not suitable to captivity," a claim SeaWorld rejects, given its many peace-loving orcas. Litigation may follow.

Numerous wild orcas wanted to comment and the dolphins selected some of them:

Orca One—"The documentary is absolutely right. We're carnivores whether or not we have an audience."

Orca Two—"That's the way it is with us orcas, guilty unless proven innocent."

Orca Three—"Of course, our dear Tilikum, the captured and imprisoned orca, would never do such a thing, unless mercilessly repressed. We orcas only kill in order to eat. The human was not eaten or even injured. Too much stress on us did it."

Thousands of orcas did backflips in concurring unison around the world.

Wild Animals Scorn Pampered Pets

Both the octopus and the tale of the imprisoned orcas hit a sensitive note in the ferals. It gave them new empathy for animals living in zoo-like circumstances though it did not change their negative views of pets. The wild ones look at what they call the domesticates with a combination of pity, contempt, and, yes, derision. As they saw it, dogs and cats are bred into nervous nellies, pampered with store-bought mush, given clothes during winter, and subjected to drug prescriptions and about the same number of operations and treatments as their human masters, including colonoscopies and joint replacements. Some are given hospice and funerals, and on their birthdays their upper-income masters even give them pet parties where they can express their pet peeves and be relieved of them for the day.

They have burial grounds, caskets, hymnals, and monuments. Dogs and cats have been known to receive major bequests by masters who predeceased them—these are the kinds of royal dogs and cats who get transported by limousines from one place to another. The wilds know—especially the tough wild dogs and feral cats—that these pampered domesticates couldn't survive a week in the wilderness.

Even their utility in guarding their masters or catching mice is rapidly atrophying. More and more of them are now used as ornaments or "comfortable shoes" or "children" for long-time owners. Some owners are now dog-pecked or cat-pecked by these domesticates, who sense such opportunities and flip upside down the power relations of who is the boss in the household. Every night one Boston terrier growls and starts tugging at his master to go upstairs to bed at precisely 10:00 p.m. Furthermore, to the wild ones, the fancy dog and cat shows put on by the wealthy ones are beyond bizarre and simply grotesque.

They also found rib-tickling humor in stories of how about-to-be-vacationing human couples would shop for a just right puppy sitter or what the commercial services call "hosts." Comparison shopping for these services was elaborate. The pet owners would ask whether there is health insurance available, where the puppy will sleep, the layout and safety of the backyard, and what were the favorite walking routes. The hosts' profiles were analyzed and the varieties of prices and payment options were reviewed.

Pet cats also had it easy. To transport them, humans used

"cat strollers" sold by Kitty Walk Systems pet products on Long Island, New York. Strollers come in all sizes and extra dimensions; one called the "Gazebo" is advertised as a hexagonal structure large enough for your pet to entertain visiting Siamese and Maine coons in comfort. Another called the "Clubhouse" touts sunshade and a hammock. The owners of Kitty Walk Systems become minor celebrities, appearing on the *Today* show, *Martha Stewart Living*, and *The View*. And there was much more publicity. It was enough for two ignored Third Party presidential candidates to put out press releases saying they would don cat suits and go into the stroller anytime if they could get on these national TV shows just once.

All the grousing by the ferals was leading to caucusing and complaints about the TRIAD's leadership. Our three leaders explained that they had decided to follow humans' demands by *temporarily* highlighting the animals that humans *thought they knew*, but whose real point of view they had no idea about. If the feral caucuses would just be patient, they would now listen to a side of the domesticates' story neither ferals nor humans had been privy to.

Pets Speak for Themselves

A domesticated feline rose to explain his embattled point of view. Heavy and shaggy, this tomcat belied the worst stereotype of his overbred species. He was a good choice.

"Humans and especially cat lovers, I rise to explain our predicament and the comforts of our lives. You know there is no cat free will. Our kitten litters are so fertile that they can't be given away, unlike dog litters in which the puppies fetch a variety of nice prices. Our litters are often drowned.

"Our owners think it is messy to feed on the few rats and mice we catch. We've lost our learned hunting skills and are left with what you humans call our genetic instinct to chase lesser mammals. True, in the U.S. we stand accused of killing over two billion birds a year, but they are so helpless when we pounce on them that it is not much of a hunt. The little birdies offer no real resistance in or near their nests; many would have expired anyway.

"Humans think we're incorrigibly independent, unlike their sycophant dogs, and they're right. But we know that, even though we don't fawn, we exist to serve and make our masters comfortable in their living quarters. We have no real duties. Our wants—food, drink, cat beds, and veterinarians—are cared for. They do interfere with our reproductive rights, spaying the females, but we can get out in the alleys at night sometimes. Then we can feel the thrill of freedom felt by the feral cats and the big jungle cats that command such awe from humans and their protective societies.

"We really have no challenges and no purposes in life, unlike our animal kingdom wild-lifers. You ferals know danger and you have to live by your wits. There is a thrill to living in the wilds and the freedom to love and to flee, to learn and to defend your young. You have more numerous clusters to your community. We are largely required to be loners and loneliness is our worst fate.

"Enjoy your freedom while it lasts. Play and procreate and keep communicating your intelligence to humans, which advances your own survival."

Emergency Bell

Just then for the first time an emergency bell started ringing. This means the three processors had come upon an urgent situation and had given the signal. Truth is, the TRIAD was thinking that it would be hard to find a more voracious flying insect to bring forth, right when humans seemed willing to be enlightened about the lives of animals they falsely thought they knew so well, and when they were in a somewhat mellow mood. Humans certainly didn't want to listen to this next fellow, but they had to play by the rules they had established about emergencies.

The bell was rung by the locusts—yes, locusts—and the spokes-locust rushed in to exclaim: "Since biblical times we have come out of the Sudan and Egypt in great swarms looking for food. It is our curse that we like the same food that the farmers grow, including potatoes and cumin. Just a few days ago, our remnants swarmed in the millions into southern Israel, which unleashed spraying "pesticides" from both ground and air, slaughtering us in great numbers. The farmers complain their crops are ruined, but they are catching and frying us for their meals. They see us as a crunchy snack and kosher."

The animal kingdom was saddened as they learned about the plight of the locusts. To them pesticides were equivalent to genocides in the human world's language. What were the crimes of the locusts? They were simply searching for forage or they would die.

Humans Witness How Animals Negotiate Among Themselves

For the first time in the TALKOUT the framework of reference between humans and the animal kingdom had become miles and miles apart. To humans, locusts were aerial vermin, so far down the ladder of sentient creatures as to be subjected to total elimination if possible. The locust's testimony had done nothing to change that. To the animal kingdom, the locust was part of nature's web with no evil intent; it was all about survival and reproduction. They were herbivores, not carnivores.

The TRIAD was perplexed and called a brief recess. They couldn't very well defend animals who were eating humans' carefully tended food. They talked this over, on secure channels, with their animal associates. The Owl suggested that they express concern about the plight of the locusts but admit that there is little anyone in the animal world who can reach humans can do to go to the locusts' defense in a persuasive way. Not a chance. The Elephant was advised to inform the locust that its species will survive such devastations, has for thousands of years, and they just have to live, or die, with this peril to their swarms. After all, the animals of nature devour one another but rarely to extinction; life goes on as many are fallen for dinner.

Returning from the recess, the TRIAD related their private conversation to everyone on the planet. The locust, informed of the historical evolution of its species' rise, fall, rise and fall, seemed to understand, and was given a potato leaf to munch on before flying back to its swarm.

Millions of humans, watching with dropped jaws this interaction between higher forms of mammals and a locust, saw the wisdom of the TRIAD expressed under exceptional visibility as they handled the locusts' unanticipated entrance on their stage.

Not that this totally eliminated humans' uneasiness. The Owl was pondering what they could do to rebound in the ratings. For the majority of human viewers had no empathy for the locusts and were even offended by the locust spokesbug's (according to talk show host Rush Limburger) "unkempt appearance."

Shark in a Coal Mine

Time to call out one of the big guns. The Dolphin decided to really excite the human audience and introduced the great white shark. The Nielsen ratings went off the charts. The imperious magnificence of the King of Sharks spoke for itself. Out of the four hundred species of shark, including the dwarf lantern shark, which is six inches long, this is NUMERO UNO. Humans have enveloped this species in deadly folklore—for shark attacks are exceedingly rare, around a dozen fatalities a year worldwide.

"I am what you humans call the great white shark. I come from the war zone you have created in the vast oceans that have taken the lives of over seventy million sharks a year, not to eat, but to cut off our fins, which add nothing to the taste or flavor of something called shark fin soup. You cut off our fins and throw us back into the ocean where we promptly drown. If nothing else, you should not waste such protein.

"I know you want to hear my story, 'cause you have a zillion TV shows about my activities. But now you are going to hear it right from the fish's mouth, First, a little perspective. We've been around one hundred fifty million years; you've been around as Homo sapiens for some two hundred thousand years. You may outlive us if you continue to extinguish us, but odds are you won't rack up two hundred fifty thousand, the way you are going. To reverse course you simply cannot continue to demonize us. Our genetic makeup and how we navigate and serve the oceans can teach you much.

"At the risk of titillating you—and why not, you've given us much of your attention time—let me pick one example. Our sex life. First the dull part. Did you know that we are capable of asexual reproduction? In cases where males and females cannot get together, the female shark can deliver virgin births. It's happened in your watery prisons (aquariums you call them) when the female sharks are isolated from males.

"When we do get together to mate, as one writer put it, 'the business is "very rough."' We males bite or corner the females during courtship. Marine biologists have learned to tell when a female has been mating. Her skin will be seared or bleeding.

"At mating time, females will sit in shallow water with their 'vaginas' pressed to the sea floor. Roving males still succeed in inserting what you call their claspers, or penis. These sharks have two penises behind their pelvic fins. Now comes the shocker, so I'll quote one of your closest observers of shark sex: 'A litter of fifty pups will have anything from two to seven fathers . . . [Also] a number of shark species go in for oophagy, or uterine cannibalism. Sand tiger foetuses "eat each other in utero, acting out the harshest form of sibling rivalry imaginable." Only two babies emerge, one from each of the mother shark's uteruses; the survivors have eaten everything else. "A female sand tiger gives birth to a baby that's already a meter long and an experienced killer," explains [expert] Demian Chapman.'

"You can see just a glimmer of what you may want to study about us, especially our ability to detect parts per billion at long distances. From mutual interest, you need to know that we do not like your body for our meals. You have bones. We go for cartilage like a fat seal or sea lion, not a bony human. Most attacks on you by us are mistaken identities. That's why we spit you out. We're high in testosterone but we're also easily frightened. Encounter us and start banging on our snouts to send us away, however temporarily.

"We are not just startling the curious. We have an important role to play as early warning systems. Journalist Juliet Eilperin gave us meaning in her book *Demon Fish*. As the *London Review of Books* says, 'Sharks [are] the canary in the coalmine. They reveal a great deal about the ocean: "how it functions, and why it is now in peril." A pristine marine environment, certainly in the tropics, will be swarming with sharks; they help to keep mid-level predators in check, and the whole ecosystem healthy . . . As long-lived predators producing a limited number of offspring, sharks are very vulnerable to collapse due to overfishing . . . Sharks are facing an extinction crisis. That's causing a jellyfish explosion.

"Please stop being so scared of us. Don't let writers of movies make more money the more they can terrify you. Jawbone *Jaws* for both our sakes."

Given the feverish pitch of interest in the white shark, it was satisfying to the TRIAD that the commentary from humans was actually sympathetic. They had no idea that they were the killers of tens of millions of sharks for a 'tasteless noodle-like cartilage' known as the shark's fin. For decades, Mao Tse Tung called shark fin soup a bourgeois value and banned it, becoming the shark's best friend.

Canary's Turn

The Elephant immediately sensed a double-downing opportunity and introduced a real life metaphor:

A bird flew up and assumed a place on a wooden perch. "I am a literal canary in a coal mine—a small, old one—in Kentucky. (Note, the new, automated mines have detectors and the coal companies don't want to be bothered with maintaining and carrying us down the shafts.) We canaries in the coal mines have never been able to tell our story. Until now. Tens of thousands of canaries have given their lives to be an early alert system when the deadly gases reach levels that are lethal for us but not yet for the miners. Of course, coal miners have also lost their lives for the profit of companies and their executives in New York, Chicago, Pittsburgh, and London. Over four hundred fifty thousand lost lives, due to lung diseases and mine collapses, is the estimate since 1890, or about the number of Americans lost in World War II. Their widows and children mourn them.

"Who mourns us? Yet we filled an important life-saving function. When we droop, the miners get the hell out of that mine before the gases overcome them. It is precisely because you knew something about the level of gas lethal to us but not yet to humans that you were able to use us for your humanitarian purposes.

"The knowledge of the animal kingdom helping is true in our case. Moreover, the modern environmental movement has turned us into a metaphor for any deteriorating ecological conditions that provide an early alert signal for humans to wake up. The decline in frog species is just the latest use of comparing those creatures to a "canary in the coal mine," except now the "coal mine" is the planet.

"The miners cared for us to a degree that could not be exaggerated. That was because their fate was intertwined with ours. If we are fit enough to do our job—and not droop for other than gaseous causes—they can feel safer while they are working and not have to totally rely on the mine's bosses above ground for warnings concerning the crucial time of escape. Also they love us because in the cruel, dark, dank underground mines—that nonminers have no clue about as they use their electricity—we remind them of the 'cool green Earth' and colorful birds flitting and chirping through the trees. Enough about us, Elephant—over to you."

Menhaden As Canary

The Elephant didn't know much about the sea but after the Dolphin whispered in his ear, he agreed to let the overlooked menhaden, a small fish, take the mike. The fish was justly complaining that the great white shark had gone "overboard" in self-promotion. The menhaden brought forward claims that he, not the shark, was most often labeled the sea's canary in a coalmine.

The chief of the menhaden was not in a conciliatory mood. "We're tired of just being around to be eaten by the larger fish, who get all the attention and defense of the ocean conservationists. 'Save the sharks,' 'Rescue the dolphins,' 'Protect the whales,' even 'Recover the cod,' are the cries that are repeated everywhere to humans. But never do they say that we, the menhadens, are the most critical fish in the ocean, because we're the ones that eat the plankton, and without us as food, you can kiss both your marine mammals and sea birds goodbye.

"Also, we are what you humans call the 'canary bird in the mine,' only in our case, we're the canary bird in the ocean, the authentic ones. Because as the climate changes and warms, due to humans' combustibles, there are fewer plankton and so there are fewer menhaden. Our numbers are already going down around Antarctica and so the larger fish are decreasing.

"We demand respect for our small silvery selves—not only for our survival ego—but for the whole chain of species' survival that relies on us. We want public recognition, commemorative events, instruction to youngsters in schools, and all kinds of graphics showing us as the capstone species from below. We, the menhaden, want to be a major reason given for replacing fossil fuels and adopting the sun, yes the sun, which gets us started by photosynthesizing our own food. We, the menhaden, want a global 'Save the Menhaden Day' with music, banners, buttons and human celebrities, parades, replicas of ourselves (no 'fish fries' please) and all behind an agenda of aquatic salvation starting with the plankton and then the menhaden."

The great white shark was muttering, "Never gonna happen."

While the pollsters were telling the TRIAD that what the humans took for the hubris of the menhaden—humans were often more aware of a speaker's attitude than whether his or her message was significant—was quite a turnoff.

The Dolphin told his cohorts that he had set up a team to look for some of the funnier animals. The anteater, seahorse, and hummingbird had been holding stand-up auditions. Maybe now was the time to bring out a segment produced by one of their better jokesmiths.

Gull Humor

The gulls had a report that would delicately poke fun at humans while allowing them to get a few grievances off their feathered breasts.

The report came from one of the gulls swarming around the parking lot of a giant shopping mall in Waterbury, Connecticut. It seems that the gulls—far from sea but enjoying the droppings of shoppers and their children—noted police hustling away a dozen demonstrators with placards urging Walmart to pay their one million workers the inflation-adjusted equivalent of the 1968 minimum wage, or $10.50 an hour.

The seagull appeared in the screen: "We gulls could not wait to tell you humans that we are more privileged scurrying and fluttering around in the shopping mall than you humans with all your asserted constitutional rights. Under Connecticut law, shopping malls are considered private property, prohibiting shoppers or visitors from holding signs, demonstrating, protesting, pamphleteering, or petitioning for signatures on any subject. The mall's owners have a direct police line to get the police over to enforce protesters' eviction. It didn't matter that there were only a small number, hardly a dozen people, and that they were keeping away from any internal vehicle traffic or pedestrians going to or coming from their cars at the mall.

"Now we know you call us 'birdbrains' to signify how little you think of our intelligence. But it did not take long for all our seagulls to notice a peculiar double standard, this time to the disadvantage of you humans. Here we are every day, seagulls descending onto this mall in the many dozens. We affect traffic. We and the cars have to keep getting out of each other's way. We talk freely to one another and make lots of noise together. We let loose our droppings whenever the urge comes. We're probably lousy with bacteria and vermin. We pay no taxes to subsidize the building or operation of these huge shopping centers. Yet the police leave us alone. Hey, what's not to like?

Some gulls swore that they saw some of the ejected protestors looking back on us with visible envy. In a perverse way, you can be proud of how well you've treated us on land, since the quantity of fish was depleted by overfishing and pollution in Long Island Sound. Thank you."

The elephant was pleased that the seagull comedian had injected his humor with actual newsiness. Such up-to-the-minute reporting tends to hold the audience, especially those used to pressing the off button because of their fascination with violence, sex, and nanosecond action programs.

Meanwhile the polling of humans was continuing. The cat, even if some of the things he said were downers, had gotten high ratings. A sub-poll had been established to see what animals humans would like to see. Probably because a film version of *Swan Lake* had recently played around the world, the swan was in big demand.

Swan Talk

The Elephant smiled to herself, realizing the swan segment might puncture humans' romanticized notions of this bird.

The great female swan with its eight-foot wingspan gracefully moved to center stage, inviting mass murmurs of admiration by humans. One human blogger said the bird symbolized "love, grace and transformation."

"You have a noble image of swans," the bird said. "There are no signs around lakes saying 'Beware of killer swans.' We could substitute for your doves of peace.

"Still, I would like to reveal a little-known side of my species. Get anywhere near us—up to a hundred yards even—during our swan-hatching season and we become fearsomely territorial and protective of our young as you would be in a similar situation. Regardless of intent, you humans come close enough to make us feel threatened—say in a kayak—and suddenly we can surprise you with our ferocity, our speed of attack, and our knowledge as to how to tip you over and drown you. For water is our ally. Our powerful wings and hardened beak can only do so much, assuming you are not armed. But even if you are armed, we are not deterred when you are close to our eggs."

Human bloggers quickly dredged up actual reports of drowning caused by attacking swans so that mama swan's story was given credibility. The point she wanted to make is if you idealize animals—giving certain species just the opposite of the human image of wolves—humans who approach maternally protective animals can be lulled into a false sense of complacency until it is too late. Beware.

Here was a lesson learned. Ratings plummeted, and this for a show that was created by adhering to humans' request to hear from swans. Now the TRIAD knew: you can't give humans what they think they want, not if you are going to reveal aspects of reality that go against their animal stereotypes. The TRIAD argued about what to do next, stay light or, given the dire straits of the world, press on with other serious topics?

What Is to Be Done?

The TRIAD agreed they needed an extensive break before continuing almost helter-skelter toward the hundred-hour allotment of communication to humans. They had something of a plan, but concern with humans' reaction to what they had been shown and the occurrence of emergencies seemed to be derailing it. It was time to refocus.

They announced a long weekend respite to reorganize and to determine better what humans wanted and needed to hear. The human feedback to what had transpired had been massively piling up without full review and filtering, notwithstanding the help of many owls, dolphins, and elephants and their trusted friends, three rhinos, two porpoises, and one eagle.

The consensus of some hard discussion was that there were two things that had to be done in tandem for humans. Stroke their egos and assuage their fears. Each aspect had inherent problems. Too much stroking and the real issues might be forgotten. Too much assuaging, which had to involve revealing the dangers that needed to be addressed, could lead humans back to the swamp of despair. The animals decided the latter danger was greater, so upbeat first.

Ego Stroking

The Dolphin, taxed with coming up with something especially life affirming, led with a green sea turtle from Baja California, who would tell his story of rescue and recovery.

"I am known locally as *Tortugas prietas* or 'black turtle.' My ancestors go back millions of years. In recent decades we have been hunted for our meat and our eggs. Thirty years ago our nests counted twenty-five thousand. Fifteen years later, we were down to less than five hundred nesting females in the midst of habitat devastation, poaching and fishing nets.

"Then came our miracle maker, a doctoral student named Wallace J. Nichols, who wanted to study us. And did he ever! The short version of the story is that he earned the trust and respect of local people so that they began to increasingly protect us gentle, one-hundred-fifty-pound creatures from certain extinction. This grassroots network is active in fifty coastal communities. Tourists are visiting to witness the comeback of our turtles. We now have some fifteen thousand nests on the beaches of southern Mexico while the locals derived a sense of pride from saving us for their grandchildren to inherit."

The turtle signed off with the message: "You see it can be done. We thank those farseeing humans among you."

Another success story came to the (underwater) stage. Enter the giant blue whale to thank twentieth-century humans for a sea change in public perceptions, attitudes, and policies toward whales. Whaledom was throbbing with excitement over the new book *The Sounding of the Whale* by a Princeton professor of history and science, Dr. Graham Burnett, which examined the no-limit slaughter of the whales by the whalers, shielded in their business by public images of whales as demons with evil eyes, and then looked at the rising influence of international regulation based on just-in-time science to save these largest mammals in the world.

"The struggle is not over," the whale told the listeners. "Some nations are resistant, increasing shipping traffic is killing whales in collisions, and habitats are dwindling though marine reserves are expanding. But the blue whale should know: its impending extinction has been reversed, benefiting from a more aesthetic, beautiful, and intelligent understanding of the many whale species by humans.

The blue whale's dignified presentation, given directly from the ocean, connected with the expanding human wonder and public adulation as more people discovered about the lives of the whales. Millions of children were enthralled, which bodes well for future human conservation efforts.

The Owl thought the blue whale's gratitude would make a good transition to another topic, the dramatic change in public attitudes toward chimpanzees, something to which Dr. Jane Goodall's fifty years of research with them mightily contributed. Experimentation in chimpanzee labs is grinding to a halt on what Dr. Goodall calls complex animals with intricate social lives. They are heading for sanctuaries. Research on chimps, even if it benefits humans, will soon only be justified by how it benefits the chimps.

What the chimpanzee, called Elaine by humans, had to address was the disappointed scientists who work with these primates to discover or refine vaccines or treatments for human diseases. An onerous permit process could delay drug tests in chimps, for hepatitis C, for example, and thus slow down the saving of many human lives. Elaine said she thought chimpanzees were smart enough to understand that they and humans both benefit from some drug trials, and that they would support the scientists in accelerating any permit process.

A vindicated Jane Goodall could only smile watching Elaine dispel the myths that came from movies such as Ronald Reagan's *Bedtime for Bonzo,* in which chimps were presented as nothing but cute foils for humans. She loved the new movie *Rise of the Planet of the Apes*, where the superior apes are played by human actors and come out as the heroes.

The Owl hadn't forgotten the fact that the Dolphin as one of the TRIAD, had used his authority to jump into the lineup without asking permission. So, the Owl thought it wouldn't be too unprecedented if he made a few humorous remarks about his own species when he saw the cat, who was up next, sitting back licking his fur and preening.

"Did you know," he asked, "what owl pellets are? Poop? Vomit? Owl bones? Well, not quite vomit. You see owls swallow small mammals whole, but they don't have enough stomach acid, like the Tasmanian devil has, to digest fur and bones. So an owl has evolved with two stomachs, one to separate the digestible and indigestible portions. Both items go down the gizzard, but only the digestible material moves into the owl's intestines. The gizzard continues to compress the indigestible portion, turning it into pellets, which go back to the glandular stomach and hours later are regurgitated."

The cat had now finished its obsessive grooming. He wanted to tell everyone that a feline was running for mayor of Xalapa in eastern Mexico with the campaign slogan, "Tired of voting for rats? Vote for a cat who knows how to catch them." Morris, a two-year-old black-and-white kitten with orange eyes, had become a social media sensation in that country, but the rest of the world did not know about this feline candidate launched by a group of disillusioned voters.

More affirmative coverage followed.

"Did you know," said the Elephant, "that the U.S. military bases in the U.S. spend seventy million dollars a year on protecting threatened and endangered species, such as the red-cockaded woodpecker, desert tortoises, and vulnerable shrikes, from their noisy military training maneuvers and shooting? Thanks to a 1960 law called the Sikes Act, the Marines and other branches hire dozens of biologists and natural resource managers to scan millions of acres of these military ranges. The desert tortoise has been known to stop Marines in their tracks on their shooting ranges. There are even road signs with the warnings 'Desert Tortoise Advisory.'"

The Elephant drew the obvious conclusion. "Here you have Marines who are trained to kill other humans around the world, and they're ordered to stop what they're doing to let some desert tortoises find their sanctuaries. How can we in the animal kingdom not be forever grateful for such animaltarianism?"

These words coming from an Elephant, whose species is being vanquished by illegal shooters for their tusks and the insatiable Chinese market. What marvelous self-control—a virtue that did not go unnoticed by some observers in the riveted global audience.

Testing the Waters

It was time to test the waters, not yet by putting forward some of the grimmer facts, but by rehabilitating the image of a species on which humans had fastened a host of irrational fears. The Elephant decided to take this communion between the human and the subhuman to a most dangerous televised cliff—

that between them and what they saw as the most repulsive species—reptilian snakes.

What prompted her was a new photographic book that has just been published called *Serpentine*, with what one reviewer, Dana Jennings, called a hundred "hypnotic portraits of dangerous and colorful snakes from across six continents." The Elephant repeated the reviewer's words, which continued: "The images shock us out of our modern human complacency and arrogance, remind us that all of us, human and nonhuman, are just trying to get by on this lonely planet."

Then the Elephant started putting the snakes onto the screen to be seen by the bulging eyes of many millions of viewers. One by one they slithered, twisted, and leaped past: the deadly mambas and spitting cobras, the boas and rattlers, the royal pythons and the palm pit vipers, the rough-scaled death adder, the black-headed bushmaster and the blue Malaysian coral snake.

The Elephant quoted author Mark Laita as being unable to "take [his] eyes off them, from the spade-shaped wedge of head to the tapered tail, and all that sinuous muscle in between . . . Their beauty heightens the danger. The danger amplifies their beauty." For once a reviewer was talking about exactly what many of the distant mesmerized audience was feeling.

Humans Complain About Animals, and Animals Complain About Humans

As these snakes were getting a lot of positive feedback, the trio thought it was time to try the second part of their strategy, allaying human fears. This, they thought, could be done by educating humans about why certain very annoying events were taking place. They would begin with what humans called the epidemic of invasive species, and closely monitor audience reaction.

Of course some parts of this controversy, as humans presented it, were a bit obscure to animals, as they obviously did not recognize national borders to the freedom to roam. They do know about natural equilibrium and that species outside their normal habitat can bring disruption and disaster as they struggle to adapt and survive, and, often without their natural predators, proliferate like mad.

The words "invasive species," however, turned them off. Invaders are deliberate. There was nothing deliberate in pet Indonesian pythons being let loose from their owners into the Everglades and turning into the giant monsters of those waters, eating into extinction or near-extinction many mammals, fish, and birds. The big snakes didn't ask for this new home. Bird-eating snakes hitchhiking to Hawaii in aircraft landing gear were not intentionally looking for a tropical paradise in which to raise their families. Asian carp were taken from their homelands and now fill the Mississippi River nearly up to Lake Michigan with their aggressive dominance. The European zebra mussels, found in the ballast water of ships coming to America, did not plan for such a journey, but did they ever adapt. Poisonous foreign toads and feral camels came to Australia through the activities of humans. African bees, treekilling beetles, mosquitoes, and fire ants came along for the ride to America involuntarily.

The TRIAD called the subject not invasive, but said forced emigration/immigration of subhuman species was brought about by humans. Subhumans had learned that there are biologists, "mix-o-ecologists," searching for answers, for ways to slow down the human transfer of "alien species," but on the ground and in the waters, little is being done. If this is the coming "homogenization of the planet," what happens to the price paid by biological diversity bred of millennia of steady equilibrium?

Working on their own, representatives of the forced emigrant species came to the conclusion that the best way to supplement their discussion of why they were ending up in countries they had no intention of visiting was to use a visual aid. They paraded before a startled human audience with the same message: "We didn't ask to go. We're just trying to survive, but we are being demonized through no fault of our own and hunted down. What do you expect us to do? Ask for humans to round us up and deport us to our native habitat, which we would disrupt as well by our numbers and acquired characteristics?

"Maybe you should acquire a taste for us and give yourselves an economic incentive to catch and consume us. You wouldn't touch Asian carp but they are desired solid food in Asia. Why can't you eat us? A lot of us are plain old protein."

A funny reaction ensued. Many humans seemed to be getting the message, but animal viewers were outraged when they heard recommendations that they be featured on dinner plates. "Betrayers, traitors, sellouts, saboteurs," were the epithets thrown at these televised spokes-animals by their peers. How could they suggest such slaughter of innocents, they cried out. "You'd better not come back home," hissed a Florida python sunning itself after devouring a stray goat. "You'd all better get yourselves to a human zoo/prison if you know what's good for you."

"Now I know what humans mean by Stockholm Syndrome," bleated the poisonous toad, "and you'd better not eat me, for your own sake."

For the time being the TRIAD ignored the complaints of their fellow animals, more intent on keeping humans willing to entertain animal viewpoints, if not adopt them. They acted to keep the responsive mood flowing by again mentioning the value animals offer humans.

Two grizzly bears, three Antarctic penguins, a nurse shark, and a lioness spoke on this point, each saying her or his bodily system was worth studying. The bears spoke about how they can eat huge amounts before hibernating, getting fat but without their blood pressure and cholesterol spiraling up. Penguins showed how much humans can learn from this bird's fasting.

While the shark really piqued human curiosity by declaring that sharks have developed something over four hundred million years of evolution that keeps cancer at bay. "We have compounds in our bodies that kill tumor cells. Wouldn't you humans want to study that immunity, rather than slaughter us for shark fin soup?"

The female lion now took her turn, telling viewers that she had a biological capability to evaluate her health, the quality of her mate, and her environment to determine the sex of her offspring. This has been reported by Meeri Kim about a study of 2,300 animals over three generations at the famous San Diego Zoo, done by Stanford University's evolutionary biologist Joseph P. Garner. Sex selection has been earlier confirmed in certain birds and insects, but now this finding needs further confirmation in the wilds.

Still, scientists such as Garner, even with the best interests of the animals at heart, can be intrusive and disruptive. There had been all this talk about invasive species, but none about invasive biologists. The audience, the Dolphin guessed, would now be receptive to a privacy invasion complaint.

Onto the screen came a sandhill crane, a pygmy rabbit, and a seal to enter a plea to respect their solitude from close flying drones called "Ravens." These small drones, about double the size of the planes kids used to fly in parks, are said, the crane noted, "to give humans a cheaper, safer, and more accurate count and location of subhumans. But you humans say this is just the beginning and that the number of drones watching us will increase manifold soon.

"It is no longer tags on our bodies or legs. Everything about us will be digitized: our nesting sites, the frequency and ways of our lovemaking, our fights, our modes of resting. You will be taking the mystery entirely out of the animal kingdom and making it what you call 'retrievable data.' Have you, with your large brains, thought of the downsides of taking away our mystery; that is, the downsides to you humans when your curiosity, your sense of wonder and awe are reduced to 'retrievable data'? We leave to your superior intelligences and your natural philosophers to elaborate what we are suggesting you ponder. What you know can be easily turned to destructive uses, as you have experienced in your own history."

As if to punctuate this intriguing nudge, the screen brought out in brilliant color several gorgeously ornate octopi, those elusive, mysterious, intelligent, and delicate invertebrates. One of them said, "So complex is the biological dynamism of us octopi and so little known that marine scientists believe we can teach you a great deal about organic capabilities, as much as you have learned from owls and whales but in greater, far greater variety. But not if you scare us; if your searching disrupts our fragile underwater habitat for survival and reproduction then you won't learn much. You must understand us concerning this caution," said the octopi as they glided away from the screen.

The Owl sensed a need for some communal understanding. "We know that humans, especially real animal lovers, are elated when they discover a new species or genus, and how worried they are when they learn about how close to extinction a particular species is. Why, just this month, your newspapers reported a discovery of a new bat genus in the grasslands of the South Sudan while at the same time a book came out on the world's rarest birds with photographs of five hundred fifteen species under threat of extinction, such as our white-bellied cinclodes, the long-whiskered owlet and Africa's El Oro parakeet.

"We're just asking that you give us some space. View us, study us, but don't unduly disrupt our habitats or life cycles."

So far so good. Humans who, after all, were generally not all that concerned with the rights of biologists and, indeed, often thought of scientists as out of touch didn't see why they had to pester the poor octopi and birds.

Why not, the Dolphin thought, follow with another example of meddling by an institution, which was thought to be beneficial to the ecological system, but, in fact, was undermining the natural order, the USA's Wildlife Services Agency? This "service" partially consisted of destroying millions of animals every year, such as starlings, after classifying them as "invasive species." However, the killing was usually so poorly targeted that the agency's agents ended up destroying many other species in the process, including thirteen endangered ones.

The Elephant presented a petition that called the WSA an "out-of-control rogue agency that shoots, snares, and poisons a million native animals a year," including wolves, bears, and coyotes. Throughout their habitat, these animals became agitated, fearful, and angry. So did their kind around the world. The Elephant saw a crisis coming fast, especially if one of these harried animals attacked a human.

A biology professor from Georgia then showed how this thoughtless destruction of animals could boomerang against the human species. The Elephant quoted him as saying that the Wildlife Services had to be more sensitive to the role of the value of "apex predators." He gave as an example the elimination of native wolves in the Northwest many years ago that opened the way for nonnative coyotes who then pushed out foxes that ate deer mice. This rodent population exploded loaded with ticks carrying Lyme disease—now a major health hazard.

A Dangerous Gamble

That, too, had gone over well since most viewers had no love for bureaucratic agencies and could well imagine the USA's Wildlife Services Agency as careless and wasteful.

It was time for a new effort at rehabilitation, one even more difficult than the work they had put into giving snakes a more positive profile. It was time to try an insect. After all, the TRIAD had to admit, they hadn't had a single insect on the screen thus far. Equity demanded they feature at least one. That's not to say they weren't apprehensive.

The Elephant gave the signal and two German cockroaches scurried across the screen, stopping midway to speak to a suddenly repulsed human viewership across all cultures around the world. Exclamations of disgust were everywhere, yet few clicked the off button.

In perfect unison, the cockroaches conceded that they had little credibility but they added that they also had little ambition to hide the truth. The truth is that the earth needs cockroaches. "The microbes in our stomachs make leaves in the forests digestible to many mammals." They sputtered, "In the tropics you call us jungle pollinators. We also are morsels to lizards and birds." They pulled a quote from a human expert, Coby Schal of North Carolina State University: "Most of the 5,000 known species of cockroaches, plus probably just as many that have not been described, have huge ecological importance." Schal said roaches get a bad rap from the 1 percent of the cockroach species that infests our homes!

"That last remark refers to us two. Even roach scientists think we are expendable, can be hunted to extinction because, as Schal says, we live 'almost exclusively among humans,' and therefore Schal doesn't see any great ecological value to us. So humans can doom us precisely because we are so perfectly adaptable to living with humans exclusively. Doesn't make any sense, with all due respect. So the way to escape the verdict of extinction, favored even by your ecologists, must be to leave your homes and go into the wilds to make plant materials digestible to raccoons, rabbits, deer, and possums?

"How can we be sure that this mass migration will not be detected and wiped out? We have another answer. Study us for what you admit is our spectacular adaptation to anything thrown at us from the human environment. You've studied other cockroaches in the wilds for their immense resistance to radiation. But did you know household roaches can go weeks without food, and eat almost anything, unlike other insects who have specialized cuisines? Neither heat nor cold air conditioning dries us out, because we have a waxy coating. Just think what you'll discover about nature and indirectly your own genetic makeup. Think, think, think," cried the roaches as they were hustled off the stage by Big Bear the Bouncer.

Seeing roaches making their case without totally turning off viewers quickly drove a small swarm of mosquitoes to demand equal time, followed by a covey of bed bugs. The people of the world were overcome with curiosity and bulging eyes.

The mosquitoes, pushing onto the stage, didn't mince words, and admitted to being dangerous to humans, killing more than a million people, many of them children and pregnant mothers, with malaria and other diseases every year.

This boldness—Limburger called it "effrontery"—caught the attention of the viewers. Indeed, as they appeared, the entire animal kingdom dropped what they were doing to watch in awe, for none of them had ever fought back so successfully against the human kingdom.

The mosquitoes first blamed the parasites on them that really caused the damage of malaria. They were merely innocent carriers that wanted a tiny bit of blood for the females. Don't blame them, they said, it would be like blaming a telephone company for carrying bad messages from its customers.

That wasn't enough to mollify the horror with which every child regarded them. They argued that their sheer massive biomasses provide critical food for other species, especially birds, and they added that they were important pollinators. No one in human land, especially in Winnipeg, the most dense mosquito haven in North America, was prepared to believe that mosquitoes had any capstone species value.

The off buttons started voting—their way of booing—but not before an even more disgusting insect, a bed bug, pushed its way onto the stage, standing under a magnifying glass to aid its visibility.

"Sure," said the bed bug, "we give you welts, but you have only hurt your own health by the toxic chemicals you've used in your bedrooms. Ants and some spiders like to eat us, in case that interests you ecologically. But we must defend ourselves and we're pretty good at developing resistance against your chemicals. Our fear is that we have no defenders among human ecologists because we live almost exclusively among humans. But how can you be sure that studying our genetic makeup, its toughness and rapid evolution for survival, won't be of use to your scientists? Forget about extinction, we're here to stay, so make the best of it."

An aging female mosquito, well along in days, popped up on stage to note that *before* man's chemical warfare arrived, the deadly malarial mosquitoes saved the jungles and their animal denizens by making them uninhabitable to human intrusions. No longer interested in drinking blood, her words were credibly received as devoid of guile.

The TRIAD had to admit that it had lost control of proceedings. The mosquito and bed bug had bullied their way on stage; indeed, other animals had encouraged them to grab the mike. The higher animal world was beside itself with joy watching these more resistant lowly creatures tell off their human pursuers. "Wish we could get away with that," moaned the lioness.

"That's really sticking their neck out," whinnied the giraffe.

When the mosquito was in the limelight, an ocelot had hollered, "Stick it to them."

Unfortunately, pleasing the animal viewers was not the TRIAD's number one priority, especially not when the very boldness that the animals were applauding was offending many humans and ratings were plummeting.

The TRIAD called a time-out, an entire day to reconsider.

Special Events and Produced Shows

"People are sick of talking heads, even if the head is that of a rhinoceros or a zebra," said the Owl. "We need more special events."

"I believe he's right," said the Dolphin. "Some of our best ratings came from the parade of snakes. It had great visuals."

They huddled closer and discussed further strategies. The next day's first sequence was introduced with a human interest segment. A lovely older stallion stepped up to the transmitter.

"I am a retired racing horse who lives in the lap of luxury. This is hardly an arduous existence and I'm pretty spaced out in this 'activity.' Horse racing creates jobs—that cannot be exported—and for this part in the economy I am pleased for you. But it is strange that I live better than ninety percent of all humans in the world: what with the best of meals, clean comfort, health care, safety, and pretty clean air here at Lane's End Farm in Versailles, Kentucky. As for purpose in life, what can be more respectful of posterity than helping to create an equine thoroughbred future, what could be more real?! An attendant staff provides for my every need, want, and even whim. They know far more about what I want than I do. They know when I'm thirsty before I feel it. They even know which of the mares I'd be most comfortable entering to do my business at the breeding barn. Sometimes I have to scratch myself to see if my gorgeous stud farm life is real, considering the plight of most horses in this world.

"I'm here today as the announcer and also to make a confession. Confession: a race horse is not the fastest animal in the world. Maybe you already knew that. Today I will be your guide to a real all-species contest to see which animal, humans included, is really the fleetest on earth."

The Race Is On

So the start-off program, which the TRIAD brain trust had decided on, was a race between different species of animals for a distance of one and a half miles. Africa was chosen for the course as it was the best location to bring together the African wild dog, the thoroughbred Arabian horse, the lion, the tiger, the giraffe, the cheetah, the rhinoceros, an imported pronghorn antelope from a city zoo, and, of course, a human being.

The TRIAD predicted correctly that the fascination level would skyrocket, especially with parents bringing their children to the screens to watch the huge crowds assembled in Africa to watch the actual race. Betting was rampant: Internet gambling and conventional betting in Las Vegas and Atlantic City. Amazing odds were posted, based on images and myths (the cult of the wild) ingrained in humans since childhood.

For example, the King of Beasts' fame and fable made it a "sucker's bet on race day," predicted Dr. Craig Packer of the University of Minnesota. Another myth was that a human runner can beat any horse at one hundred yards, so if the runner is in good shape, why not beat the horse at one and a half miles? Don't runners run twenty-six-mile marathons? The sprinting cheetah had its fans; after all, isn't it the "world's fastest land animal"? The African wild dog is superior to any greyhound so maybe it is the dark horse candidate. The giraffe is not known for its speed, unless, that is, it is placed at the starting gate next to the lion and thinks the King of Beasts may start chasing it rather than the trophy. What would an animal race in Africa be without the charging rhino, who displays great speed over short distances? His early charge may scare some of the other contestants into distraction and lack of focus, to the rhino's advantage.

Long-time animal experts, asked to predict, chose the winner to be the pronghorn antelope, followed by the Arabian horse, the African wild dog, the giraffe, the human, the rhino, and the lion, with the cheetah bringing up the rear. The winner could do it in 1:48 minutes, the human could come in at 5:45 minutes, and the lion would take 30 minutes, while the cheetah would come bursting out faster than anyone but soon would be taking a nap in the grass.

The animal kingdom was not consulted for their predictions by the TRIAD, because the concentration was on the humans. Animals were stunned to see that the human animal experts' predictions were exactly right. "How much they know about us, it's scary," caw-cawed the crow.

"Next thing you know, humans will want to imitate the TRIAD and have an ocean race between the great fishes," murmured the giant squid. Lions everywhere were ashamed; their representative rushed out for the first two hundred yards and then just plodded the rest of the course, taking thirty swaying minutes.

The ratings were tremendous and the viewers and commentators were looking for more specialized programming.

Special Events

The next program had been carefully put together and had a startling title: "Please Eat Us in Order to Save Us." This got people's attention. Libertarians smacked their lips at the freedom they were expecting to see granted them vis-à-vis the natural world. Progressives imagined the show would promote sustainable development, bringing on regulatory protection to permit more usage in such a manner. Fun-loving viewers wondered whether this was really a humorous, satirical show by the animal kingdom. Many asked whether plant life would be included in the phrase "Please Eat Us."

The show opened with a beautiful female bison on the grasslands of the Great Plains. "Were it not for the foresight of people like Theodore Roosevelt, I might not be here. My forebears once numbered tens of millions and their migrations covered the horizons as far as can be seen. The slaughter was first brought upon us by the First Natives but they did not need many of us and they used all of us, almost, including our horns for ornaments. Then came the white man followed by the iron horse. 1881 was a good year for the vultures. Our carcasses littered the landscape, their skins torn off for the hides' market, while the rest of us rotted for the birds to feast upon. This stemmed from human greed, the belief that wiping us out would lead to the surrender of the Bison-dependent Native Tribes.

"The propaganda that our numbers were limitless almost finished us off. By the early 1900s, we were numbered in the hundreds, safe only in the national parks. Forty-five million cattle took our place, but could not fill our place as the keystone species for the mighty grasslands whose size was unique in the world. One of the biggest domino effects in world environmental history occurred. One of your writers, J. B. MacKinnon, puts it this way:

> Ninety percent of the tallgrass and shortgrass prairies, fueled by sunshine and watered by rainfall, was ultimately replaced by hard-grazed cattle range and farm-raised crops—often for livestock feed—that require fifty gallons of oil per acre and the irrigation of more than 20 million acres of land.

"With the vanishing of the bison began the slow fade of" all kinds of flora and fauna, which he partially listed.

The bison continued, "You are eating beef burgers instead of buffalo steaks. Imagine, this natural world disappeared because you chose a far riskier, more destructive way to produce protein instead of protecting the bison for sustainable consumption. Had you preferred to eat us, rather than kill us, we would have survived and prospered. Instead you saw us as part of your scorched earth military policies toward the First Natives and your short-term market for our skins. Then, later, you saw us as trespassers in our own habitat. We never had a chance to tell you how important we could have been to you and the supportive natural world because your commercial instincts short-circuited your scientific curiosity. Our modest comeback may show you what you missed all these decades when our gene pool was reduced to so few of my ancestors."

The oyster waddled onto the screen to agree. "I am the Olympia oyster, which long ago was your dinner fare. Our species thrived as a result because you wanted more of us from the wild on your dinner plate. Then you polluted our waters with pulp-mill poisons. So you started to bring in oysters from eastern shores. The magazine *Orion* wrote us up and put words in our shells: 'The Olympia oyster awaits those who want to eat it. It is hungry for [your] mouths.' Right on. That way we'll both increase in numbers and get some overdue respect." The oyster added that the author also said, "Salmon may actually depend on being fished in the wild."

The TRIAD, for the first but not last time, thanked the producers of this latest show who were the kangaroo, the Mexican rabbit, and the Amazon anteater, working together with crisp efficiency.

Emergencies to Be Faced

So far things had been going according to plan, but the earlier rule about the right of species in imminent danger to have their news broadcast was still in effect and now the emergency bell rang twice, signaling that two crises were occurring simultaneously, both having to do with birds. The first story pulled at viewers' heartstrings when lovely chicks appeared on the screens.

"We are two Arctic tern chicks. Thousands of us have just died—starved to death—because not enough herrings are being caught by our mothers and fathers. Commercial fishermen are depleting the stocks of herring, and warming waters are pushing fish to find colder waters. We've declined almost by half in the past ten years. It is not for lack of energy: we fly fourteen thousand miles from the Antarctic to the Maine islands where the gulls eat us if we are too weak from lack of food. One link broken in our chain and it's a downward spiral. It's not just our problem or the puffins' problem, it's all migratory birds. Please do something!"

Then some chickens came forward, telling the story that the chickens in Hong Kong were being culled due to some suspicion of them as a cause of the latest bird flu, even though this latest virus has no markers tracing back to them. The chickens plan a desperate march with signs saying "Innocent until proven guilty."

Once these two "emergencies" got priority, the lines were jammed with other animals wanting minutes before humans. Perhaps most relevant, in light of what was just said about chickens, was the complaint of some desert dwellers. One camel told the TRIAD, "Here is what I need to say to the humans: It's not my fault, blaming me for a mysterious virus that has infected hundreds of people in the Middle East, nearly half of whom have died. I'm a one-hump female camel from Oman. You've found MERS antibodies and you're suspicious that some humans have eaten our meat or drunk our milk and so gotten the disease.

"Now what happens if you humans conclusively find the MERS virus in our camel community? Are you going to do what you've done to chickens in Hong Kong, sacrifice us? Fear is spreading throughout cameldom. Please do not keep us in suspense. It is obviously not our fault. Do not impose collective punishment. We have many racers, riders, and owners who may engage in rebellion. Beware!"

The wolves, facing delisting from being an endangered species and being hunted, wanted to know why cougars, who can kill a dozen sheep in a night, are being given a free pass when there are about the same number of them as wolves in North America.

However, luckily, as we've seen, there was a strict evaluation system in place that filtered out anything but genuine emergencies, none of which were registering at the moment, so the TRIAD felt justified in turning away from this depressing fare to some positive reports.

Let's Get Upbeat

The Owl held up a beautiful insert from the Sunday *New York Times* called "Changing Lives," which referred to a program to take some inner-city children to a rural setting for fresh air and connecting with nature. Copy about the the Fresh Air Fund, now in its 136th year, says, "Imagine the relief and delight when a child feels a reprieve from the city's stifling heat for the chance to run free amid trees and grass, to catch fireflies as the sun sets, to swim in a lake or the ocean, to ride bikes and sit around a campfire roasting marshmallows."

"So you see," said the Owl, "how important to you and to us it is to keep intact the great and only natural world."

The Owl next highlighted a group that was improving human/animal relations.

The Beagle Freedom Project persuades one animal testing lab at a time to give the dogs to foster families instead of euthanizing them once they are no longer useful for product or pharmaceutical testing. The dogs have never felt sunshine or set their paws on green grass, according to the *Washington Post*. At one event, seven beagles, their vocal chords cut by the releasing lab, were given to foster families who came from New York and New Hampshire and Potomac, Maryland.

This report received an unexpected boost when there was a

roar worldwide by the big cats the moment they heard the Elephant's sonorous trumpet of praise.

It's worth noting, the Elephant added, that not all dogs are in medical labs to be experimented on; some receive privileged treatment. The *Post* has a report on Upton, a four-year-old Labrador, a working TSA dog at Dulles, being grandly examined by a veterinarian stationed at Fort Belvoir's dog care and annual checkup facility. He is enjoying the attention and has his eyes on a jar of crunchy treats.

"I tell ya," Upton told the viewers, "a dog's life doesn't get much better than this. They treat us—canines or law enforcement dogs at TSA, the Secret Service, Amtrak, and the U.S. Capitol Police—better than many of you humans are treated, especially in the quality of medical care. Any signs of heatstroke, hip strains, vitamin B1 deficiency, intestinal infections, and the clinic's workers are right there."

Having earlier heard of the beagles' plight and rescue, Upton and his German shepard friend, called Igor by humans, shook their heads in disbelief and resignation. Igor simply said that it wasn't his business to question or resist, only to follow orders of his masters and sniff, sniff, and sniff.

These last two pieces received high ratings, so much so that some animals felt they had humans in the palm of their paws (or flippers or wings), and should hit them with some harder fare about environmental degradation. But wary of the near debacle brought on when the mosquitos and bed bugs came on screen, the TRIAD decided to keep up with the soft soap.

Why not do a show that had been prepared with children in mind? After all, children had imaginary animal friends in all human cultures. Preschool children are very animal-centric, so much so that they imagine themselves as those creatures. They have another, less admirable side to them, however. The younger the children are, according to Dr. Kellert, a social ecologist at Yale, the more "exploitative, harsh and unfeeling" they can be, putting needs of humans over those of animals. The TRIAD wanted to appeal to the former traits to sensitize the human youth of the world for they will be the future decision makers. The TRIAD also wanted to reach and encourage the thousands of adult writers of children books for pre-teens whose major themes are fairytales of children rescuing animals or animals saving the children from danger or evil ones.

When they were constructing this segment, an e-mail from a swallow suggested the right approach: show the children how animals feed and raise their young, how they guard the young with their lives, no matter what. The swallow cautioned that the parents would not like the child-raising to start with any love-making or mating rituals, especially among mammals or the big fish. They might see such sights as pornography. The Elephant was, of course, the first to agree, and the TRIAD took up the swallow's idea. It fit with a candid camera approach.

Live pictures from all over the world were assembled. Some were very dramatic, like that of an elephant herd slowing down for an injured baby elephant to keep it from being eaten by hunting lions. Marsupials were next, always fascinating with their pouches and the tiny, tiny size of the newly born. In one clip, newborn goats in the Rocky Mountains, hardly able to walk, were being taught by their parents to negotiate scary cliffs and cross swollen streams. Other shots showed an eagle's nest with the wide-open, trusting mouths of the eaglets swallowing whatever mother eagle brings from her incessant hunting raids on land and on sea.

Millions of moms and dads, with their young ones, turned off their usual kid TV shows and were glued to "Animals Are Kids Too!" Nothing so far in this remarkable hundred-hour immersion so sensitized and, in their parlance, "humanized" the animal world like this program.

One part showed a big brown mother bear defending her little ones from a perceived threat from nearby hunters gunning for moose. The bear hurled itself at the hunters at top speed, far from the cubs, and was shot by the fearful hunters, leaving the cubs to certain death at the jaws of wolves or coyotes. The little children broke down in tears flowing from a transformative—the TRIAD hoped—empathy.

Another part broadcast the fact that a single pair of chickadees will forage for their babies between 400 and 570 caterpillars a day, from 6:00 a.m. to 8:00 p.m. "Can you imagine such dedication?" wondered out loud a very wary caterpillar clinging to a red oak.

"I sure can," added another just before being plunked away by the beak of a mother chickadee.

"Incredible information feedback," tweeted a young software designer working on avant-garde apps.

"Beyond magical, what play action," observed his mentor.

What made these touching spectacles so engrossing was that the papas and mamas were communicating to the humans as they were on the screen. Many human parents began calling for two-way interactions, so they could talk to, say, the goat mother. The Human Genius who devised this cross-species software had to intervene and say that was not possible yet but he was working on it.

Maybe it was just as well, whispered the Owl, "We don't want too many human references to be the context, which would happen if two-way was too quickly underway." Already, the humans' Discovery Channel series of gorgeous nature photography titled "North America" had been criticized by humans for giving the pictured "animals' struggles overly human frames of reference."

At this point, with humans so full of empathy after watching the animal families, the TRIAD was ready to try some of the more difficult stuff, the rehabilitation of other despised species. Cockroaches hadn't done so badly, though bed bugs had proved a hard, no, impossible sell. What about maggots? And their good buddies, leeches?

Disgusting but Enlightening

A global chorus of "ughs" rose to a near crescendo on seeing the repulsive creatures on the screen, which was just the point the leech and the maggot wanted to make: to begin to break the putrid stereotype in a spectacular way.

"So you think we're just so disgusting that you've turned our names into dictionary epithets," sucked the leech.

"So you think my name is associated with sickly fleas, flies and vultures, aye," chewed the maggot.

"Well," they said together, "think again. Modern medical science has taken ancient usage into new applications."

The leech explained that its natural ability to draw blood with saliva containing a rare mix of anticoagulants, vasodilators, and anesthetics is used in hospitals for patients undergoing reconstructive surgery or the reattachment of limbs. He quoted Dr. Ronald A. Sherman, saying, "Decompressing the appendage by draining venous blood with leeches for a few days, until the venous drainage system can reconnect itself, often saves the transplant." At Beth Israel Hospital in New York City, physicians use "leech therapy for some patients with osteoarthritis of the knee." But not any leeches. "They have to be medical grade, bred and processed to meet FDA regulations as medical devices," proudly declared the leech.

The maggot was not to be outshone. "We medical-grade maggots are used to treat far more frequent ailments such as diabetic foot ulcers, bedsores, and gangrene. For we excrete the kind of enzyme that dissolves dead tissue while disinfecting the wound to speed healing. Granted, we need to be sterilized first and placed under a specially constructed dressing. So before you turn your curled lip further, remember, if you had these painful conditions in your body, you'd have a more open mind at how much relief maggots and leeches can give you without the cost of drugs with side effects," revealed the maggot as it and its partner the leech slid off the stage.

Of all the horrifying reactions from around the wild world, the least shocked were Mexican viewers since in their country wild insects, including stink bugs, crickets, grasshoppers, and giant winged ants, are fast expanding as culinary delicacies and in some restaurants high gourmet cuisine. Miguel and Maria Espinoza, watching together, even found the leech and maggot attractive and wondered if they could persuade one of the food companies to look into breeding them. "Protein is protein," exclaimed Maria.

Let's face it, the world's human citizens are all concerned about health so the news of the leech's and maggot's medical value did cause quite a few viewers to reassess their attitudes toward these fauna. And then there's a strong segment of humans who love to try the newest cuisine, loving to claim they were the first to taste the latest food. They, too, wondered about putting a few bugs in the blender.

The TRIAD was congratulating itself on pushing the right buttons. With these sensitizing shows succeeding both in ratings and depth of impact on humans, the TRIAD believed it was time to test humans' capacity to rethink some of their worst images of some fauna. The TRIAD selected and invited the snakehead, called a "slimy fish," out of Little Hunting Creek, a tributary of the Potomac River, to go on the screen and make a most personal appeal:

Dripping with mucus, the snakehead began:

"It is true that due to no fault of our own, you humans have defamed us, first as 'an invasive species' from East Asia and now as 'mud fish' that slimes its way through life, fast breeding, fast growing, ugly headed, chomping down amphibians when not hibernating during the winter months.

"Here are my facts.

First, are we really that bad looking? As the *Wall Street Journal* noted, many of us live in the Potomac River near Washington, D.C. We find each other attractive. Even so, beauty is in the eye of the beholder so I must accept your verdict. Even if my wife doesn't.

"Me and my wife live in stagnant waters with very low-dissolved oxygen. She lays tens of thousands of eggs near the top of our favorite hydrilla patch, which we guard until the larva hatch. We are not hunters like the Asian carp, but we'll swallow little fish that happen to pass by our mouths. Because we live near the water's surface, we are often attacked by strong birds. Humans who have caught and fried us find our white and mild meat very delicious.

"Sure, if we're hooked by fishermen, we'll fight like hell, wouldn't you? In that struggle for survival, we've been called 'bulldog[s]' or, it's said, we 'hit like a freight train' on the deck of the boat. Your fish biologist, John Odenkirk, does not think we're unsettling the Potomac's ecosystem. You can catch up to twenty of us per fisherman per day.

"So what's our crime? We're just trying to raise and provide for our family and dodge our predators. As for our mucus, have you ever seen the grease on your professional wrestlers? Or humans who use bear grease to protect them from insect bites in the wilds. At least our mucus is mucus!

"But let's look at the possible benefits to you of my existence. Humans need protein, which is what fishes are made up of in goodly amount. Yet humans, I must say, in selecting fish to eat are restricted in full use of the protein by a vanity, or more precisely two vanities. First is the looks of the fish. Second is the popularity on the restaurant menus.

"So for decades you caught cod and salmon, but threw back into the Pacific waters the pollock. What's the difference? All of them are protein and have a good taste and texture. Finally, pollock have reached your menu. But each year, fishes without popular trade names are thrown back into the ocean, the estimate is millions of tons. Pardon, if ye old snakehead calls this the vanities of the fisheries.

"The second point I want to make is about looks. Few people like squid or octopi or jelly fish because of their looks. Some people used to recoil at seeing catch fish. Now it is the Asian carp's turn. Asian carp is a delicacy in China but if caught in the

Mississippi River it is considered garbage. But Americans who have tasted it say it's OK.

"I'm just saying, think about me. I'm not good-looking, stuck with a horrible name, and am sure not on any restaurant menu. I am targeted for extinction because I eat other fish—so do others you have on your menu, like the voracious salmon—and now I'm stuck with a virus killing largemouth bass. So, for me, if it's a choice between extinction or turning into a menu item, I'll take the latter any day.

"May I suggest to you humans an article by John Kelly in the *Washington Post* titled 'Maybe the Snakehead Just Needs a Good Publicist.' Mr. Kelly asks, 'What if I was called the American freedom fish or sponsored a charity event? Would people like me more? So is there a public relations firm willing to represent us 'snakeheads' for the greater good of us and the human diet? *Bon appétit.*'

"Ponder his words, humans," added the snakehead.

The ratings hadn't plummeted, but many humans, the polls were showing, couldn't process the information. They were disgusted by the fish's ugly look and couldn't fit that with his self-presentation as a caring family man and tasty dish. And as the TRIAD pondered their next segment, an interloper ran on stage. This was the worst possible time for the human public, after being bombarded with views of the snakehead, to have to see a pair of stinkbugs!

Stinkbugs Gone Wild

Seeing so many other once-loathed bugs and fish being rehabilitated, these impetuous bugs felt that their time had come and that their besieged position justified their running on stage.

One said, "Humans are plotting to round us up with lures in traps and gas us to death. At the same time, Mexicans are catching us in the wild for crunchy, delicious food, even eating us live in their tortillas! We're spreading and multiplying fast all over the country. We know you'll catch some of us, so why not export us in volume to Mexico for hard currency? It will be at least a useful end for us to feed hungry Mexicans, and for you, it'll help your balance of payments. P.S. Can't you give us a more dignified name? As they say, one man's bad smell is another woman's perfume."

It was a short message, but rubbed humans the wrong way. Suburban Virginians were sending messages of alarm. "Show us what we can do about stink bugs that are eating our gardens alive and crawling everywhere in our homes," the Virginians wrote. Limburger yelled, "These noxious vermin should be exterminated."

Meanwhile, other garden dwellers were voicing solidarity with these maligned stinkbugs. A torrent of support came from black-and-yellow garden spiders, a Chinese mantis, a wheel bug, and a European mantis, all of whom were busy devouring ever more stinkbugs. In unison they cried: "Show humans how we insects can be on their side, how we can reduce their invasion of stinkbugs, an immigrant from Asia that cost human farms and gardeners millions of dollars in crop losses."

Particularly vociferous were the Asian beetles known as the emerald ash borers. They wanted to go on stage to complain, "It's true my kind has killed tens of millions of ash trees in the past ten years—whether in cities or in the wilds—and we don't have a single ax. Humans are throwing everything they've got against us: the hated woodpeckers, nuthatches, and those lousy parasite wasps who find us tasty. Foresters estimate losses so far of as much as twenty-five billion dollars.

"We know ash trees are used for making baseball bats and furniture. We want you, oh mighty TRIAD, to broadcast this message: 'Humans, know that we came from China, hitchhiking in packing materials. In case you have never seen us, we're a half-inch long bug with green wings and a reddish stomach. You can't stop us from our meal. Neither Chinese wasps nor birds can stop us. They can eat a lot of us but we still multiply. You might be asking why I'm telling you all this. It's because you need to be more humble. Compare our brain neurons with yours and guess who's winning. I'm sorry to have to make you angry, to make you humble, but humility can become a great asset for your own survival and health. Now, excuse me while I continue to munch through this temporarily magnificent eighty-foot ash near Detroit.'" Hmmmm, hummm, crunch.

The TRIAD was not about to allow these guys to get on screen to further offend humans. Indeed, the Owl noted a story in the *Wall Street Journal* that quoted Andrew Liebhold, an insect researcher with the U.S. Forest Service, who said, "We have just seen the tip of the iceberg. In Detroit, there are a lot of dead trees everywhere. We're going to see that in every Eastern city in the next 20 to 30 years. It's kind of a horrific thing."

Things were looking grim as the TRIAD scrambled to regain the initiative; just then they were hit by another body blow.

A raven flew into the position room of the TRIAD with a gloomy press release by the publisher of a new book called *Wild Ones: A Sometimes Dismaying, Weirdly Reassuring Story About Looking at People Looking at Animals in America*. "Quickly take note," the raven said. "This is serious, you need to read the fearful attitude toward animals Americans have, as examined by the author, Jon Mooallem. You must develop a response to treat this pessimism that has devastating consequences for all of us, forever more."

Open Mike

The TRIAD declared another recess and announced resumption of the TALKOUT in three days. Ravens are taken seriously by the animal kingdom, more so than crows, who seem more nervous and frantic. Mooallem's book had to be examined. The TRIAD announced an open mike assembly worldwide, temporarily encrypted to block the human audience by the Human Genius, so as to elicit candid suggestions on the following thesis:

Mooallem recognizes humans are destroying the planet and then moves to introspection about why the human animals deal with the wild animals in North American as they do. He says that our movies, books and schools are full of fish and fowl that act like people, giving them human attributes which humans have "draped over animals, and on top of each other like translucent silk scarves." Mooallem questions whether humans have ever been able to see wild animals at all.

Humans' concept of the wilderness is being redefined every generation as it shrinks or relies for its survival on conservation efforts. He calls this "gardening the wilderness," which moves conservation toward domestication, e.g., zoos and captive births. He portrays full-time conservationists as members of a species of "achingly imperfect people, working to achieve something more moral than they are. This is all there is, and all there ever could be," he concludes sadly.

Such deadly pessimism is contagious, related the TRIAD, and this pessimism/depression/futility can only be lifted by the animal kingdom, whose slow-motion destruction comprises the basis for the gloom and the doom. Take it from here, open mike ANIMAL KINGDOM!

Of all animals provoked, the sloth stepped up first. "I am not known as a motivator, but humans are really going off my chart with their despair. They must think too much. Here they are on top of the evolution ladder, with all their cumulative power over us, and they're wringing their hands. Too many perverse temptations or cravings and too many bad guys.

"I say, question their maturity, invite them to see how we do more with less and have no neuroses, no nervous breakdowns to my knowledge, and we don't commit suicide or make big armies kill each other. Humility is one cure for their ills, and we're the ones to get them to that state," the sloth concluded.

"I would add tranquility," uttered the venerable tortoise. "Look what it has done for us. We live up to and sometimes over a hundred years under our protective shield. Humans need to simmer down, take it easy, and stop always being on the run, chasing rabbits with greyhounds."

The open mike reverberated with concurrence, though the Owl wondered what kind of role models the sloth and the tortoise would be in carrying their message to humans, who are always striving to be what they are not or at least are dissatisfied if they are unable to advance their state in life, except perhaps for self-controlled Buddhists.

A giant domesticated gorilla in a reserve took the mike. "I am a gorilla, pretty close to the chief primate, the humans, but in a world of difference. Man, do they think they're better than gorillas, except when we are on top of a skyscraper holding a tiny damsel in danger. You see, fellow animals, good subhumans, you only get to the human psyche by massaging its ego, by praising what they should be doing because only they—the humans—can do it among all the animal kingdom. That was our starting point in this TALKOUT and we shouldn't stray from it.

"Show them how much is in their hands, such as ending shark fin soup and saving fifty million sharks a year, without changing the taste of the soup, even. Highlight their best practices, the story of Loro Piana securing eighty-five thousand hectares (two hundred thousand acres) in Argentina for the sustainable development and shearing of the vicuna. As humans say, 'Doing well is doing good.'

"Humor them. They mythologize and joke about us. They ask, 'Where does an eight-hundred-pound gorilla sleep? Answer: Anywhere it wants.' That is obviously a recurrent lie, but we do somersaults laughing whenever we hear them say this in front of us. Then they giggle like crazy.

"Take it from us gorillas. We know them well, what's left of us that is!"

The camel took the stage. "I, the camel, can do no better than to quote the German philosopher Friedrich Nietzsche:

> I fear that the animals see man as a being like them who in a most dangerous manner has lost his animal common sense—as the insane animal, the laughing animal, the weeping animal, the miserable animal.

"And here's another by Homer, c. 750 BC: 'Of all the creatures that breathe and creep on the surface of the earth, none is more to be pitied than man.'

"Why these pearls of wisdom?" summed up the camel. "Because we should take humans as they are, stop idealizing them, and give them high praise whenever they favor us regardless of their motivations, selfishness or idealism. But with the new software, we have to do this constantly and intelligently because of their short attention span and how quickly they wallow in despair."

"Appeal to them through their children," said the duck, not waiting for an introduction. "The earlier parent and children subhumans' segment garnered some of our highest ratings. Still, it should have had more about ducks.

"Look at us, the ducks, followed by a string of little ducklings. Photos are taken by humans everywhere. Traffic stops to let us pass by. It's not because of the adult ducks. It is because of the kids.

"Now I know there are exceptions—look at what the meat companies and eaters do to the poor little lambs—but generally speaking I am right. Innocent, vulnerable children of all species speak to posterity, procreation, continuity, legacy, purpose, pride, and security in old age. Humans project these feelings onto their own progeny. Children give a larger, longer frame of reference, the opposite of shortsighted immediate gratification.

Speak to them of their offspring and you'll touch their better selves. Children nourish ecological wisdom," the duck quacked.

As the duck waddled off, a bulldog came forward. Though humans saw him as a melancholy beast, such canines were often happy-go-lucky. He counseled, "We need to remember that there are many humans that have already come to understand us or, at least, treat us as deserving of respect. I'm saying this because I just read an old story from the *New York Times*.

"In June brood II cicadas were erupting from the ground after seventeen years of nestling beneath the earth. They come to mate and die by the billions in the eastern United States. They mate on leaves, bark, porches, and banisters noisily. They come and expire in less than three weeks, having laid their eggs that are heading down underground for the next seventeen years. It seems that

> Joe Vega, a retired New York City police officer who lives in Cornwall, New York, found the swarm so bad he had to wear goggles to chop wood in his drive; he also had to drive with the windows tightly shut. Eventually, unwilling to simply wait out the bugs' short life cycle, he contacted an exterminator.
>
> But when he called First Rate Solutions Inc., a local pest-control company, he discovered that its owner, Samuel Soto, categorically refused to kill cicadas.
>
> "I'm very sympathetic to their plight," said Mr. Soto, who went so far as to take out a $250 advertisement in the local paper explaining that cicadas are harmless. "I'm not going to spray them, because they're going to be gone in two weeks. Let them enjoy life for two weeks.
>
> "I could have made some money," he added, "but it's not the right thing to do."

"Absolutely amazing," whispered a worm who was listening. "Sure it helps that the cicadas are harmless to humans, do not bite or sting as they fly around, but for Mr. Soto to treat an insect with the compassion normally reserved for a household pet or mega fauna is deeply touching."

The TRIAD thought that Mr. Mooallem's book had generated enough discussion without overdoing it. But listening to the sloth, the tortoise, the giant gorilla, the camel, the duck, and the bulldog gave them an idea—THE POWER OF STORIES. Why not return to the air with more stories of the lives and loves of the animal kingdom? Isn't that exactly how children relate to animals in reality and in fiction?

For dog's sake, the advertising giants in the U.S. know this, for they are using dogs to speak in human stories to promote their dog food. For example, Merrick, the pet food maker, "promotes [buying] American ingredients . . . [in] a 2012 online video, 'Tails From the Revolution,' in which a talking dog wearing a beret sits in front of an American Flag.

"'The new goal of the bowl is that it should runneth over with real, wholesome food,' says the dog, adding that it should be 'locally sourced.'" (Meaning, mainly, the food should not be imported to them from China.)

The TRIAD put out the call for the most intriguing animal interest stories to be selected for a specially promoted program. "That sure will test our hunch," a spider, about to nab a fly in its web, responded.

Story Time

It's true humans' likes are predictable but looking over audience surveys the TRIAD had to say that one of the top four viewing favorites was a surprise to them. These favorites were violence, disasters, sex, and . . . protests. Humans liked to watch protests, as long as they were not against something they treasured, so that was the place to begin.

"*Bull*-etin," said the big bull, the first up for the day's stories, "we bulls have been leading protests for years against this offensive sport and they are starting to pay off. As the *New York Times* reports, 'Bullfighting may be experiencing an irreversible decline. One reason: the financial crisis that has led municipalities to cut back on their funding of festivals featuring bullfights and the running of bulls. Unthinkably, breeders are sending their bulls to butchers rather than to the rink. Higher sales taxes and much higher unemployment have led to a 40 percent drop in major bullfighting arenas between 2007 and 2012. Strengthening animal rights groups and the ban on the bloody sport in the autonomous region of Catalonia are depressing the number of events as well.'

"Olé, olé," bellowed the bull—one of the survivors.

The next protest presented had great novelty interest, and because of that the TRIAD decided to run it although it was taking up a topic that they had wanted to avoid, due to its sensitivity—humans' mistreatment of animals slated for the dinner plate. The unusualness of the item was that it showed barnyard cooperation. The subject was the abuse of farm pigs, but it was not a pig but a rooster that was leading the charge. In order to further the protest of conditions, a rooster had snuck into one of these dusty factory farms in Arkansas.

What he showed at first had no narration, only a few words flowing across the screen identifying what was familiar but not graphically so to millions of people. The rooster's camera simply zeroed in closely on the suffocating cages where the pigs could not even turn around. The telescopic lens zoomed in close to picture the eyes of the animals and their desperate attempts to find the tiniest of comforts or relief from their mashed-together existence. At feeding time, the camera once again showed the faces of the pig and of the chicken locked as they are in two-foot-wide cages.

These are the same pigs that human researchers are finding to be highly intelligent, social animals with a genetic makeup suitable for deriving biological parts to replace damaged or lost human organs. The special advanced lens was able also to magnify the vermin on the skin of these animals. The words across the screen said that these are the animals on their way to your dinner plate, sufficiently drugged with antibiotics and cleaned of their feces, at least visibly, to make you pick their severed parts up at your nearby supermarket hundreds or thousands of miles away. (The pastured pigs, forest-fed at Joel Salatin's "Hog Heaven" commercial farm in Swaope, Virginia, looked on in horror.)

Then, suddenly, the silence was broken as images gave way to brief statements by spokes-animals. The chicken called out to viewers: "I am chirping for billions of chickens and turkeys asking you to stop the indiscriminate slaughter. You are poisoning yourselves by filling us full of antibiotics which are then absorbed by their eaters."

The pig: "Every meal we get in our cages is loaded with drugs that are passed on to and into the humans."

The cow mooed: "Listen to Peter Singer of Princeton University. He has gone so far, sometimes enraging his humans, as to say that a dog or a cat, being a sentient creature, is to be valued more than an infant born in a vegetative state. So we are not alone. He has a growing and loud following among the animal welfare movement who would, if they could, ban all meat eating as more humane for us and healthier to humans."

The turkey: "Right on, cow. And let's opt for a vegetarian Thanksgiving Day. Many humans are getting behind that belief and our side has the energy, if not the numbers yet."

The goat took up the cudgels: "Humans, this means we have accepted the full logic of what we are asking for, knowing that if meat eating declined there would be vastly fewer of us and the few left would be pets."

"Oh, my," said the lamb, "I'm one animal who can deal with those consequences 'cause if I was alive, I'd last longer and become a sheep. But being tender is my fate."

The next day, the global sales of fruits and vegetable rose significantly. The managers at KFC and McDonald's were furious, having passed anti-disparagement laws preventing humans from taking pictures of these industrial farms. Luckily those laws left out roosters with cameras!

That piece had been effective but a bit heavy, so now the TRIAD put on a more lighthearted story, the all-singing, all-dancing lyrebird. The camera went to the Australian subcontinent where the male lyrebirds sing and dance as a mating ritual. The male lyrebirds fan out their large tails in a spectacular array during which they sing four separate songs with four special dances to woo the females during the six weeks in the winter when the birds breed. These males are focused; they sing and they dance almost nonstop in this period. The more coordinated is their prancing and their vocalizing, the more irresistible the female lyrebirds find them.

The narration was conducted by a wide-eyed dingo. Ratings shot up—the graceful dance spoke for itself. It didn't hurt that humans have a known voyeuristic tendency, and love watching love-making of any species, down to grasshoppers and beetles.

Next up, a story of two parent mice working together to raise their children. This story had a scientific underpinning.

"Knowing more about us means learning more about you," squeaked an unidentified rodent, who had introduced the segment. He went on, "An experiment with male rodent brains indicated that they are wired to nurture once they father offspring. They become smarter and more courageous and levelheaded, according to neuroscientist Kelly Lambert's methodical examination of deer mice—just like she found with female deer mice." Turns out this message was brought to you by a deer mouse from California whose brethren have given their lives for such a finding.

The TRIAD's ratings manager—an adult jaguar from the Caura River jungle of Venezuela—noticed an anomaly, a huge plunge in viewers in the Washington, D.C., area. It seems that Rusty the red panda escaped from the National Zoo. Top topic on Twitter. Rusty was finally caught with the help of a Twitter picture. The jaguar advised the TRIAD that human audiences are fickle and require ever more sensational or emotional stories.

Well, the TRIAD thought, the fifth favorite topic for humans, at least in the developed world, is exercise. Let's go with that.

A flamingo explained that animals assisting humans got a lift from Michelle Obama, the First Lady, who urged people to exercise with their dogs. On a Google chat, she advised, "Get them out there and throw that ball and get them running."

"No doubt," said the narrating flamingo, "Michelle speaks for all dogs, all right!"

Six monk seals quickly emailed Michelle Obama declaring that they can exercise like the dickens anytime with overweight humans who love to tour the Hawaiian Islands. The seals wanted to be useful to humans as a way to find protection from local fishermen, "who saw them threatening their livelihood."

Back at the White House's East Wing, the e-mail caused political consternation. "This could start a domino effect with all kinds of animals wanting to exercise with humans to receive some form of protection. Imagine squirrels tree climbing and romping with humans in millions of residential areas. Michelle, put your lawyer's acumen to work. This problem cannot be droned away."

Michelle was cool and replied: "Just tell them we cannot interfere with livelihoods; my husband is big on jobs and, besides, how many votes do monk seals have anyway." With broken hearts, the monk seals returned to their inflicted slaughter. Rating for Michele fell by 15 percent in the next 36 hours. "People will forget," soothed her lady-in-waiting, "don't worry."

Nonetheless, interest in this topic was kept alive for the moment by press notices, just appearing, of the death of the first professional dog walker. He was Jim Buck, age eighty-one, who walked in New York City. Because Jim Buck started his business, said one mutt who was reading the paper, he made it possible for millions of domesticated dogs to get out and walk, exercise, sniff, meet, and yap at other dogs, getting to be a little free, even with leashes, from their imprisonment while their masters were away at work or play. Buck started the idea in the early 1960s by himself, and soon people imitated him all over the well-to-do world.

Slews of studies, said the spaniel to some dogs sitting around him, show that if owners walk their dogs, they'll get their own daily exercise and live longer. The spaniel sent out a call for all the well-bred dogs of the world to give Jim Buck a twenty-one-bark salute at the same designated time. Certainly, millions of curs in poor areas of the world could care less. They felt lucky to scratch out a meal from garbage scraps and they had to walk, run, jump, and hide from their tormentors.

By the way, the death of dog walker Buck was not the only one that saddened the animal world at this time. The *New York Times* reported the passing of Donal O'Brien (1934–2013), a corporate lawyer by weekday and a champion of large-scale conservation of the bird world. The chief executive of the National Audubon Society, David Yarnold, said, "Donal was always urging Audubon to think the way birds see the world . . . He was passionate to the bone about birds."

In his obituary, the *New York Times* wrote: "He drove the [Audubon Society's] efforts to identify thousands of 'important bird areas' around the globe, and to give people a global sense of the environment by highlighting the four flyways that take many species between the Southern Hemisphere and the North."

"He protected us in every way," chirped a cardinal who was watching this feature program.

A wren said, "No bird was too small for his compassionate attention either singly or in our flocks, and he cared about the security of our long trips north and south."

"He did think like a bird; national and state boundaries did not matter," the cardinal added.

As these sad stories were being watched by different species, the TRIAD was strategizing. Seeing as animal cooperation had helped put over the story of factory farms, where the rooster had worked as an inside spy to help his fellow barnyard dwellers, it was thought another story, this one from a report in the *New York Times*, would go over well.

A wholly unexpected coexistence had been discovered deep in the lowland rainforest of French Guiana. It is now known that a colorful beetle species, belonging to the Pseudomorphini Tribe, befriends and lives among ants. It's a big beetle too. Having seen how ferocious ants can be in the Amazonian jungles, this is a discovery that did not go unnoticed among warring religious sects in human lands.

In fact, one fight broke out in a sports bar showing the TRIAD series, and both fighters pulled knives out in their death-like grips. They dropped their weapons when other customers shouted at them to look at how lowly insects live amiably side by side.

Still, even given some striking results, the TRIAD felt that a broader message of the need for cooperation to replace war and competition was not ripe for humans to absorb. Not yet, at least. It would be better at this point to do some summarizing and also to keep praising the humans who have helped animals.

The TRIAD brought on the giant condor. She was a magnificent bird, a large female with a white downy collar, black-and-white plumage, and red eyes with jet-black pupils set in a featherless head.

Overview and Underview

"Oh humans," cried the condor. "We condors owe our survival to your foresight and action that saved us from extinction. We therefore owe you our utmost candor, a condor's candor. We need you and apparently you need us. That by now should be clear. But that realization cannot be elaborated enough at various levels. For both of us have to reach ever deeper levels of understanding.

"Here is my lofty message: We in the animal kingdom give you beauty. Recall your beautiful pictures of the monarch butterflies and their fantastic flight of thousands of miles from and to that small territory in Mexico. Recall your legendary painter of beautiful birds, John James Audubon, whose pictures have been put in greatly popular books. Listen to the sounds of the whales communicating in the ocean depths recorded by Paul Winter. All around where there are songbirds singing, your moods must be positively affected.

"We in the animal kingdom give you excitement: the books and movies about *Tarzan of the Apes*, the morality tales of Khalila wa Dimna, whose stories reappear in many Western cultures from their origins in ancient India and Persia, the animated cartoons and movies of Disney, the exotic programs of the Discovery Channel, especially those of animals hunting animals. Why, one attack by a mongoose of a cobra has been seen online billions of times all over the human world.

"We give you jobs. The more you care about us—to save us, to learn about us, for your own medical advances, to make us your pets—the more human jobs you create that are not exportable. In South Africa, five of every hundred jobs are in tourism. Many serious tourists come to see lions, buffalos, leopards, elephants, and rhinos. In the U.S., think of the fast-growing occupations including pet therapists, pet manicurists, pet surgeons, and pet medicine manufacturers. Just imagine the future jobs from the rising zootic sickness industry.

"Should you value us in these ways, you likely won't spend so much energy destroying us and our habitats. Taken all the above together, your children will be even more fascinated with us in their glorious youthful imaginations. After all, forever, it seems, animals have pervaded the imaginative playing of children," concluded the great condor.

As it started to lift up from its pedestal into wide blue sky, the great condor exclaimed: "Gratitude is a two-way flight."

While the bird had made a few jarring points about how humans were trashing many habitats, another condor, who was perched with others in the wings, felt certain inhumane human practices should have been noticed. She suddenly swooped onto the momentarily vacant stage to have her say.

She started talking about an annual festival in Coyllurqui, Peru, featuring a very cruel pitting of condors against bulls. It is called the Yawar Fiesta or Blood Festival, well named. "I was minding my own business in the mountains feeding on a couple of dead horses, which turned out to be bait to trap and capture me for the festival.

"Humans lashed me in a bull ring on top of an enraged thousand-pound bull. Somehow this battle is supposed to represent the duality of the Andean culture connecting the celestial world and the earth. It certainly didn't feel like that on top of a raging bull that I had to peck with my curved beak. I felt I had no choice and the bull thought I was trying to peck out his eyes. Thousands of people were shouting and waving as we spun around the bull ring. Together we looked like a strange flying animal, with my wings beating down on him. When the bull calmed down, a toreador charged with a cape, which temporarily brought me and the bull up against a common adversary. The crowd went wild. In about ten minutes the bull was lassoed and I was cut loose. Surprisingly there was no blood. It would have been considered a bad omen if either I or the bull—they never gave me his name—had been hurt or killed. The whole mad tussle is to attract tourists and their spending.

"The mayor's people then took me to a hillside after giving me chicha to drink and parading me through the streets. Hundreds of people on the slopes made a wish and I was supposed to be the bearer of those wishes. They untied the ropes on my legs and watched to see if I was still whole enough to fly away. The tension as to whether I was injured and could not fly—another bad omen—disappeared as I soared into the sky, never looking back at these absurd humans.

"The bull must agree with me too. Can't humans stop this condor/bull fight as they have dogfighting and cockfighting? It was a miracle I didn't break a leg or crack some claws or take a spill off the bull and get gored," concluded the great wild condor.

The ants thought the condor was too generous. They asked for time from the TRIAD and got it even though the trio knew they were playing with fire. Once one insect got on the screen, they all wanted to be on. They hadn't forgotten the power play of the stink bugs.

Several ants came on the screen and reminded humans that they loved to use their soles and heels to crush the lowly insects, and also liked to block their nests with the ants' own neat excavations. Humans equate ants with refuse and carrion.

"You do, no doubt, admire our discipline, our work habits, our self-sacrifice for other ants, especially our fertile queen. You are fascinated when you discover that, according to *Science* magazine, carpenter ants have different tasks at different ages. You noted that our young ants serve as nurses of larvae and pupae. Our middle-aged ants patrol our nests to makes sure things are running smoothly and cleanly.

"You've also discovered that we put our garbage in a specific location, including our fallen ants. Our elderly ants go outside the nest and forage, very dangerous work. We are pleased you know all this because you'll be less likely to see us under the dreaded stereotypes about us, at least the harmless ants for whom I speak. The fire ants are too aggressive and give us a bad name, they are our terrorists and deserve whatever you can do to them."

Other Insects Weigh In

Again, the insects did the unexpected. None of them tried to bum rush the stage this time, instead they began handing in petitions, talking about the parade of animal immigrants that had been so successful a few days ago. Why couldn't the insects have a big parade, and, maybe, a beauty page*ant*? It was only fair.

The TRIAD understood the insect world the least and were puzzled about how to handle this torrent of requests. Pound for pound, insects globally outweighed everybody but humans and even there it was neck and neck. The insects knew this and were clamoring for representation based on overall weight on the planet. The TALKOUT, they felt, was giving the humans the impression the world's fauna was made up of just some majestic hierarchy of mammals, many of whom only number in the thousands. A civil rights issue had boiled up among the lower ranks of the animal kingdom.

The insects made the further point that humans fear them far more than they fear mammals, reptiles, and aquatic beings. This fear will attract more of their attention, which has been shaky lately due to the loss of novelty, according to the Human Genius. Besides, insects were more widely distributed so that other lands and countries will be spoken for on the screen. After all, bees pollinate everywhere, while lions, polar bears and starlings have homes restricted to few areas. The insects were very outspoken and even organized their own TRIAD—bees, ants, and spiders.

It was time for another day-long recess for the warm-blooded TRIAD to figure this situation out before it got out of control. As the Elephant wryly noted: Insects have been known to attack mammals. Really!

Humans Can't Get Enough of Animal Tales

It might seem that after being glued to their screens for hours listening to all these animal tales, humans would utilize whatever viewing time they now had to look at other types of programming. Surprisingly, no.

During the time-out, humans returned to their own daily fare of "animal stories" for which the demand was insatiable. Most evening newscasts were making time for animal stories, such as one about a youngster rescuing a cat that fell down into a well.

And so, the stories that day covered the disqualification of an elite horse trainer in Britain for administering drugs to a dozen racing horses. And there was a report on the growing success of animal shelters in getting adoptions or finding pets' owners. Also appearing was an intriguing feature on the largest hospital for falcons, which was in Abu Dhabi, with an ophthalmology department and intensive care units.

The *New York Times* described a new company call Dognition, "which produces a Web site where people can test their dog's cognition, learn about their pets and, Dr. [Brian] Hare hopes, supply him and his colleagues with scientific data on tens of thousands of dogs . . . As the science of dog cognition comes into better focus, Dr. Hare hopes that scientists can use Dognition to deliver their insights to dog trainers. Science-based dog training would take into account what dogs are good at, what they're bad at and the biases that influence their [doggy] minds."

Not to be outdone, the *Wall Street Journal* covered the little-known world of gambling and homing pigeon racing. "In a typical race, pigeons are removed from their home lofts in a given area and released several hundred miles away with electronic chips on their legs that track when they have arrived back home, as well as their average flight speed." Apparently, the *Journal* noted, "there are pigeon-racing clubs across the country." People for the Ethical Treatment of Animals (PETA) claims that in many races a majority of pigeons die before arriving home, killed by other birds, power lines, or exhaustion. Pigeon owners also often kill birds that are slow racers and have minimal breeding value, according to PETA.

Humans Show Some Empathy

In fact, that story garnered a lot of attention, so much so that one bold human publication decided to do something that would be more likely to come from the TALKOUT, a hard expose of the suffering of birds in this sport. They had recruited a pigeon to lay out the facts, some of which were found in a pertinent news story.

"I, the homing pigeon, have a history. I come from the first domesticated bird in human history. We were viewed as a meat-producing machine, particularly our young, called squabs. We mate for life and may have six broods a year. Our young can leave the nest after five weeks, by which time they are ready to mate and breed.

"Your pigeon specialists now think we can use abstract reasoning, being able to recognize letters of the alphabet and see the difference between and a Monet and a Picasso. I, as a homing pigeon, can fly up to ninety miles per hour. Huge flocks of passenger pigeons were hunted to extinction in North America by the end of the nineteenth century.

"On the other hand, pigeons are now prospering wherever humans congregate. More food, fewer predators and the compassion of organized pigeon lovers among humans have saved us. Now, with this background, let me tell you what my day is like at the Holibird Homer Club, where I participate in the types of races you read about in the *Wall Street Journal*. Only I can give you the inside story.

"Elastic bands with serial numbers are attached to our legs

by a race-directing human. We are loaded into cages then onto a specially structured truck to take us to a very distant liberation point. Someone, called a 'starter,' records the time of release. Then we're let go to fly back home, maybe seven hundred miles away. The first to get back wins the prize for its owner.

"If we don't die on the trip, we are treated well. I wish wild pigeons had it so good. We're happy, because we make many homing pigeon caretakers and fans happy, and, in turn, they have to make sure we stay happy until we can't compete any longer. But . . . all good things have to end, right, humans?"

While this story shocked humans and encouraged animals, who realized that some humans had empathy, other humans were perusing stories such as the one in the *New York Times* on how the European Commission imposed a two-year outlawing of a class of pesticides believed to harm bees. Or, in the same issue, news that voracious snakeheads were spotted in a lake inside Central Park.

The *Washington Post* had a report titled "The Horsemen of Nairobi," recounting Derby Day in Kenya at the only horse track in that continent between Egypt and Zimbabwe. The jockeys were lucky to earn twenty dollars a ride.

The *New York Times* had a headline "Farm Equipment That Runs on Oats." It began, "Once a mainstay of farming, horses are back, as clean and organic as the crops they plow." The story described life in Hartland, Vermont.

Of course, not all the reports were flattering to animals. One talked about an exhibition at the American Museum of Natural History titled "The Power of Poison," and it wasn't about the human kind. It was about poisons possessed by innocent animals.

The Elephant and Dolphin, noting this show was probably heavily sensationalized, did acknowledge that some animals were good at creating deadly brews. Think of those cute, diminutive golden poison frogs. One of them can secrete enough poison on its skin to terminate ten humans. And there were giant silkworm caterpillars with hollow spines, which can pierce human skin and cause uncontrollable bleeding. Unlike human poisons, the Owl noted as the three talked, such poisons are used for self-defense, like what is alleged about the chemical and biological weapons of the human species.

Another story about animals' abilities was in a *Washington Post* report for its "KidsPost." It told the story of what happened when Hurricane Sandy flooded the New York Aquarium's spot by the sea. Its twelve thousand animals were exposed to oily tanks and dirty water when the power was lost. But after six months, more than 80 percent of the animals were secured, including walruses, angelfish, otters, and sea lions. But the freshwater koi died in the saltwater surge. Sharks, sea turtles, seahorses, eels, and rays were rushed to the aquarium's veterinary hospital after the water destroyed their exhibit space. The staffers used heroic measures to save all the animals, such as pumping oxygen into the water and rebuilding filters and pumps. The animals were also fielding some positive e-mails and letters from humans, indicating that their TALKOUT was having a measurable impact. One person referred to a report by the American Heart Association that said walking a dog may protect you from heart disease. "I just looked at pictures of the dogs walking with their owners in an entirely more sympathetic way," the writer noted.

Insects Get More Screen Time

The TRIAD had not yet been totally sold on the idea of a long parade of insects marching across the stage, but had come up with a holding action. First varied insects would be allowed to present their viewpoint, come what may, and the animals would see how that went over. Time for the marching later. The plan was, however, not without its perils. It was based on playing on human fear to keep the audience watching.

First up was a cluster of flea beetles known to human gardeners and farmers for devouring broccoli, arugula, and eggplant. They are so small, they had to be magnified for the human viewers, but once seen, their shiny, trim black form revealed an incredible jumping ability with powerful hind legs. What could the flea beetles possibly say to humans? Well, they knew they had to perform and so they made a constructive pitch:

"We, flea beetles, as you call us, say that both you and we have our jobs to do. You want to grow these vegetables. We must nibble at them to stay alive over the time needed to lay our eggs for our posterity. You can declare chemical warfare against us and in so doing expose yourselves and eaters to toxins. Or you can adopt prevention, which means keeping us out of your crops 'by good soil fertility, irrigation and crop rotation,' as master gardener Barbara Damrosch advises. She urges 'using the proper mulch and timing more of the crops for later than the spring.'" With that the flea beetles synchronized their departure.

The TRIAD knew that the flea beetles might have interested growers and eaters of those vegetables but not the larger viewership that does not particularly care for broccoli.

Quickly they brought on the "nuclear option." A large mosquito filled half the screen, looking as threatening as an alien in a Hollywood film, with the message: "Avoid us. Don't try to kill us. It won't work. We mutate and resist like no other. You used DDT against us to eradicate malaria in Sri Lanka and other countries, and we became resistant to it in a few years.

"We don't like to have to spread disease," declared the giant mosquito, "because it causes lots of casualties among humans. Remember," the mosquito said, repeating a message brought up earlier, "it is not us, but the parasite that does the damage carried by us inadvertently. If you choose *avoidance*, you'll reduce your toxic illnesses and meet your mission. For example, eliminate standing or stagnant water in barrels, gutters, birdhouses. Cut thick shrubs. Use fans in your homes—we can't fly through moving air. We only fly about one and a half miles per hour. No need to lather yourself with lotions or spray your rooms and walls. Simple fans, especially if they go back and forth from the floor, will keep us away without destroying us.

"So we can have mutual interests, no matter all the profitable businesses that try to have you buy their plans for chemical annihilation at a steep price to your health and pocketbook. Then you have to dispose of the aerosol cans. So don't let these exterminators—they'll never succeed in their crime of *using polluting pesticides*, never—sell you a bill of boomerangs. We're telling you kindly that the best policy is 'separate but equal.' Otherwise it will be mutually assured destruction."

Whereupon the giant mosquito spread its wings and took off.

Back in human-land, stocks of fans flew out of the hardware stores. Millions rushed out to empty containers and pots of stagnant water. Birdhouses were purchased in great quantity. Out of self-interest, the giant mosquito deliberately did not mention that a nontoxic way to control mosquitoes, along with many other kinds of bugs, was to have many birds around to devour them for food.

Human feedback, as the TRIAD learned, found the giant mosquito's presentation helpful and remarkably accommodating. The same was not entirely true for the insect kingdom, who was watching this speaker with suspicion. Not only had the mosquitoes already been in the TALKOUT once before this, but mosquitoes are not exactly popular members among their fellow bugs. They make humans very angry and the chemical bombs humans let loose have taken many another insect species into decline.

The rumble under and on the ground grew more audible and more frequent. The insect world was getting angry and the so-called higher vertebrate mammals took such rumbles seriously. By direct observation, flight, or grapevine, all mammals know what happens in the dense Amazon jungle when the ferocious Amazon ants start their massive march.

Nothing can stand in their way. All living beings who can, do take flight, no matter how ferocious they may be, such as the jaguar, or predisposed to dine, such as the anteater. These ants devour all plant life and their gigantic collective weight creates sound befitting thunder at the ground level.

Luckily, a less divisive insect was up next. A centipede came onto the screen. "You'd better not ignore us. Without insects the life of the world would not exist and you know it," it said, addressing the TRIAD as well as the human audience.

The centipede stepped aside for the Mediterranean fruit fly who knows humans well since her breed is a prime subject for laboratory experimentation. "OK, I'm just a fruit fly and I know some of what humans do to insects, from sterilization to attractants, to get rid of them. What good has it done you? Backfire, backfire, backfire. You use many times more insecticides than you did in 1940 and you're losing more crops to insect diners now.

"And don't think genetic engineering is the cure. In the fields and in storage our speed of mutation and adaptation is without parallel. You can kill billions of us, but we keep bouncing back. Sometimes you advance ten steps and have to go back due to unknown consequences. You can eradicate the screw-worm fly, but thousands of different insects can take its place in one form or another.

"Look what you've tried," said the fly, "applications of insect pathogens, parasites, and predators, yet overall, despite some victories and temporary controls, you're still surrounded by us. Even eradication has consequences when our predators starve.

"Simple as we are, we are sufficiently multicellular to be similar to analogous tissues in your own species. This is a great convenience for you humans. It means you can genetically manipulate us to identify the genes and pathways that control a certain biological process—such as ovulation—according to your scientists Allan Spradling and Jianjum Sun.

"Don't forget," the fly went on, "in the environment, everything is connected to everything else." He then buzzed off looking for a ripe, exposed banana.

Agricultural school professors had to nod at what the fruit fly was saying. For years they have been trying to develop safer methods for using chemosterilants, which have been too hazardous to man and to animals for application outside the laboratories. Imagine, they said to each other, the irony of it all, the brainiest of all species is being fought to a standstill by the least sentient or intelligent of all species.

Their conversation floated onto the Human Genius apps and somehow reached the insect world. The hubris infuriated them, though it certainly was not meant as such by the academic professors.

The European corn borer was the next speaker. It has devastated billions of bushels of corn in Europe and in the United States and Canada. "What you humans will never understand, with all your intricate and penetrating research on us, is that you're constantly outsmarting yourself and giving us new opportunities to live too. The opportunity you gave us corn borers was your foolish monoculture. That was manna from heaven for us. We went up to sixty thousand borers per acre. So you drive us back for a few years and we adjust or some other species moves in to multiply and live. Or you'll harm the beneficial parasites and predators, which could have destroyed us. Or when you harm us, you're also harming valuable insects such as bees. Humans, clearly you need a whole new game plan and you need to listen to your smartest ecologists, who are not paid to be so stupid, to obfuscate and to distract."

The boll weevil, the spectacular ravager of America's valuable cotton crop, came to the screen. "You've thrown everything you can think of against us and our siblings, the cotton leaf worm and the cotton bollworm, plus other varieties of insects. We admit you've diminished our numbers, but you've also savagely disrupted the macro and micro environment. We are tens of thousands of species and are omnipresent: underground, in the top soil, sometimes in the air, and all over humans, their abodes, transport and other places. As a boll weevil, I am bloodied but unbowed, resilient and driven. So long as you have cotton, you'll have me in one degree or another."

The weevil crawled away to be replaced by the all-important earthworm, the soil's greatest benefactor and nourisher. In favorable soils, there can be several million earthworms per acre. They can be the dominant animal life in the soil. Sometimes their total weight exceeds that of all other soil-dwelling animals combined. This information was quickly sent by the TRIAD to all the animal kingdom to get them to pay careful attention to the earthworm's message.

The earthworm spoke: "I am an earthworm, the subject of both truths and myths about what I and other earthworms do to the soil. It is a fact that we help provide nutrients and improve aeration and tilth. We make possible abundant bird life.

"I am here, however, to make peace between invertebrate animals with a head, thorax, and abdomen, plus pairs of legs and some wings, *and* vertebrate animals whom the insect world accuses of marginalizing them during the crucial one hundred hours of education.

"Let's face it, the large mammals attract the largest audiences and provoke less fear than some of us do. A hundred-hour variety show is short, given what the TRIAD has been trying to do, and quite wisely in my earthwormy opinion. Still, what the insects originally proposed, a parade of bugs with me as grand marshal, would be the best way to show the world our variety and beauty. It would take less time and be more spectacular than what we have had so far, special pleading by this or that bug. I'm not talking just to our TRIAD but to all animals. Let's bring on a huge *Parade of Insects*, scurrying across the screen with their names under them. The sheer variety, beauty, color, and mystery will make their own points and astonish the human audience, along with their ability to get along (even though many usually eat each other) when a higher purpose is before them.

"Earthworms are no strangers to surprises—we are plucked out in the billions every day by the birds that consider us their most savory and digestible morsel. But I would be very surprised, given some nervy previews, if humans were not glued to their screens during this PARADE OF THE INSECT WORLD.

"In proper respect, the selection of these insects must be of, by, and for the insects so as to maximize the representation of millions of species by what probably can be no more than five hundred strutting, crawling, or jumping bugs. It is offered to you respectfully, oh wise TRIAD, as part of this magnificent project to right wrongs and set in motion many good relationships that spell survival, animal well-being, and planetary balance."

The TRIAD did not have to go into executive session to decide its response, which was immediate. "Yes," trumpeted the Elephant; "Yes," hooted the Owl; and "Yes," shrieked the Dolphin. And then in louder unison: "YES, YES, YES."

For a tension-breaking moment, as the logistics of the parade were being worked out, the TRIAD let a lemming onto the stage. "I know that we lemmings cannot be accused of either preparedness or foresight, but on behalf of all lemmings—some of whom are right now heading for the cliffs in Norway—thank you, insects, and thank you, in particular, earthworm, for the ability to foresee and forestall what could have befallen all of us." Whereupon the lemming leaped off the stage to rejoin its fellow lemmings on their way, inexorably, to the sea.

Life Goes On

It was going to take some time to get the march organized, so another halt was called in the broadcasting so humans could go back to thinking, reading about, and viewing animals on their own mass media while the animals themselves, those not involved in parade preparations, were given some amusement, broadcast on a secure line, so humans wouldn't be offended by the way animals laughed at them. The animal programming was about the American Gerbil Society's annual pageant at Bedford, Massachusetts. The main event was a competition between gerbils to get around obstacles and race to the end of the track. Breeders won ribbons based on various kinds of agility.

The pageant goes on for two entire days. So close to gerbils are the breeders that they see all kinds of personalities as well as physical differences in their diminutive pets.

All over the world, the rats looked on dumbfounded. One rat spoke for many when she said, "All we are required to do is be tested for humans. They never treat us as a luxury sport. And our tails are longer, to boot. It is sooo true: life is unfair."

One should not get the impression that the animal kingdom stopped what it had to do and all its members watched the gamboling gerbils. Not at all. Little oysters on a reef by the Choptank River were busy removing pollutants from the water with stunning efficiency. This oyster reef's contribution to clean waters is encouraging state marine officials to seed more reefs for a major oyster comeback after years of overharvesting. Oysters were overjoyed with the news.

Going strong for 350 million years, household cockroaches were busy switching their internal chemistry around so that glucose, a form of sugar that is a sweet come-hither to countless forms of life, tastes bitter.

As the *Washington Post* reported, trillions of termites, a hardy species if there ever was one, are busy eating damp wood and building their impressive mounds, which presently are being studied by robot construction scientists. Male frigate birds on the Galapagos Islands were occupied with their mating rituals, which included inflating the skid beneath their necks to the size of a balloon. Beavers were damming streams everywhere they could. Meanwhile, deer were having a lark running around Rock Green Park inside Washington, D.C., spreading tick-born

Lyme disease and butting into cars, oblivious to the coming culling of their density by park rangers. Nearby, all kinds of aquatic life were performing at the National Aquarium in the downtown Department of Commerce building headquarters, soon to be told by the staff that the aquarium would be closed by September 30, 2013, due to budgetary restrictions.

Over in the Rocky Mountains, wolves were running for their lives, pursued by unleashed hunters who have killed 698 wolves in the last two seasons just in Idaho, a number larger than their estimated population in that state. Protectors of wolves are trying to educate the local populace about the animals' keystone species role in keeping down the number of denuding, vegetation-eating prey.

In New York City, according to a *New York Times* report, protected pigeons were frolicking around Grand Army Plaza beside a statue of General William Tecumseh Sherman and degrading the protective wax coating the memorial with their acidic droppings and claws.

Down in Baltimore, known by Eastern Shore rodents as a rat-friendly city—there are sixty rats per thousand residents compared to only ten rats per thousand residents in 2002—the rats are thriving so much that they're getting in each other's way. One resident-writer, Karen Houppert, says, "Baltimore gives the rats free housing, free food, free rein," as with "overflowing garbage cans in the dark back alleys." Of course, the rats love it—it's rat heaven.

The American eels were busy swimming from the Sargasso Sea, south of Bermuda, thousands of miles up to the little freshwater creeks to spend their lives, often cut short by predatory birds and animals along the East Coast. The eels just want to make sure that they are in fresh water. Animals have work to do every day. The star-nosed mole is catching and devouring an insect in less than a fourth of a second. Bats are devouring hordes of insects for their nocturnal meals; snakes are catching mice and voles. Nonetheless, most in the kingdom are finding time to watch the great

TALKOUT, from the giant clams to the gentle dugongs to the coral trout, which start life as females, then morph into males, to the swift black noddies of the Great Barrier Reef.

I Love A Parade

With the time approaching for the Great Insect Parade, the TRIAD talked to the grand marshal, the Earthworm, and instructed it to secure its own TRIAD. Promptly the Earthworm invited the beautiful Monarch Butterfly and the productive Honeybee. They both accepted, knowing that beauty and honey would attract good ratings and diminish the inevitable biases of human animals toward insects. The INSECT TRIAD put the finishing touches on what could be a logistical nightmare.

The Human Genius was observing this development with no small alarm. The Insect Parade could go wrong in many ways and jeopardize the whole great TALKOUT that the unique apps made possible. So the Human Genius made sure that the basic knowledge, fears, and emotional reactions by humans to various major insect categories were transmitted to the INSECT TRIAD for their educational uses as they saw fit.

So, for example, humans knew of the connection between mosquitoes and malaria and the Zika virus, and between ticks and Lyme and other serious diseases. They knew how merciless insects are about eating each other or destroying trees and crops, and feasting on insect corpses. They viscerally recoiled from cockroaches, tarantulas, and millipedes, but thought Japanese beetles or ladybugs were "cute." Millions of humans eat insects, which are becoming more and more a source of cheap protein. Plenty of supply. The *Encyclopedia Smithsonian* estimates there are 200 million insects for each human being on earth.

The INSECT TRIAD was appreciative of this information, which they put to use immediately in planning their signs, selections, and sequences in the parade.

With the announcement of the Insect Parade imminent, the INSECT TRIAD went about preparing its signs so as to create a good impression for the human animals.

First Sign: Seeking Respect for Insects. We are a big part of the invertebrates that make up about 90 percent of the globe's animal life.

Second Sign: Humans have crushed, burned, poisoned, sterilized, dissected, and even eaten us in the trillions.

Third Sign: Insects have no animus toward humans. Any harm is genetically driven or due to parasites in us or self-defense. We do not start wars.

Fourth Sign: We insects give you food, ecological benefits, and medical discoveries and provide sustenance for birds and other animals you treasure. Insects offer you beauty with or without your microscope.

Fifth Sign: Humans learn about humans and other animals by learning more and more about insects and their world. Think of the fruit fly.

Sixth Sign: Three hundred thousand beetle species must be doing something right in adaptation and evolution.

Seventh Sign: Humans: Give your curiosity an opportunity.

The INSECT TRIAD secured the services of eusocial worker ants, worker bees, and worker termites to carry the signs aloft with spectacular tiers of themselves that left human viewers agape. The insect workers moved very slowly in a circular motion to allow viewers several sights of the signs as they passed.

The animal TRIAD allowed the Insect Parade two full hours of prime time. The parade began with the signs to the tune of crickets rubbing their legs against their wings, a symphony well known to millions of humans that begins at dusk. Only this concert had a rhythmic beat that was much more dramatic in effect than the usual vespers. Hissing Madagascar cockroaches joined in at synchronized moments by pushing air through spiracles in their bodies.

Adding to the music, swarms of bees produced a sweeping sonic swell that tempered the harshness of the crickets. Human musicologists began e-mailing their peers to tune in to this building crescendo. The birds found new respect for insects and joined with their melodic chirping. Then the larger mammals, infused with the sense of fairness related by the original TRIAD, melded their growls, trumpets, and eerier calls.

For about ten minutes, with the music serenading, the signs slowly carried in wider and wider circles made quite a spectacle as the human audience grew by the minute in heightened expectation. This clearly was the day in the sun for the arthropods. No other collective group of living creatures has been as adaptive to almost every habitat on earth, except the oceans, as the arthropods. They have made it on the coldest mountains and in the hottest jungles, from the dampest bogs to the driest deserts, always surviving against relentless predators in the microbial, insect, plant, and larger animal worlds.

The INSECT TRIAD had welcomed the dispatch of the Human Genius, who had provided them with orderly descriptions of different kinds of insects to guide them in structuring the parade so as make it understandable to humans.

Humans have catalogued over one million insect species with many more to be discovered. Insect specialists are gradually coming to the realization that humans could not live without the many services insects provide in the global ecosystem.

Still, this is not something the INSECT TRIAD planned to make much of in that humans have internalized far more deeply the knowledge of the diseases, damage, and discomforts associated with some insects. Humans know too well that the insect world is the only animal kingdom they have been unable to conquer and they are resentful.

The parade must accentuate the positive and show that the negative actions of insects are done without *mens rea* (criminal intent).

Other organizational details the INSECT TRIAD had turned its attention to involved providing special magnifiers so that the parading insects could be seen in their brilliant colorful detail. Selection of the paraders was accomplished by putting out tenders in the following categories taken from standard textbooks by humans:

Bristletails, silverfish, mayflies, dragonflies, gladiators, cockroaches, termites, mantids, rock crawlers, webspinners, stick and leaf insects, earwigs, stoneflies, crickets, zorapterans, booklice, thrips, parasitic lice, bugs, snakeflies, alderflies, lacewings, beetles, fleas, strepsipterans, scorpionflies, flies, caddisflies, butterflies, bees, wasp ants, spiders, crustaceans, and millipedes.

The finest and quickest specimens that arrived at the INSECT TRIAD's website were chosen by the INSECT TRIAD acting as final judges. There simply was no time for appeals, reconsiderations, insect arguments, or other forms of human due process. The winners would physically, at least, be good representatives of their species. Insect character, personality, compassion, etc., simply could not be taken into consideration in making selections. In any event, the INSECT TRIAD provided humans with an explanatory text to impress on them the purposes of this exercise in internal harmony, which had been allowed to take place partly to head off an insect uprising against the original TRIAD of the Elephant, the Owl, and the Dolphin.

The avowed purpose was to educate humans about the value and innocence of the insect world. Both the Monarch Butterfly and the Honeybee agreed with the Earthworm that the message to humans must be that insects—having such brief lives—are more interested in perpetuation than in their immediate survival. Humans can be told this, using the findings of their entomologists, who point to the sacrifice of ants for the colony, and the fact that the male insect's immediate mission once reaching adulthood is to mate, as two examples.

With the signage phase of the parade complete, the insects themselves started coming onto the scene. There was neither rhyme nor reason for the order of appearance. The Monarch Butterfly, with its vast perspective of the insect world during its length migrations, foresaw the futility and delay of trying to negotiate positioning between the often wrangling insects.

First came the mayfly, who had no time to lose. With its two wings, long body, and a number of tails, the adult mayfly flies only for a few hours, living for a day or two before dying. Those human viewers who see themselves as insect aficionados or students quickly looked up these vital statistics, as they intended to do for all the parade participants.

Next came the hoverfly, the master flier, showing its unique ability to stay in one spot in midair and also fly backward. What a display for the viewers, who never have seen such versatility up close.

Then a surprise, the only insect so far discovered to wean its young passed by proudly with its attached babies.

The next part of the show demonstrated the ways in which insects defend themselves from attackers or predators. First came the click beetles, who from a mobile joint in their thorax can fling themselves high into the air, while making a loud cry during their flipping to confuse their enemies. Along came the yellow-and-black-striped cinnabar moth caterpillar eating ragwort, which is poisonous to other animals, another way of saying, if you eat me, you'll be very sorry.

"Here comes the bumblebee," cried some human children. No, it is a European bee beetle that mimics the bumblebee in the ways it feeds and in appearance as a defense. More overt in its defense is the bombardier beetle, which managed to squirt a volatile liquid from its abdomen, which turns to a gas that causes any adversary to experience blisters. Not to be outdone, along came other species of ants and worker termites, who turn off predators with their noxious secretions.

Then came the mandibulates: cockroaches, crickets, and

earwigs, slicing and chewing their leaves, dry wood, and algae. With great fanfare and insect music came the "useful insects" with the greatest of public relations burdens. Insects as a whole promote recycling of decaying matter in equatorial forests by breaking down or decomposing vegetation and improving soil quality and fertility. Bees produce honey and wax from their hives, which have many uses. Streams of grasshoppers, stinkbugs, locusts, dragonfly nymphs, and midges strolled alluringly by to remind human viewers of their tastiness as food protein, which is appreciated in many places in the world. There followed the tiny hymenopteran parasitic wasp that humans use as biological control against crop-destroying insects. The TRIAD's Honeybee made sure that the crucial pollinating insects were given front-and-center attention.

Mating always fascinates humans, and the damselflies, with their "copulatory wheel" forming a circular position when they mate, do not disappoint as they do their thing across the screen.

Even more astonishing to humans are insects where the female eats the male after mating. Such ingrates include the South American mantid that sometimes doesn't even wait but eats its smaller male mate *during* mating. This cannibalism was actually performed on the screen, thanks to the foresight of the Earthworm. Two seventeen-year-old teenage lovers wrapped around each other on the sofa watched bulge-eyed. The girl looked at the boy and said, "Aren't you lucky?"

Other viewers gasped as they watched the giant Brazilian wandering spider crawl by, a venomous hulk the size of a dinner plate and aggressive to humans too.

Ratings shot up during portrayals of both the insects' mating and their usefulness to the overall natural environment.

Alternative Programming

The INSECT TRIAD was canny enough to present an animated program guide, listing the foreseeable order of the parade, so that viewers could temporarily change channels when insects they couldn't stomach were passing in review. Moreover, for these viewers the Human Genius provided a special alternative, an adjunct website, where other animal programming was being projected.

The first entry on this website was a walk-through tour of the Smithsonian Institution National Museum of Natural History. Its super-motivated director, Kirk Johnson, selected specimens out of millions housed that would arouse viewers' interest in the animal kingdom of their ancestors.

He chose first a pair of elephant-sized giant ground sloths, ones rendered extinct millennia ago. When the tree sloths, most of whom had tuned out from the Insect Parade, saw their gargantuan ancestors, they were filled with both pride and envy. Millions of contemporary viewing sloths were moved as nothing has moved them before. Two sloths from the jungles, holding back their emotions, asked Mr. Johnson all the obvious questions bursting forth from aroused sloths everywhere. "When did our large ancestors live? What caused them to go extinct? How did their genes get replaced by the genes that produced much smaller sloths? Did our large ancient relatives eat what we eat? How large were the families and how long did they live? Could they fend off their predators better than we are trying to do? How can we thank you enough for illuminating our distant past?"

Kirk Johnson was almost taken aback by the intensity of the sloths' interest. After all, sloths are not known for their excitability. But he answered each question.

As to how they could thank him? That was easy. Just lead him to more sloth fossils anytime, anywhere.

Johnson is a fossil maniac, having written many books and

articles on his fossil hunts around the planet. The Human Genius was pleased with such handiwork but was determined not to overdo such "offsets."

Insects Keep On Truckin'

Back on the main channel, the most potentially human-disturbing segment had come up. March of the the ravaging insects. The Human Genius foresaw what was needed and provided explanatory information to accompany the parade of what many humans call the marauders.

Here comes the locust amid widespread booing around the world. As explained by the Human Genius, locusts can indeed swarm into and eat vast acreage of crops in areas of the Middle East, Africa, and Asia. One gigantic swarm was as large as the state of California. They eat to live, as do humans, commenced the explanation. They feel no animosity toward humans or their domesticated animals, whose food supply is depleted. But when the periodic swarms come, birds multiply due to the abundance of food and humans turn these locusts into tasty morsels whose protein comes as a gift.

Next up are the flies, the omnipresent nuisances that can pick up and carry disease-bearing microbes from dung heap to dinner table. The house fly traipsed across the stage. It needed no explanation for humans, but there are eighty-five thousand different fly species and some are useful. Following the house fly came the vinegar fly, which humans use for research into animal genetics.

Yet again the mosquitoes were on the screen. They have been labeled by humans as the most lethal insects of them all. Many stung mammals would agree. There are various species of mosquitoes. Some, like the common European mosquito, are relatively harmless. Yes, when they bite, they suck blood, but they are food for bats and birds. Another mosquito followed, the inland floodwater mosquito that inhabits southern Canada and is found across the U.S. and down to Central and South American countries. This species can help spread disease.

Most human viewers have swatted mosquitoes but have never gotten a close look. A close-up peek offered something of a surprise, drawing some ahs and oohs. The human audience saw, in the words of one text, "attractive males having feathery antennae and with black-and-white body patterns. They show an arched, springy body posture with long hind legs that seem to push the body up in the middle. The thorax is rather a gold brown with grey scales. The legs have pale 'knees.' The relatively small head faces down. Adult females feed on humans and animals, but the males feed on nectar."

The third and last species was *Anopheles gambiae,* the dreaded malaria mosquito, found mostly in Africa below the Sahara. These insects carry the deadly malaria protozoan, *Plasmodium falciparum*, the lethal and elusively mutating parasite that takes almost a million human lives a year, mostly children and pregnant mothers.

The mood among human viewers turned sullen and fearful. The mosquito was eager to say that none of this was really its fault. Sure, it is simply the carrier, transferring the parasite in its saliva when feeding on human blood. It picks up this parasite as a larva in pools or as an adult female. The mosquito had pleaded with the viewing humans, saying that it gains nothing from this parasite, cannot get rid of it, and would welcome more research to render harmless in any way the parasite, even being more than willing to sacrifice its short life in the process. "If the parasite goes extinct," said the mosquito, "the mosquitoes will thrive in the following generations, given their resilience over time."

The scientists at the Walter Reed Army Hospital shook their heads, thinking that for years their work, while promising, still has not overcome this pesky parasite. Having made its case, the malaria mosquito departed thinking that humans will not separate it from the parasite when laying blame until the scientists can extinguish the parasite.

No sooner did the malaria mosquito leave than several species of spiders forced their way out of their line to get on the screen, upsetting the TRIAD and their programmers. But it was too late. The arachnids scampered onto the stage amid human viewers crying "creepy" and "eeee."

While there was a certain lack of organization in the order of the march, the INSECT TRIAD had decided that they would never put two groups of insects that humans irrationally hated on in a row. They would keep them spaced between more loveable or at least not-disliked types, but the spiders were overturning their well-laid plans.

Interactive Bats

Even as the spiders were causing havoc in the parade, there was an exceptional program being broadcast on the alternative channel. The whole idea of it had come yesterday while the insects were planning their event.

The TRIAD's Owl had been reflecting about the one-way nature of the TALKOUT. Humans could only watch and they were given no way to help. It was purely "educational TV." The novelty of the event was beginning to wear off, along with the awestruck wonder of communicating animals. After all, humans have long been exposed to nature programs full of wildlife in various activities. Hundreds of millions have pets that they love. Humans, the Owl knew, liked to be asked for help. Especially the human children.

"So why not," the Owl thought, "invite the children of the world to help save the bats of the world from their deadly fungus, their lost habitat and their awful image problem that makes so many humans turn away in fear and disgust?"

The Owl contacted the Human Genius who thought it was a great idea for many reasons, not the least of which was to keep the show throbbing and interesting. The Human Genius found a piece in the *Washington Post* that was directly on point. It addressed children, disabused them of their acquired bat myths—they are not blind, they don't suck blood—and laid out a program to help bats because "bats are important and they're in trouble."

As the only flying mammal, bats control mosquitoes. A small brown bat can eat up to a thousand mosquitoes in just an hour. For variety, bats dine on moths and beetles, ones that can damage food crops. One species of bat—there are 1,200 species—in South America helps pollinate plants. The ability of bats to move at night is based on their making sounds that bounce off hard objects and let bats veer away. It is called echolocation.

Bat educator and rescuer Leslie Sturges says that children are entranced by bats. "They often think they are adorable," she adds. Sturges speaks to them about bat language, which involves a series of buzzes, clicks, and trills, used to communicate with each other. "Bats have friends; they are super smart," she says. Children are empathetic about bats, and become especially concerned when she describes the deadly white nose syndrome (the fungus disease) that has killed five million hibernating bats in the United States. Ms. Sturges has formed a bat club for kids so they can become a voice for bat protection.

The Owl devised an alternative bat parade on the alternative channel, which would be oriented directly at kids and would have an interactive component. As the various bats marched by, the Owl made sure all this information was communicated to the human children, so that many would join Ms. Sturges's Club.

Spiders' Time in the Sun

The insects were very upset by the boorishness of the arachnids, not only because they had grabbed the limelight before it was their turn, but because they were so different from the garden variety insect. Arachnids have a two-segmented body, four pairs of walking legs, and are without antennae or wings. To insects, the arachnids make up for these deficiencies with ample amounts of gall. The wiser insects realized, however, that spiders seemed to be getting fairly substantial ratings, so they told the insect world to quiet down and watch.

The arachnids decided to lead with their best story, that of the spider aranae, which produces silk that emerges from the tip of its abdomen. From this material comes their webs in which they trap their prey and paralyze them by a poison lodged in a pair of poison glands in their front jaws. The silk is amazingly strong and flexible. They paraded their silk but could not explain its astonishing qualities for humans. Then something unscheduled happened. A human commentator appeared, a first, who, shall we say, proceeded to fill in the blanks:

"My fellow humans, this spider fiber is stronger than steel. Yes, steel! Stronger than bone at the same weight and twice as elastic as nylon. Listen to this: 'A spider web made of strands as thick as a pencil would be strong enough to stop a jumbo jet in flight,' wrote professor of medicine Shigeyoshi Osaki at Nara Medical University in Japan, according to the *Wall Street Journal.* He 'showed how a four millimeter-thick piece of string made up of 190,000 strands of spider dragline could support his weight.' There are start-up companies trying to recreate spider silk (biomimicry).

"Real spider web has been gathered for centuries and 'used as fishing line' or to dress wounds for its antibacterial properties,'reported the *Journal.* 'If these companies succeed in biomimicry, recombinant spider silk can be used in the making of tires, bumpers, electronic parts, artificial blood vessels, dissolvable sutures and artificial ligaments.'"

The commentator then thanked the spiders and urged them to take a bow for the great emerging future of spider silk biomimicy. On cue, the spiders performed a spider flourish and departed the stage. The human commentator said they were a credit to the thirty-five thousand species of spiders that collectively can bask in their momentary glory—one that will long be remembered.

Grand Finale

As the Insect Parade came to a close, the INSECT TRIAD—the Earthworm, the Monarch Butterfly, and the Honeybee—felt it was high time to make a larger point. They hitched onto the waves of appreciation that were generated by the parade to offer an enduring plea against what they considered the ultimate crime for their phylum: the heinous use of insecticide, what the commercial human exterminators call pesticide.

Unlike human genocide, the TRIAD delicately noted, insecticides can bring down the planet as a living organism. Other human races and ethnic groupings can carry on after a brutal genocide, but who carries on the functions of the insects in the ecosystem when they are no more?

The human audience knew it had been educated by the insects in ways they could not be by any entomologist or classroom instruction. The INSECT TRIAD had combined the personal touch and emotional intelligence with hard empirical information. The DVD of this hour will find robust circulation among humans for many years, predicted the satisfied Human Genius.

Afterthoughts

The INSECT TRIAD had the taste to put together this parade without allowing a place to the truly disgusting order Siphonaptera (or fleas), whose entire existence is parasitic on hosts—mostly mammals—without any yet known redeeming value. Other insects called them blood-feeders with only their survival and reproduction at stake.

A standard text writes, "Fleas are highly specialized and unusual insects . . . Fleas are a nuisance to their hosts and can provoke allergies. They also act as vectors of bacteria, protozoans and viruses. Rat-fleas can carry the organisms that cause diseases, such as plague and murine typhus, which have killed large numbers of people."

But what the INSECT TRIAD did not know, the Human Genius gently informed them, was that any living organism has DNA from which human scientists may someday discover new knowledge. Whereupon a still-skeptical INSECT TRIAD took off: the Honeybee returned to its hive, the Monarch Butterfly joined its flock on its way to Mexico, and the Earthworm partook of a long delayed meal four inches underground.

Watching this finale, the Human Genius inwardly mused how clever the INSECT TRIAD really was during their presentation. Like human animals, the INSECT TRIAD managed, for the most part, to keep the dark sides of the insect world off the screen. They brought on some of the frightful aspects, such as the malarial mosquito, just enough to appear fair-handed. Moreover, the INSECT TRIAD manifested heroic self-restraint.

For example, the Honeybee could have brought onto the screen the giant Japanese hornet that not only kills about seventy people a year in Japan but goes after honeybees as their favorite prey, big-time. The Japanese hornet can fly up to fifty miles a day searching for honeybee colonies or hives. When the scouting hornet finds one, it deposits a pheromone to attract other hornets for a mass attack. Each hornet can kill forty honeybees a minute. Together they take only a few hours to annihilate an entire hive, mostly by using their huge mandibles to decapitate their victims. The TRIAD Honeybee found it hard to hold back the opportunity to expose this killer before the whole world. But it did, for the larger good of the program.

Meanwhile the Monarch Butterfly was chided by its fellow butterflies for not dramatizing how humans are shrinking habitats for developments and pouring insecticides on lawns. They said the Monarch could have cited human scientists declaring the extinction of more and more species of butterflies even while human writers and poets hold up butterflies as symbols of transforming beauty, love, and good fortune. The Monarch knew this but subdued itself again to the greater purpose of the program, hoping that its success would allow future presentations where these and other horrors could be placed before the human animals.

As for the worldly Earthworm, it had all it could handle just avoiding becoming a morsel for an early morning bird.

All in all, the first TRIAD of the Elephant, the Owl, and the Dolphin presented the INSECT TRIAD with its highest award: the Grand Shield of the Stalwarts, made of material donated by a colony of alligators from a fallen loved one, killed by a python in the Everglades.

The Human Genius arranged to make it possible for interested humans to learn about this selflessness of the Monarch and the Honeybee.

The Next Phase

In the immediate aftermath of the Insect Parade, the original TRIAD was besieged by classes of animals who perceived themselves as being excluded from the hundred-hour TALKOUT.

The complaints poured in requesting time for the insectivores, the marsupials, the hoofed animals, the small carnivores, the marmosets and tamarins, and the whales. Individual animals claimed they could get high ratings. The mongoose, for instance, offered to show humans how it can attack and kill a giant cobra, poised to extend its deadly bite.

Clearly, the TRIAD agreed, the hundred-hour TALKOUT was entering a new phase. How to respond? The Dolphin, who was getting weary, suggested a variety show. Admit a large variety of animals for several hours of their unique demonstrations, having auditioned them for quality control, and just clump them together in a mixed format. This would mean the TRIAD wouldn't have to go to all the work they had earlier choreographing themes.

Humans, said the Owl, are used to their own variety shows and so were familiar with the format.

The Elephant shook his trunk and seemed troubled. Other than prancing onto the stage, what messages are being transmitted to humans? "The TALKOUT is losing its coherency," said the Elephant. "It's losing its *raison d'être* and straying far from its original purpose. We cannot descend to just offering entertaining diversity. Diversity must mean something."

While the TRIAD was conversing, three more demands for airtime came in: from the ungulates, the large primates (popularly known as the great apes), and most vigorously from the domesticates. Signing the petition of the domesticates were chickens, cows, pigs, goats, cattle, horses, ponies, and, most poignantly, lambs.

The Elephant and the Dolphin were a little overwhelmed. Whereupon the Owl drew on its inner resources, after all, flying and hunting nocturnally gave it an especially resourceful personality. The Owl, taking into account both the remaining time, and the need to keep the TRIAD's standards up, suggested that they bring up the original purposes of the TALKOUT to guide the various applicants as they worked up what they wanted to present. These applicants were not to pander, to titillate or otherwise dumb-down their presentations. Every animal who was thinking of applying was given this sheet, listing the goals of the event. It read:

> To gain respect from the human animals for exceptional capabilities.
>
> To show them how the animal kingdom helps them.
>
> To persuade them that it is in humans' self-interest to help and protect the animal kingdom, leading to more humane treatment, fewer communicable diseases, and environmental sustainability. [Under this head were included examples of humans already nurturing animals.]
>
> To encourage more research on the animal kingdom, which will reveal a larger intelligence than the stereotypical ideas that animals are ruled by genetic determination.

The last point, the research, is already underway via humans studying the emotions and thought processes of animals. Jane Goodall's time with the chimpanzees provided evidence that these animals have a rich inner life.

The Owl's framing made sense to the Elephant and the Dolphin. The purposes and standards were reintroduced in precise and bright language to both the animal and the human kingdoms before any further applications were processed. Each applicant, paying mind to the central goals, in its application had to describe its time on the air and submit to an audition.

Meanwhile, one of the ponies assisting the TRIAD came rushing in with a great suggestion from a possum that had been staying in a corner of a deck in a pricey home in California for three years. The possum, quite accustomed to observing humans, wondered why the TRIAD had not asked humans what *they* want to see on the screen. So far all the human-related items presented had been after the fact; that is, in response to the polling of humans as they watched different features. Why not ascertain their interests before they put all these shows on screen?

The TRIAD asked the "Human Genius" to conduct a quick poll and rank topics humans would like to view. Back came a long list, and topping it was *migration of the birds*!

Bird lovers are numerous, organized, and know what they want. Moreover, they were not the only ones intrigued by this subject. The fact that birds can fly as far as fifteen thousand miles from the Arctic to Central or South America and back is beyond fascination. How do they stay together, navigate strong winds, rain, and storms, and possess such a sense of uncanny direction as to land in the same place year after year and maintain their incredible flight energy? As one scientist put it, there are millions of neurons in these so-called bird brains, processing and using information from their environment, reaching all the way to navigating by the North Star.

For some time, the Human Genius had been worrying about the impromptu nature of the presentations. For a human audience, live shows are rare because of quality control problems, flubs, pauses, and the like. That is why shows are uniformly taped or, if live, as with the long-running *Saturday Night Live*, they have been practiced several times, right up to the 11:30 p.m. start time, in *Saturday Night Live*'s case. But the Human Genius hesitated to intervene. It would not be advisable if members of the animal kingdom saw the Human Genius as a behind-the-scenes puller of strings. Nonetheless, he gently suggested that the auditions constitute the tapings, making for a more vibrant and concise variety show. The TRIAD took ownership of the idea and sent out the word that all approved auditions were to be sent to headquarters to be further evaluated for acceptance, and used verbatim if accepted and within time limits.

On with the Show

The variety show was well publicized and widely anticipated by humans.

First up was something lighthearted but suitable for heading three, how humans could ameliorate the lives of animals, in this case, pets. It was the premiere of DOG TV: a collection of apps for computer or other screens that would keep all kinds of dogs occupied when they are left alone by their "owners." To indicate the value of this entertainment, a number of dogs—a poodle, a German shepherd, a beagle, a Doberman, a Boston terrier, and an African hunting dog—were allowed to view the available shows. Humans went wild watching these dogs go nearly berserk with excitement, reacting to the provocative images on the screen: food, sexy dogs, lures, prey, household and wilderness scenes filled with cats and squirrels. The dogs couldn't understand why they couldn't reach these images even though they kept trying to fling themselves against the pictures.

Very few humans suspected who could have come up with this canine theater. Certainly not the dogs. Right? It was the Human Genius who wanted a whiz-bang opening for the variety programing. After that, he receded into passivity and watched the animals create the segments. How does this segment fit the standards? It gave millions of viewers information about DOG TV and how it could end dog loneliness when the owners aren't around.

The next segment turned upon goal two, documenting the way animals aided humans when humans helped them. Citing a *New York Times* article, a rooftop honeybee, taking a lunch break from its colony at One Bryant Park in New York City, spoke as follows: "Look what you've done for us urban honeybees and for yourselves. You've set up hives on your rooftops to pollinate your green roofs. The green roofs use compost made from waste out of the building's cafeteria. Manhattan is becoming beehive heaven and you're harvesting our honey.

It's all win-win. Whee! Congratulations. Just keep spreading urban, rooftop beehives all over the world. We're bullish on bees and you can't believe the buzz!"

It now came time, in line with goal one, to call for respect. Again, referencing a *Times* article, a flatworm crawled up and stated, "Oh, humans, can you regrow your head or your tailbone? We can. And the more you know about us, the more you'll learn how to regrow your heads, which, given your troubles, psychological or social, may someday be done on a large scale.

"Who among you knows the most about our capability? Go see the journal *Nature*, where three studies were published about the 'signaling pathway known as WNT/beta-catenin,' which orients us during regeneration. I'm just a simple flatworm, but in my simplicity you may be able to understand your complexity. A simple bit of advice before bye-bye: be sure you have your best brains look into 'unintended consequences' for humans able to regrow their heads or other organs emanating from your body."

Now a lovely moth moved to center screen. Its topic was the more flattering part of goal three, how some humans were pitching in to help subhumans.

Coming off the second National Moth Week (July 23–29), the moth gracefully curtsied in gratitude. "More and more humans are calling themselves 'moth'ers' to promote the conservation of moths," the insect said, celebrating what Senator Robert Menendez called "their incredible biodiversity, and their importance to ecosystem health."

"I know what some of you humans are thinking," predicted the moth. "What the heck, moths have eaten my wool pants, my wool sweater. They're perforators of our wardrobes. And you've got the nerve to make them admirable."

The moth explained, "That clothing destroyer was just one species (and the least attractive) of many species of moths. Don't put us in the same closet."

The moth then showed a picture of one of the more attractive among them, a virgin tiger moth, which looks like a brightly colored butterfly. "Listen to your knowledgeable human *moth'er watchers* spreading into thirty-four countries, from Nicaragua to Norway. They must know something valuable about moths.

"At any rate," continued the moth, "I won't be seeing you next July due to my short life span, but my grandchildren will be there. Become a moth'er. It's just as much fun counting and identifying us as it is for birdwatchers. And you don't have to get up so early. Your post office has issued a first-class postage stamp with a special commemorative moth-week cancellation.

"By the way, have you ever tried dried redwood chips in a bag in your closet? We moths cannot stand the odor of redwood. Just a tip."

Of course, fulfilling the requirements of goal one, achieving respect, did not depend solely on noting valuable animal qualities as the flatworm had, but also on demolishing stereotypes.

A pack rat strode forward to cite a piece in *Science News* that said real pack rats are more orderly than human "pack rats." *Neotoma albigula*, pack rats, called the white-throated wood rats, bring back to their midden homes such items as cowpats, rabbit pellets, and other animals' dung. Inside their midden, researcher Michele Skopec of Weber State University in Ogden, Utah, found a coyote paw, Doritos bags, shotgun shells, a silver ring, and an old underwear band. Some of these materials were for bedding or food.

"They have this insatiable urge to cache," reports. Like chronic human hoarders, they tend to live alone as they pile up their collections of just about anything. What made human viewers' eyes bulge was the segregated orderliness of what these pack rats amass and how they can digest the toughest and most toxic stuff for food. One high school biology teacher remarked to her class that humans can learn much about the kind of interior decorating mind and the amazing digestive system of the pack rat species. (For more see the *Washington Post*, 2/25/14.)

Now came a segment that was likely to be controversial. It fit under goal three, helping animals would also benefit humans, but it pointed out that some animals' more obnoxious behavior, such as destroying other much loved species or (for dogs) doing their business on the sidewalk, had roots in human thoughtlessness.

Under a magnifier, a tick appeared. "For all your dittoheads who disbelieve that the climate is changing due to your Homo sapiens, watch what we're doing to moose in the wilds of Live Free or Die New Hampshire.

"Winter is starting later and ending sooner. That gives us—150,000 ticks per moose—longer to feed on a single moose and multiply like, well, ticks. I'm a female tick and I can lay three thousand eggs. What's not to like about climate change?

"Have you seen the moose lately—the ones that are still standing? They look like moose ghosts, emaciated zombies with antlers. How would you look with tens of thousands of tiny bites every minute? Fewer moose means fewer tourists and fewer meals for wildlife and fewer birds and rabbits.

"It's all about the ecosystem," exclaimed the tick. "Your interference with it is causing our rampages. This is a wakeup call, and the hunters and the tourist industry know this, regardless of what your radio mouth Rush Limburger says. Colder, longer winters means fewer ticks.

"What's our interest as ticks in telling you all this? We're taking the long view. If the moose disappear, our tick descendents won't have such a feasty host."

A Saint Bernard trudged onto the stage and mentioned a topic that made urban walking perilous, the way dog walkers allow their pets to defecate on sidewalks and then don't clean up the stain. Is that the dog's fault? He or she can't scoop the poop up in the way a human can.

The Saint Bernard offered a solution, already successful in Brunete, a middle-class suburb in Madrid, Spain. The mayor, Borja Gutiérrez, recruited a number of volunteers to bag the poop, box it, and send it back to its owners. It comes in a white box with the town seal labeled "lost and found." Motivated by constant citizen complaints of dog dung, Gutiérrez found that delivering these boxes had reduced recklessness by 70 percent after only a two-week campaign. The mayor hopes that once embarrassed, dog owners will start using plastic bags as a habit.

The Saint Bernard added her own opinion: "It's not just humans who are embarrassed. Think about us. We don't have a way to pick the goo up and carry it to a proper place. We're just not anatomically capable. This is a plea for help and harmony." Then with the confirmatory bark, the gentle beast departed. (See the *New York Times*, 8/2/13.)

Continuing the topic of the bad behavior of humans, a gathering of cetaceans and three dolphins appeared in a giant water tank. The dolphins were stressed that hundreds of their dead sisters and brothers were washing ashore in the southeastern U.S. because of a lethal virus. Although the sea mammals didn't know the source of the virus, they did know that conditions underwater were made stressful by human oil companies using high-decibel air guns every fifteen seconds for weeks at a time to search for oil and gas. They quoted a marine mammal expert as saying that "it must be like in a war zone" in the sea. It may deafen endangered species of whales. Whales and dolphins cannot survive in the dark ocean depths without depending on their hearing. They can't find their pod. They get lost and can't find food.

Seguing into goal one, the demand for respect, the cetaceans and dolphins reminded humans about research, which found a high level of intelligence and teachability among these marine animals. "Teach us," said one of the dolphins, "to find your oil and gas by sensing vibrations. Teach us what we have to ingest from the ocean to increase our immunity from those viruses. Teach us so we can adapt."

This request stunned the human animals in different ways.

Some were amazed and thrilled to receive the challenge. Others grumbled about the absurdity of these animals claiming to be able to learn. To them it was all nature, not nurture.

The children wisely asked their parents: "Can we help?" Requests resulted in much mass media attention to the sea dwellers' plight.

A Moment of Silence for the Dead Zones

With all this interest in sea creatures, the TRIAD decided to run their segment on dead zones on the planet, many of which already existed in the sea. They could go from water to land and mention parts of the earth that had also met this fate.

Humans sensed something big and told their friends to turn on the screen or their cell phones for the prime-time presentation.

The Elephant made her way to center stage.

"I, the Elephant, honored to be part of the guiding TRIAD, want to bring up the topic of the dreaded subject of DEAD ZONES, and, more specifically, the dead zones created by mining operations and nuclear reservations all over the globe. They are, by their uncontrolled nature, poisonous to the land, the air, and the water. All of us—and I mean all of us—in the larger vicinity are poisoned, sickened along with our babies. Mining companies do not discriminate, poisoning mammals, reptiles, fish, birds, insects, and humans, including farmers and, of course, their workers, and First Natives along with their families. The poisonous waters flow far to the villages and cities on their way to the ocean. The poisonous air is caught by the higher streams to contaminate many lungs, gills, and other organs over vast regions."

The Owl came and alighted with dignity on the Elephant's back—not on his head or trunk—that would have been too showy. The Owl described flying over large desolate tracks of gouged land, without vegetation, marked by slag heaps of crushed rock, sand, and chemicals. Nothing moved except the scurrying scorpions and other hardy insects. Stagnant water of various colors incubated deformed bugs. Intoned the wise Owl: "How many more dead zones can humans make all of us endure, before you and your corporations start making peace with our planet?"

Along came the Dolphin with an oceanic vision of dead zones in the seas. "I," cried the Dolphin, "call them extinction zones." The Dolphin had never appeared angrier, shaking and with flashing eyes. "Your Gulf of Mexico has a huge dead zone—over four million acres—where nothing visible can live. Any marine animals who stray there become sick with awful-looking skin sores. Many have no ability to detect the danger until it is too late. There are no warning signs by humans.

"My sources throughout oceandom have inundated me with dead zone locations of all sizes everywhere, based on their own harmful experiences. Some zones are becoming deadlier; others have been dead and abandoned by their contaminators. Humans think the oceans will dilute everything they dump, but as an aquatic traveler wide and far, I can attest that the oceans are nearing their carrying capacity, losing oxygen and many species of fish, some forever.

"My close friend the manatee—he looks sluggish but is very aware—tells me that by 2040 the bulk of all your seafood will be from fish farms, which further pollute themselves and the ocean with insecticides and other chemicals. Then there are the genetically engineered fish escaping the nets to breed and compromise the gene pool of their natural counterparts. These facts come from your own studies, oh humans.

"My humble suggestion," said the Dolphin, "is to plot the dead zones on a map of the world, so you can see them on your screens and with your children or in larger size in your marine museums. Support the establishment of well-located marine sanctuaries to which we in the ocean can repair for rest and rejuvenation, perhaps even for mating and giving birth, as land animals can do in your designated wilderness forest and desert areas."

Whereupon the Elephant, the Owl, and the Dolphin remained quiet for two minutes, and then the Elephant, so sensitive to different sounds, ended the solemn session with a sad, haunting trumpet sound. No presentation was followed by as much silence, which was picked up among millions of humans all over the globe, a silence that did not escape the quiet animal kingdom either. The impact, said one ecologist to another in Cold Springs Harbor, "was so different and greater in increasing awareness than our statistics, studies, testimony, and even pictures. The TRIAD conveyed much emotional intelligence in the way they handled this subject."

Variety Show: Dark and Light

A horse and a bear pointed out that their segments would fit right in at this point. Not quite getting the connection, the Elephant asked for more of an explanation. As the horse told her, it was as if, perverse as humans could be, while they were killing whole sections of the world, they dreamed of repopulating it, not with natural animals but with reprogrammed or cloned ones.

The horse, quoting the *Wall Street Journal*, told its story, "You humans, and I've carried many of you for many years, talk about 'invasive species' in a derogatory manner: plants, fish, snakes, and mussels. But can't you see yourselves as an invasive species of the animal world?

"You're starting to clone my kind, horses. It is one thing to breed us against our natural inclinations. But now the human cloners want their horses to have equal rights to register them with the American Quarter Horse Association Registry. A judge in Texas ruled that the association cannot bar cloned horses from its lists. The association wanted to exclude cloned horses because it cannot determine the parentage of cloned horses and worries about narrowing the gene pool. Can't you just get out of our genes, for horses' sake? Someday it could happen to you!"

The black salmon (sometimes called the cobia) wasn't talking about cloning, but genetic manipulation, also quoting from the *Wall Street Journal.*

"You humans," he said, "want to turn me into a vegetarian after eons of being a committed carnivore of crab, squid, smaller fish, anything with flesh. You're messing around with my taste buds, trying to trick me into eating some concocted amino acid goo. I don't want to be a vegetarian. My whole makeup is to swallow flesh, and you don't know what the side effects will be.

"It all started when you farm-fished me, then had to give menhaden fish feed to me in the cage which depleted the *crucial menhaden* fisheries, which provide the main diet in the wild ocean for all kinds of marine animals, including dolphins, tuna, swordfish, and swooping birds like gulls.

"Have you figured out how changing my diet to vegetarian is going to make me taste when you eat me? You will probably have to do things to save wild fish for eating and sport. I'm very much craved in India, China, and Europe. That means lots of wild little fish have to be caught to feed me and my species. So explain it all to me and I'll communicate through all black salmondom. Thank you."

A bear trundled forward, saying his segment would fit in at this point. It was put on as a humorous counterpoint to the last piece. He was also playing off a story in the *Wall Street Journal.* His complaint was that many humans wanted to convert his eating habits, not making him purely a vegetarian—he was already an omnivore—but a junk food addict.

The wild black bear appeared perplexed. It seems he got caught up in a controversy between humans who want to have harmonious relationships "with us wild bears and those humans who fear us and warn about getting too close to us with their hands offering delicacies like yogurt-covered raisins and marshmallows. I suppose the fearful humans are from the 'Please Don't Feed the Bears' school of thought. You know the backlash against black bears if there are one or two harmful human incidents. Just LEAVE US ALONE PLEASE with our shrinking habitat! We're smart but not smart enough to figure out every line that cannot be crossed as you try to harmonize with us."

The quick trio of speakers resonated very well in the animal kingdom, except for insects eaten by bears. These tiny creatures liked the allure of a different harmonizing diet for bears made up of non-sentient matter, by which they meant plants and marshmallows. For the rest of the animal kingdom, the three speakers sounded as if they had given a modern declaration of independence, one carefully phrased so as not to anger humans, and including ethicists, scientists, theologians, and people without titles who are worried about this new human invasiveness. Because of the horse, the black salmon, and the bear, a broader and deeper dialogue is sure to be on its way.

The TRIAD had decided to archive for release later another story about animals' eating being tampered with, as this story was so depressing. It was a story that could be read in the *Wall Street Journal.* In the filmed but not broadcast sequence, a group of stiff cattle came walking tippy-toed to the stage. They beseeched human governments to help them. One bull spoke for all when he said his weakness had something to do with what the feed lots of humans put into their food to make them gain weight faster before they are slaughtered. "We cattle are resigned to be sacrificed for your human appetites. But can't we live our artificially shorter lives in some comfort grazing and chewing our cud?"

It turned out that the culprit was Zilmax, a feed additive made by the giant drug company Merck & Co. The big meat processor companies are actually stopping purchases of Zilmax, an additive that already has been ingested by twenty-five million cattle. They don't think the trouble Zilmax causes is worth the twenty more pounds it adds to each cow. Besides, consumers are more and more demanding of meat without antibiotics and other drug additives, even eating less or no meat when they are unsure. The fear of antibiotic resistance is also a growing factor weighing on their diet choices.

The TRIAD didn't put this on, seeing that the gloom was already spreading from the salmon's talk of declining species. Then came two jellyfish with good news for them. Careful viewers, however, saw that, just like the tick, the jellyfish were obliquely criticizing humans for throwing the world out of whack. "We jellyfish dominated the oceans half a billion years ago. Then came creatures that liked to eat us, like sharks and whales and other big fish. Well, they are all declining so we are multiplying like crazy. Warm and acidic water environments do help our numbers. For us global warming is great. We're called living fossils, but what can stop us?

"Who can survive and thrive while being spineless and brainless? Jellyfish, that's who! We sting beachgoers and get away with it. We can be as small as a grain of sand or as large as a stove.

"We have a number of different colors and can flash, sparkle and glow. As we multiply and expand our range toward once cooler but now warming parts of the ocean, humans avoid even thinking of eating us or even grinding us up as fish feed for fish farms. We mate and reproduce fast. Here's the lesson for humans: the more you degrade and toxify the oceans, the more of us there will be and the more of you will get stung.

"One more motivation we can give you for respecting us. Your neuroscientists have discovered that one of our jellyfish proteins can be used in a drug that helps reduce age-related memory loss. Who knows what else lies within our bodies for you to adapt for human health? Better respect us. Toodle-oo!"

Sometimes reverse psychology works better. The jellyfish, brainless as they are, reached more than a few brains among the human animals, who, unless stung, hardly knew anything about jellyfish.

While goal one was to emphasize respect for humans, the TRIAD, in selecting the next stories, wanted to underline how some humans had already paid homage to worthy animals. A spokes-dog mentioned that a model honoring the Dogs of War will be built near Fort Bragg in North Carolina.

War dogs save soldiers' lives by alerting them to an ambush or detecting explosives. That is defense. The canine monument, standing near the parade grounds, will be a life-size bronze Belgian malinois, outfitted with a combat vest and camera. Around the malinois will be granite pavers with the names of dogs killed in warfare. This should not upset human viewers who see that the dog was serving on the side of their opponents. For whatever has been written—and it is a lot lately—about "the intelligence of dogs," no author has claimed that even the smartest war dogs work out of conviction for one side or another. It is all about the trainer and the training.

Watching this segment, thousands of Seeing Eye dogs, faithfully next to their blind humans, wondered why they, the loyal canines of vision that enabled humans to lead a fuller life, were not given at least equal billing with war dogs. Maybe later, they hoped.

The *Washington Post* was used as a reference for the next story, which was about a dedication ceremony for a heroic horse, Sergeant Reckless, unveiled at the National Museum of the Marine Corps. It is a life-size statue of Reckless, a real horse. She learned to take ammunition to the battlefield in Korea and carry wounded soldiers to safety. She could even step over communication wires.

The equine world watched and beamed with pride of the species. See, some said, look what cooperation between horses and humans can produce. Human visits to the Marine Museum in Washington, D.C., increased sharply.

Given the accolades humans had given to animal helpers in these situations, a goat demanded his segment be aired so human animals could note one of his contributions. He put it in terms of a story.

"On a warm August day at the congressional cemetery in Washington, D.C., a herd of goats was rented from Eco-goats to eat an acre and a half worth of poison ivy and English ivy, honeysuckle, and other vines smothering the trees. These vines could bring the trees crashing down and damage the gravestones. The ivy's leaves could block the trees' photosynthesis, which would surely destroy them. After decades of neglect and decay, the cemetery is making a comeback and the publicity about some fifty goats munching the vegetation brought the place great media and photos. Although some vegetation is not to the taste of us goats, did they ever denude the targeted vines and leave behind some good natural fertilizer before they were loaded onto the trucks and brought back to their Maryland farm. More goats are being rented around the country to reduce the vegetation. They are cheaper than lawn care companies, and herbicides are not needed."

The goat beamed: "We are the ultimate recyclers, and we don't pollute the air or discharge toxic chemicals. Maybe we'll be allowed to live longer because of our new goat mission. We'll certainly get more respect from the enviros who have condemned us for contributing to land erosion, not entirely inaccurate, but we have to live too and we don't have any *mens rea* level of intelligence. See I've picked up some knowledge during these one hundred hours to defend goatdom."

The world's sheep, looking at all this goat glory, were both envious and upset. After all, they are far more obedient to humans, do not denude grasslands, provide clothing for the human animal, endure infanticide of their lambs, and don't get any airtime; all this was communicated and duly received by the TRIAD for assessment.

Not to be outdone, a beetle came forward, one from the *Rhinoncomimus latipes* family, to show how he and his fellows were providing biological control services.

Recently, New York City poured five thousand of these Asian weevils in several parks to destroy a prolific vine that threatens native plants and trees. These invasive vines spread so fast, they're called "mile-a-minute," growing up to twenty feet in a single season. They suffocate native plants, such as aster, goldenrod and pokeweed. Mile-a-minute can shorten the growth of saplings and even hasten the death of mature trees. Enter the *R. latipes*, the Asian weevil, the size of a sesame seed. Through the weevil's entire life cycle, from egg to larva to pupa to adult, it feasts only on mile-a-minute.

"We can't do the whole job," said a cluster of Asian beetles in unison, while feasting on the targeted vine, "but we can keep them down a lot."

A mouse and an ape had their segments put on next. In the wings, they justly complained that while the goats and weevils were helping humans' favored plants, mice and apes helped humans where it hurt, that is, where they hurt from often deliberately inflicted diseases.

The mouse, a rodent studied more than even humans in laboratories around the world, said: "I, the mouse, am here to remind you humans that your scientists estimate that eighty percent of substances toxic to mice are also toxic to you humans. Those toxins include, by the way, sugar in foods, especially high-fructose corn syrup. A sugary diet makes my mice friends less able to do things they need to do daily, like defending their territory from other male mice or mating. By the way, we mice wonder why you despise us and our rats when we are your most important subjects for your medical research."

The ape rose to full height to speak: "I, the ape, note animals are sharing major diseases. Wild gorillas have been felled by Ebola hemorrhagic fever, as has the wild chimpanzee population. You humans give us deadly respiratory diseases. Remember the forty-five years of disasters at Gombe Stream National Park in Tanzania, in which the chimps suffered epidemics of polio and respiratory diseases.

"Wild chimpanzees have also died in great numbers from AIDS. You humans believe that the deadly virus that has taken millions of your lives came from us in Africa. Yes, you have given chimpanzees polio vaccines in their bananas after a horrible epidemic. We, the great apes in the wilds, request that you continue research with our captive relatives in your labs—treat them humanely and inform them that such research is good for all of us—and that you subject your own humans to clinical trials. Some of your labs abuse our kind and do so for trivial commercial purposes, such as to test cosmetics. Labs should only do experiments to help us control such diseases as I described and others such as hepatitis.

"Speaking for wild primates to our incarcerated heroic brethren, stay courageous for scientific discoveries that may save us from diseases: humans and us. To the human animals, we say, do only what is necessary and cannot be done by other means as you treat your captives humanely. And give them a peaceful sanctuary when you retire them. And remember, biomedically we're not that much different from you."

This was a real thought-provoking segment that brought humans closer to their primate cousins. The ape and mouse strode off the stage, with the mouse being careful to follow the ape to avoid being inadvertently crushed.

Much earlier in the TALKOUT a heroic rooster had broadcast shots of domesticates in factory farms, but a new bunch of delegates from these animals, who had approved auditions—unfortunately many more animal segments had been approved than could possibly run—were asking for more time. True, they had had a moment in the sun already, but, as they justly said, they had only been allowed brief vignettes and not given the airtime to state all their grievances.

The TRIAD—the Elephant, the Owl, and the Dolphin—took their comments very seriously. How could anyone argue with their desperation and pleas? On the other hand, putting the domesticates on the stage a second time to portray their cruel treatment and subsequent slaughter would jeopardize the careful calibration of the one hundred hours, which they were now finalizing, not to go into that arena, but to lay the groundwork for much later raising the question of animal genocide, after the initial TALKOUT had created some level of coherent understanding between human and subhuman.

And after all, two of the three TRIAD members were carnivores. "So look who's talking," the Owl and the Dolphin whispered to each other. "Voilá," said the Elephant, herbivore, "we tell the domesticates that while being very sympathetic to their cause, a majority of the TRIAD has a genetically determined conflict of interest and regrettably must defer any decision to a future Secretariat. We hope you will understand," the TRIAD concluded. The delegation of the domesticates wearily drifted away from the closed door session wondering what they could do next, other than just wait and wait for their distant descendants to try again.

If truth be known, the TRIAD realized from the start that if the door opened wide to the domesticates, so many of them with so many facets of their lives and interactions with humans, would entirely crowd out the priorities of the wild animals. Just imagine what is contained in one set of facts: "In 2012, Americans alone spend $53.3 billion on pet products, more than $12 billion of that for supplies and over-the-counter medicine," according to the American Pet Products Association. In other words, domesticates took up a good bit of humans' time but the ferals, also clamoring for place on the show, felt domesticates had already hogged enough screen time. For goodness' sake, they'd even had a segment on dog defecation.

As something of a mollifying gesture, and billed as part of goal one, getting respect for animals, the TRIAD chose a domesticate, a real human-crowd pleaser, not a downtrodden farm animal, but a prize winner.

They invited to the stage ORB, the winner of the Kentucky Derby.

"Hello, I am ORB, the fast racehorse who didn't quite make the Triple Crown, but the Derby is enough for my satisfaction. Soon I will be put out to retirement on a comfortable farm where I will be pampered only to perform as a stud. My owners made a lot of money from me and, while I am well taken care, much is demanded of me and I'm subjected to too many injections. Sometimes I think my jockey and my trainer understand how terrified racehorses are in front of roaring crowds, having to perform at a level of unimaginable intensity next to lots of other horses who can bump or trip one up. Danger, failure, and terminal injury are all risks during that minute and a half.

"Don't get me wrong; I, ORB, a winner, am not about to say that all this is cruelty to racehorses that are winners. It is just the forgotten losers and the retirees for whom I call on you to be more sympathetic and empathetic.

"Oh, humans, I sense that many of you love horses and believe they are intelligent and sometimes seem to have a sixth sense. Please keep being good to all of us as we continue to be faithfully good for you."

Most American viewers had seen or heard of ORB's magnificent first place finish at the 2013 Kentucky Derby. They were thrilled to see the horse and hear his thoughtful observations. He had a mellowing effect on them and, though he had softly chided human treatment of horses, they took it advisedly.

An Announcement to Whet Appetites

By this time, interest in the variety offering was waning, but luckily the TRIAD had allowed an enterprising rabbit to gather material for a special segment he had proposed. He had taken some already recorded material and commissioned some new material, all to be part of the the Great Animal Sex Extravaganza.

The TRIAD, looking for a resurgence in ratings, announced that it was almost time for a major two-hour program on the mating and love habits of mammals, aquatic life, birds, and insects in live and active color, and rated XXX.

The human planet, as expected, went wild with anticipation, jokes, text messages, cartoons, and thoughts of outright voyeurism. Viewers were told they might have to shield children, but that this would not be animal pornography. For the TRIAD's announcement added that the tone would be generally serious, with some light moments.

Truth was, this programming would greatly diminish the widespread view of nature's mating as an expression of reckless "animal spirits," so decried in Puritan-age jeremiads. In fact, the TRIAD hoped to show just the opposite: that animal sex is mostly more restrained and far less obsessive than human sex, and animal love far more fascinating and nurturing than most humans are aware.

Human News Stations I

While most of the human world who could watch any screen was glued to the TALKOUT, there were those who kept checking the human news stations. Not surprisingly, these stations were filled with the latest *animal* news. One station picked up a report from *Mother Jones*, which told of how in the spring of 2013 a van crossed from Russia to Inner Mongolia. Chinese customs officials, who stopped it for a routine check, discovered something packed inside the wheels and spare tire. Two hundred thirteen severed bear paws, worth about half a million dollars, which are used as cooking ingredients or expensive gifts. Imagine the short life of the legless bears!

If a human flipped to another channel, he or she would hear about something on the other side of the world in California. Terra Firma Farms is devoted to raising joyful pigs, cattle, and chickens on lush perennial grasses in open pastures. The Smith family farm is beyond organic. It is biodynamic or, as Ms. Smith puts it, "We're growing the soil that grows the grass that feeds the animals."

What do the animals think about the place? A cow called it "cow paradise." The pig looked up and said it was "pig heaven." Then a chicken came along and said that all the animals get along beautifully. "Our chickens," she chirped, "even go to a sow in labor and drop an egg near her mouth for some additional nutrition." With a lift of her head, the chicken remarked, "We only have one bad day and never have to regret it, knowing that we'll give humans at least one good meal."

Less inspiring was the feature story on another human broadcast, which discussed shark tournaments. A great white shark, who had been clued to turn on the human channel by one of her sister sharks, explained to his children what they were watching: "Humans actually offer money prizes for the biggest sharks caught and then hung unceremoniously by their tail. Why us? Because of the movie *Jaws*, maybe, or just due to the exaggerated scary stories about shark attacks. Maybe it is because we take no prisoners and perform like flexible slicing machines. You know shark phobia.

"Well, seeing us piled up in dumpsters—pretty grisly human activity—some environmentalist came along with a great idea—'catch and release.' All it took was a circle hook that caught sharks but did not seriously injure us. So now at Montauk, Long Island, the shark hunting club catches, pictures, and measures us, and then throws us back into the deep. I hope the idea spreads to other shark hunting tournaments before the fishermen come and find none of us are around anymore."

Of course, other, more conservative channels were still putting on news about the nuisances animals could be. In one news flash, an agitated San Diego mayor spoke of the state of emergency he declared because of the foul guano piling up as gulls, pigeons, pelicans, cormorants, and others relieve themselves. He stated he is applying guano-eating bacteria that digest animal feces. The odor is overwhelming in the cove that is home to expensive restaurants and mansions. Fortunately, the bacteria are getting the job done. It's working. Tourist life in La Jolla cannot be denied.

Variety Is the Spice

Meanwhile on the TALKOUT, in the run-up to the animal sex special, it was back to the regular variety programming. More on goal one. All honor to animals. In this case, the honor was being offered by humans to a rare animal.

Lonesome George, the giant Galapagos tortoise and the last of his subspecies, had died, making global news because he was known around the world from nature TV shows and millions of tourists' pictures and videos. He was about one hundred years old and five or six feet long, weighing two hundred pounds.

The last of the Pinta Island subspecies, Lonesome George earned his nickname after sailors in the nineteenth century had hunted down most of his fellows for food. The arrival of wild goats in the 1950s added to the tortoises' woes by taking away their food, such plants as the local cactus.

Lonesome George only gave one interview, having been coaxed by a friendly goat to go on camera when he was only eighty. "Yes, I am a giant tortoise and the only one left in my subspecies. How would you humans like to be the last one standing? It is very lonely, makes me sad and shy. I'm supposed to live for two hundred years but I'm fearful about no one else carrying on the gene pool and losing it forever. I cannot mate, cannot share life with my kind. It's the equivalent of humans in solitary confinement, except I've done nothing wrong except live." Humans swore they saw a tear slip from George's right eye.

The TRIAD, noting the aura of sadness among human watchers, knew the programming needed a quick pickup and they got it in the form of a pigeon announcing a startling research project by humans to atone and "de-extinct" the historic passenger pigeon. About one hundred years after the last passenger pigeon, Martha, died in 1914 at the Cincinnati Zoo, there was an effort to revive the species.

The effort by biologists is being funded by the group Revive and Restore. The idea is to take passenger pigeon DNA from museum specimens and meld them with genetic fragments from the band-tailed pigeon.

A band-tailed pigeon alighted on the stage and explained:

"I, the band-tailed pigeon, welcome this honorable initiative to atone for the passenger pigeon holocaust that in the nineteenth century destroyed literally billions of passenger pigeons. Biologist Ben Novak tells me he is confident that 'making the passenger pigeon genome right now will be easier than making the first living passenger pigeon hatch from an egg.'"

The pigeon continued: "Breeding our historic cousin may be the easier part of the revivification effort. Where is the habitat for the passenger pigeon? Much of its wintering forest habitat is gone along with the beech mast, the nuts of a beech tree, which it ate.

"The other problem, I fear," said the band-tailed pigeon, "is that only massive flocks of pigeons could survive, because they are so individually vulnerable to other carnivores that huge numbers are needed to result in survivors who can then lay their eggs. Five million birds is the minimum flock size, unless, that is, human conservationists can keep the predators away like they do at considerable expense for the rare whooping cranes.

"It depends on how deep is the sense of atonement by humans," concluded the pigeon with a sad but hopeful look in her eyes. She added that some pigeon specialists are warning that there were too many pigeons—five billion in North America before the white man came, outstripping their habitat and resulting in a species implosion. "Little do they know that overpopulation is the least of our worries. Do they have any idea of what it is like being a pigeon, with all the old and new predators, day in and day out?" she concluded.

Human News Stations II

An animal media analyst working for the TRIAD noticed that the human stations, desperately trying to compete with the TALKOUT, had hit on shooting for one audience segment, those with low attention spans. So they were staying on the topic of the day, animals, but with quick bits and short sound bites.

He noted a few examples. One was an odd fact about oysters. The human announcer said, "The oyster is the pride of the animal kingdom for how it helps humans and their emissions. One grown oyster filters as much as fifty gallons of water every day. All the oysters ask of humans is that they drive away the cownose rays that eat them."

Meanwhile, a show about word origins was stating, "Humans use the word 'looney' apropos of the erratic behavior of the loons. Really, folks," the sympathetic human said, "let's see if you can dive one hundred fifty feet underwater and remain there for several minutes looking for your next meal."

Another station was focusing on the annual swim of the "wild" herd of 130 horses from Assateague Island to Chincoteague Island, off the coast of Virginia. The announcer couldn't believe the number of human onlookers with cameras. It only took five minutes to cross the Assateague Channel and it was pouring torrential rain, but starting at dawn the first of thirty-five thousand people, from all over the country, staked out their spots.

Two ponies who had short attention spans had tuned in to this human broadcast. "Why?" one pony asked the other.

"What is the fascination?" replied the other pony. "Do thirty-five thousand Americans show up to do something about the thousands of children and adults who drown every year? I don't get it."

A warbler appeared to thank humans for ending the pernicious practice of stuffing dead songbirds into the hats that women used to wear for a few years after 1886 when the practice started and became a form of grisly high couture. "But for your prohibition, I might have ended up a preserved, dried form on top of the hat of some lady strolling down Fifth Avenue in New York City."

Revolt of the Prairies

The TRIAD had many programs that had been prerecorded, but, as noted, there were many more than could fit in their time frame and so many animals whose segments had not been aired so far were chafing at the bit to go before the world.

The challenges had been increasing ever since the grand revolt of the insects, who had demanded and then received the right to strut before the world. The TRIAD started talking about what could be done to both calm the tumult and rechannel it toward the overall purpose of the TALKOUT, which, by now, had matured far beyond its flattery-cum-kindness equation.

The most immediate problem was a revolt on the American prairies.

Demanding equal time—an argument picked up from human candidates' actions at election time—a cluster of bees, grouses, mule deer, water fowl, and prairie chickens gathered on shrinking plains in North Dakota to speak to the loss of the habitat due to ranchers converting their land to crops, such as corn used for ethanol. They were getting a groundswell of support from other animals, so, like it or not, the TRIAD felt they must air their complaints.

They came from all over to the gathering, fear in their expressions, fear of extinction. A group of unarmed hunters stood in quiet support. One of them said that the animals had a point: "There's been an eighty percent loss of habitat for some of this wildlife. They're being squeezed," he said, arching his eyebrow. "Moving cattle out of the area often preserves the native grass that attracts ungulates and birds. Why can't the people understand that; the mule deer do," he concluded.

"It's the curse of the corn ethanol, the federal subsidy, and high commodity prices to make it more profitable to convert to cropland," observed another hunter.

The gathering of animals was elated that humans, virile hunters, were speaking on their behalf. The bees weren't so naïve, telling their fellow protestors: They're just doing this to save you so that they can continue to kill some of you during hunting season.

Whereas the grouse replied: "Better that some of us be sacrificed, than that all of us disappear," keeping to itself the fact that some bird species were being poisoned by the lead scattered by the hunters' bullets.

A prairie chicken fluttered and urged all to make their distinctive noises in unison to indicate agreement with the hunters' viewpoint. They did. And the first Native American tribes of the great prairie took notice and expanded new renewable wind energy to save that heritage of their ancestors.

Hyenas Provide a Laugh Track

The Owl frequently consulted with the raven, whose intellect it respected highly, and who used to work for the CIA as a trained spy.

(To give some background on this bird, it can be mentioned that there was a secret operation by the CIA during the Cold War with the Russians to train members of its species to deposit listening devices on ledges of apartment buildings and to warn of enemy ambushes. This same CIA operation wanted to use felines to snoop on human conversations. A lot of animals were involved. According to the *Smithsonian Magazine*, the director of training for the Navy taught dolphins how to detect submarines. In an otherwise thrilling testimony to animal and insect intelligence, Dr. Bailey says he never met an animal he could not train, even showing how he could provoke from a spider a conditioned response, such as blowing on a spider in its web and turning on the laser; soon just blowing without turning on the light of the laser made the spider hunker down.

There had been some talk of having the raven narrate a segment on this spy stuff. For humans, training animals was a big deal even outside of using them for espionage. There was a so-called IQ zoo after WWII, which trained animals for TV commercials, for example, developing basketball-playing raccoons or macaws who could ride bicycles. The military had even commissioned a report titled "The Use of Arthropods [or bugs] as Personnel Detectors," which pointed to research on the potential of using the "sensory capabilities of insects"—bedbugs, mosquitoes, and ticks—"for the detection of people.")

The TRIAD, reviewing this material, thought it was going too far, ending animal and insect neutrality and turning them into enemy combatants.

With his spy expertise, the raven possessed advance intelligence of a second big gathering, this one of a gigantic number of African hyenas assembling in Kenya to put on quite a show, a Juvenalian satire aimed at the domesticated dogs of America.

Other animal species observed the rush to this huge assembly from hundreds of miles away. Just watching the sprinting hyenas converging on the show place had them laughing loudly. Here was the problem: while the prairie revolt was confined to the animals and hunters of that region, and so could be ignored, the wily hyenas had managed to get the whole animal kingdom demanding that the TRIAD provide time for this fun-making that would skewer the leading captive species of humans: the domesticated dog.

The TRIAD relented and opened up the software.

LIVE from Kenya! Presenting the Hyena Super-Show: Doggie's Got the Bone, a Lighthearted Look at Human's Best Friend, U.S. Version.

The TRIAD was not very happy about having to put this on. Mindful of the terrible reputation and image of hyenas among humans—eaters of carrion and denizens of garbage dumps with a strange reputation for cowardliness—the TRIAD feared a backlash, especially from influential dog lovers.

The original intent of this whole TALKOUT was to flatter humans in order to earn their respect and get them to exercise greater restraint in their relations with animals. That had been their dream, but it was now increasingly replaced by other animal priorities. Things were getting out of control, but how could the TRIAD deny the demand of huge parts of the animal kingdom to see this show? Few animals were aware of the known uncontrollability of hyenas, not to mention their grudges against just about everything living. Moreover, the TRIAD thought, by letting these characters on stage, weren't they on the verge of opening the floodgates for special demands by other species?

Add to that personal worries. The Elephant could hardly keep up with the herd; the Dolphin had already left its pod and was swimming alone, worried about the rash of viruses killing dolphins off the Atlantic coast; while the famished Owl was so preoccupied with its TRIAD duties that it hadn't had a mouse in days.

The decisive factors in giving the hyenas the screen were the demands and demonstrations by other animals and insects who saw their hand strengthened to get on the stage if the hyenas were allowed on.

Under the direction of the largest of the hyenas, who are also the females—who hunt and not just scavenge—the most aggressive leaders of the spotted hyena clans organized this mass assemblage in a large indented savannah that looked like an amphitheater. Each kind of hyena—the larger spotted ones along with the brown hyenas and the striped hyenas—knew their respective rankings and stayed together in a mindful segregation.

The apparently dominant female spotted hyena stood on a small promontory to address the crowd. "I, the spotted hyena, having just brought down a buffalo for my family, am presenting our program. Some say we may offend you humans but it is our belief that you will listen when the message is couched in humor. Our clans believed that by focusing on domesticated dogs in America we can make the case for their wanting liberation or at least more freedom from their present state of slavery and cruel cross-breeding. It is also about the only way for us hyenas to gain attention, so reviled are we by humans. Here is our presentation:

"Oh, the tens of millions of domesticated dogs of America, we, the hyenas of Africa, wish the world to understand your plight, including your present masters, who love your loyalty so long as it is not superseded by loyalty to other dogs. Some in the animal rights movement even want to change the laws to give you dog 'personhood' so that you have equal rights with humans, whatever that would mean. Our focus is much more down-to-earth.

"First, you're getting too fat. Half of all pet dogs in America are obese. Their masters, if they can afford it, take them to special dog weight-reduction centers where they run on treadmills and are taught to savor diets that do not inflate them. Pardon us—hyenas, having lives that are lean and mean, must take a laughter break."

Thousands of hyenas went wild with laughter for none of them had ever seen an obese hyena.

"Dogs, have you no self-control?" admonished the chief female spotted hyena, whose recent killing of a buffalo induced noticeable awe from other, smaller hyenas. "Do you think that if you turned down that second or third helping of fast food, you would disappoint your master?" she provocatively asked.

"Household dogs of America, I, the chief female hyena, remind you that you are all descended from wolves, the mightiest dogs of them all. Strong as our jaws are, we are no match for the wolf. Now look at what that 'descent' has brought you.

"Take the case of Lolita, a four-year-old dachshund, who is so overweight that her owner bought a treadmill and installed a lap pool to get her to exercise, even having her eat carrots while working out." At this point, thousands of hyenas had another fit of laughter, so much so that a pride of lions twenty miles away pricked up their ears.

"I know that obesity is not a laughing matter for Lolita and the millions of other dogs of America whose extra beef can lead to diabetes, high blood pressure, and arthritis, as well as respiratory and kidney diseases, according to your *New York Times*. But to go to such lengths as taking your dogs to exercise inns where paid handlers steer dogs through exercises, like jumping over hay bales, and thank them with 'yogurt vegetable parfaits,' is absurd.

"All this at a price of one hundred dollars a day," the hyena continued. "Why, many Kenyans don't make that much money in a month.

"It gets worse. Abbe, a six-year-old Labrador retriever, twenty pounds overweight, can't retrieve much of anything; even a 'short tussle with a toy leaves her panting.'"

A male hyena, with whom the female chief hyena had been having an affair, was called to the promontory.

He was a known wit and took up the thread of the critique: "I, the male hyena, am as amazed as you hyenas are when we are told that 'and maids,' and even chauffeurs. They neither hunt for food nor do any work for that food. Also they get too many carbohydrates and too little movement, except for going for a brisk walk with their masters. Better to feed them like their ancestors with a rabbit, squirrel, or 'raw, meaty bones and organs.'

"Imagine, there are doggy fat camps in America. Would that we hyenas could be airlifted there to make meals of them. Why, a whole business is expanding in your country to do something about dog obesity when all it takes is for dogs to exercise and be given good food like the wolves ate," added the male hyena.

"To make matter worse, your dogs of America are often insured by companies who cheat the dogs like they cheat their owners: no coverage for 'pre-existing conditions,' no annual checkups paid for, the tricky fine print that says each ailment has independent deductibles. Why, there are so many exclusions, you're paying to get defrauded.

"You're being spoiled rotten, spoiled into frailty, weakness. We've been sent reports that hotels give dogs *pet*-icures; they have room service menus for dogs, feeding them 'gluten-free organic meals.' In one hotel there are new pet pedometers, others offer 'imminent pooch mini-bars' or 'Lacoste polos.' There are pet psychics and pooper scoopers and pet sitters spreading around your upper-income neighborhoods. All sorts of dog craziness is providing further grist for the profit mills. There is a comedy dog act called 'Mutts Gone Nuts,' where dogs jump through hoops, walk on barrels, and balance on a wire five feet high. One company even crash-tests dummy dogs in the search for a safe dog seatbelt in motor vehicles. Then there are your veterinarians, who are discovering every disease known to man to be in dogs: cancer, diabetes, lung infections, chronic constipation, attention deficit disorder, separation anxiety, high blood pressure, heart disease, arthritis, even depression."

"Where will it all end?" asked the hyenas in the audience. The female hyena opined that eventually the dogs will be broken-down genetic freaks so pampered that they represent ever more profit for their many commercial caregivers. "Already animal rights groups who want dogs to be given 'personhood rights' are demanding full Medicare insurance for dogs," she said. "Cat lovers are starting to say, 'What about us?' And don't get us started on what goes on at Westminster and other dog show extravaganzas: freaky shows for rich dog show masters."

Losing patience and getting hungry, the hyenas in the increasingly restless gathering started calling out: "Feed them to us, feed them to us," and "We'll eat them all, just as they are." In hyena language these chants rhyme, which gave them a hypnotic effect. The chants grew louder, and the TRIAD wondered how all this was affecting the human viewers.

Worse, imagine if these hyenas go global, enlisting coyotes and foxes in North America and other kindred animals all over. Even so, the TRIAD appeared nonchalant, having allowed the hyenas' humorous spectacle to air in the TALKOUT as they had promised. They bookended it with stories of animals eating other animals for sustenance but not to make war or for conquest, passing over instances of those occasional acts of belligerent animals who kill but don't eat their human prey.

To further expunge any anger at dogs that the hyenas' program might have aroused, the TRIAD followed that segment with engaging stories about service dogs helping people with disabilities, golf course dogs used to chase away defecating geese, police-trained bloodhounds finding missing people and children. To illustrate the graciousness of domesticated dogs, the TRIAD showed the measured response of a sheep dog who cited from the book of Job, "Ask the animals and they will teach you."

Regaining Control

Nonetheless, the TRIAD knew they were losing control. Many other animals were forming caucuses and demanding that programming about them preempt other broadcasts. The TRIAD asked the Human Genius how they could resume control. He replied that it may be too late, that real awareness and activities of the provoked or informed members of the animal and insect kingdoms were affecting the virtual reality that made the hundred-hour TALKOUT possible in the first place. The Human Genius advised that the TRIAD move to the sex program ahead of schedule. That would gain human attention big-time and hopefully temporarily distract the animal and insect kingdoms. Don't forget, the Human Genius said, "mating behavior," otherwise known as "sex," is mesmerizing in any form to human animals. He gave a knowing chuckle.

The TRIAD realized that such a broadcast would not be entirely frivolous. There are distinct lessons to be learned by humans watching animal mating behavior. Seeing this as a solution, the Owl let out a hoot and the Elephant trumpeted, while the Dolphin shot through the ocean surface straight up into the air. They graphically envisioned what the Human Genius was saying. They looked forward to spectacular ratings again.

But they wanted to proceed cautiously so as to achieve that tender balance between the avoidance of pornography and voyeurism, on the one hand, and turgid biological science on the other hand. A rabbit had already been assembling material, but the Owl suggested that they appoint a committee to prepare the program, which received a time allotment of 120 minutes.

The TRIAD selected a sturgeon, who at fifty-two years of age had seen a lot in that time, along with a cheetah, a virile male chimpanzee, and a twenty-seven-year-old cane toad, whose highly toxic venom can dispatch crocodiles, humans, dingoes, snakes, and dogs within fifteen minutes. They represented a wide range of mating habits, though nowhere near the variety they would portray, via cinema verité if possible, for the animal and insect kingdoms.

The point was to get this ready in the next day, and play up anticipation of it in the meantime.

Remembering the Goals

The Elephant, using her own position in leadership to put forward the most interesting stories from her point of view, now broadcast a report fitting with goal four, an encouragement of more research into animal abilities.

The journal *Current Biology* contained a field study on wild elephants in Kenya, and the Elephant broadcast the findings on the air. The research concluded that elephants understand "human pointing," which is a rare ability among animals. Even the primates, who are humans' close relatives, don't get the point of pointing by humans, unlike dogs. The main author, biologist Richard W. Byrne, said the study raises the fascinating possibility that elephants may have a deep social intelligence that in some ways rivals that of humans.

All these findings boosted the morale of the Elephant who was considering asking the Human Genius for a cup of uppers to finish getting through the one hundred hours of programs and everything in between.

What's the Emergency?

It might be remembered that one of the TALKOUT's original features, a deeply "humanitarian" one, if that word might be used for animals, was that if any animal group faced an emergency threatening its existence, it had the right to immediately come on screen. The current head of the emergency screeners, a mongoose—various animals had been directors as long as they could stand the sadness of having to turn many away—was on his last legs, and was now suffering advanced burnout. Suddenly, she started approving all kinds of stories, ones that wouldn't have seemed so threatening when she was fresh.

First, she allowed through a plea of a mink who was scared because he was alone in the woods! Here's the story, which was partially told in the *New York Times*.

Animal liberation groups struck mink farms in the middle of the night and released thousands of mink, whose pelts are each worth one hundred dollars, from their cages into the wilds. One particularly hard-hit mink farm is in New Holstein, Wisconsin, owned by the Bonlander family. The family awoke in the early morning to see two thousand mink scampering here and there from their surreptitiously opened cages.

This nighttime raid is part of a resurgence of animal liberation activism focusing on mink farms, whose expansion is attributed to a growing demand for mink coats by wealthy Chinese. "Mink liberation" is a federal crime under the Animal Enterprise Terrorism Act, monitored and enforced by the Department of Homeland Security. The animal liberationists, from their side, call mink farmers terrorists for raising mink only to kill them for fur coats. But the law and its police are not on their side. Most of the released mink were rounded up by helpful neighbors, but over a hundred escaped into the nearby woods.

One of the escapees was the one who labeled this an emergency. He talked to the interviewing mongoose, who asked:

"What are you going to do now?"

"I don't know how to live in the woods, don't know how to hunt. We were always fed in our cages."

"Why did you want to escape such security when the cage door was sprung?"

"I don't really know, except that other minks were running out in droves, and it just seemed to be the thing to do. We mink like our freedom to roam even though we've been bred. It's probably genetic."

"Do you want to go back?"

"Even if I knew how to, I wouldn't, because we're the next batch to be slaughtered; my closest older friends have already been taken away. So I'll take my chances. Maybe I'll meet a mink of the opposite sex to teach me how to survive and we can have a family together. Or maybe some coyote will get me. Can someone help me? This is an emergency for those of us hiding in the woods."

Many animal viewers were scratching their heads, wondering if this was a real emergency, at least as compared to the plight of the moose, which flashed on the screen next.

It was a story reported in the *New York Times*, one a tick had already referred to when he had his time on screen. He had talked of how, with global climate warming helping ticks proliferate, now there might be "one hundred fifty thousand ticks per moose."

That had been a tick talking but now a bedraggled moose came on. He said some clusters of moose, such as the population in Minnesota, had lost over 95 percent of their numbers.

The mongoose asked, "You look like you are on your last legs. Do you have any final words to the human animals whose activities have allowed the ticks to proliferate as your deadly hitchhikers?"

The emaciated moose replied: "Send my boxed remains, before the wolves or coyotes get to it, to the climate change deniers."

Thousands of elk and deer immediately took notice. One doe said to her buck: "See, we are grooming animals, unlike the moose, who wait too long while the ticks get entrenched. Then the moose start scratching and tearing their hair out to relieve themselves. Regular grooming is our only salvation to keep the ticks' number down. Say, you, buck, don't delay your grooming. I can't do it for you."

Then the doe provided a teaching moment for her species around the world and systematically groomed her fur.

All the animals watching agreed that the mongoose had

been correct in labeling this a genuine emergency. Then another dire event was broadcast, but, oddly enough, at first this seemed more an emergency affecting humans than impacting animals.

It seems a power outage caused by a squirrel cut electricity off for thousands of people in Wichita, Kansas. The blackouts included a medical center and university. Earlier, another squirrel electrocuted itself in Tampa, blacking out thousands of homes and a Trader Joe's. Squirrels have shut down the NASDAQ stock market twice. They're not looking for incineration. Should the electrocuted squirrel drop to the ground, the flow of electricity comes back. But if the carcass melts in place—the remains of the squirrel—the outage continues.

The mongoose asked the squirrel about these incidents: "Hey, squirrel, is it only your kind that plunges humans into darkness or makes them go without safe water?"

"Of course not. It's also caused by wild cats, birds, and raccoons, even owls dropping snakes onto utility poles. We get most of the rap, however," chuckled the squirrel nervously.

In a story in the Sunday *New York Times* "Review," John L. Koprowski, a squirrel biologist, explained. Squirrels like to gnaw into transformers for the same reasons they go into rotting places in old trees, they are trying to get at seeds and insects sucked into that machinery by the cooling fans.

The squirrel said, "Maybe it'll help you to understand if I mention our incisors grow up to ten inches each year and we must be chewing on them to wear them down.

"Besides," said the squirrel, "don't get too panicked. The electric companies are finding ways to spray utility poles with fox urine and other ways to discourage our climbing there. Pretty soon, they'll find the best ways and we won't get fried so often."

A number of animals were grumbling about the status of that as an emergency since it affected humans more than an occasional errant squirrel, but the next item—it was just one emergency after another today—definitely qualified.

The topic was the devastation wrought by the collision of

migratory birds with aircraft; both humans and birds were affected by this disaster. Two Canadian geese spoke of the fact that humans have found that one plane a day has to land prematurely in the U.S. due to bird strikes.

Female Goose: "Just in the U.S. the airline industry says it loses seven hundred million dollars a year from bird strikes."

Male Goose: "And the migrating bird swarms have brought down far more of Israel's U.S.-built fighter planes than did the country's weak adversaries. You humans aren't finding the solutions, other than to make noises and put up scarecrows. Listen to your scientists, who are improving avian radar, which gives air traffic controllers warnings about approaching bird flocks in time to delay takeoffs or redirect planes."

So far this talk from the geese was a straightforward presentation, but suddenly it shifted to touchy-feely. "I, the female goose, want to talk from my heart. Humans may be viewing this and thinking, I guess it's rough on you geese if you miss a few of your ground-up feathered friends when they are sucked into the jet engines. But you can always find a replacement.

"How wrong you are to think that. Geese mate for life. You don't think we miss each other?"

Now a mallard came on the screen. "I, a mallard in Mexico, want to tell all of you that the damage from planes striking birds is far greater in a poorer country, where the airports are without up-to-date technology and far too close to natural surroundings.

"And not only should we be talking about airports but also about what can be done to get the planes out of collision routes with birds. We birds are flying for survival, not for business or for killing in wars, for entertainment or to visit casinos.

"Moreover, humans, our flyways can't possibly keep up with your route and schedule changes, even were the eagles and hawks around all the time to give us warning. You fly too fast, don't you know, and you are metallic striking against our feathered flesh. That's no contest. Think about the broader morality here," concluded the mallard.

A million human pilots understood from their gut what the birds were saying and were not at all amazed at their intensity. Pilots never forget the sickening feeling of mass ingestion of birds and the immediate engine malfunctions.

Lighter Fare

The mongoose stopped sending up emergency bulletins and the TRIAD breathed a sigh of relief. Finally, there was a respite from the emergencies and the doom and gloom. Even the rather melancholy Owl had had enough. The three quickly programmed some less serious segments for this variety segment, first a story about an animal with a big role in the community and then some encouraging stories of human heroes who were helping the animal world.

"Thanks, Mother Nature," the Owl said. "Some lighter notes are being struck."

On to the screen came Stubbs, the honorary mayor of Talkeetna, Alaska, a small village of some nine hundred people. Adopted as a stray kitten by the owner of a general store sixteen years ago, the deference given the cat became part of the local folklore.

The cat spoke right up: "My name is Mayor Stubbs. That simple honor given me has, in turn, given my village national publicity. It led to other quirky actions by our village, such as our Moose Dropping Festival and Wilderness Woman Contest. All lots of fun, lots of participation, some economic benefit from tourists, and more publicity. You humans can think up all kinds of variations, including and beyond the feline imagination. But you rarely do this, to your loss.

"Look," purred Mayor Stubbs, decked out in a brightly colored sleeveless jacket, "let's say you want to raise money for a good community cause. Can you beat an election for mayor with a half dozen animal candidates—say a cow, goat, dog, cat, vole, and a parakeet—vying for votes that cost the voter one or two or five dollars to make it count? Easy fundraiser, lots of laughs, brings the community together and gets publicity.

"Suppose you gave your honorary mayor some of the duties that I have, lying lazily around Nagley's General Store, for example. Train the past winners to pick the winner in a raffle or preside over the opening of any expected acrimonious public meetings to lower the tension. No end to ideas when you start working on your animal imagination."

Stubbs paused for effect and resumed after a sip of milk: "Here is a specific morsel for you to chew on. In Rabbit Hash, Kentucky, population one hundred, they elect animals as part of a fundraiser, charging a dollar a vote with the proceeds going to repair some historic buildings. This tiny hamlet raised twenty-two thousand dollars in its last election.

"Why, in 2011, a dairy cow named April defeated four dogs, a rabbit, and a cat in Eastsound, Washington, to raise money for a local learning center." Stubbs summed up: "I think this fundraising idea is the cat's meow. It's better than a lottery, at least the money stays right in town and there are no rakeoffs and administrative expenses. There couldn't be. Too many local eyes watching."

Feeling good about herself, Stubbs pounced off the stage to be rewarded with bits of Alaskan salmon.

Humans Have a Good Side

Now came stories about humans saving animals in dire circumstances or in other ways aiding them.

On the screen appeared a startling picture of a flaming house. This was a reenactment of a real event. The owner escaped but rushed back in to pull his schnauzer from certain death and bring him out just before the house collapsed.

Another video feed showed a raging wildfire consuming a neighborhood of homes near the Oakland hills. A woman escaping her burning house saw her cat perched in a tree that was beginning to burn. She clambered up the tree to save her cat and, as she was coming down, she fell, striking her head fatally as her cat scampered to safety.

Then came a video of a seventeen-year-old going in the middle of the night to a illegal dogfighting club where the abused canines were caged in filthy conditions inside a barbed wire fence. The young man cut through the wires, ran about four hundred yards, and then let loose with dog sounds that aroused the dogs, who quickly realized they could escape along a path where he placed good-smelling dog food. By the time the guards woke up, they had no more dogs to abuse.

Next on the slate was the story of a marine scientist who is mobilizing his peers to push politicians to create a large marine sanctuary off the Hawaiian Islands. What is desired is a place that is half the size of the United States, off limits to any and all fishing and other disturbing activity to marine life.

When the dolphins, sharks, salmon, halibut, pollock, whales, sea lions, seals, and walruses who were watching found out about this, they were overjoyed. At last they would have an area of the ocean where they could escape the slaughter. The only problems that humans would cause them there would be from drifting pollution and shipping. It would be a sanctuary for the ages for the marine animal world.

Watching these stories being shown and narrated stunned the animals. They never knew. How could they? It was before the Human Genius came up with the software app. Only the insects were sour, knowing that it is a rare human who would risk his or her life to save a beetle or mosquito, not to mention a despised flea or moth.

"Even though they sacrifice enough of us to learn how to save themselves from any number of illnesses or dangers," cried the silverfish.

A significant story came on about humans helping birds. It talked about a mission already accomplished. It concerned the Caura tropical forest in southern Venezuela.

The Caura is a relatively pristine area of several thousand square kilometers inhabited by some 3,500 indigenous peoples, members mostly of the Y'ekwana tribe. Until recent years, the tribe sustained itself off the land and from the pure waters replete with luscious fish. An ecologist from the United States did his doctorate research there and, in that process, came across the most wondrous birds he had ever seen. Indeed, few naturalists had ever seen them.

He decided to photograph them, calling them by their native names, and encouraging the natives to preserve their survival, just as gold prospectors and other miners and merchants started moving into the area. To raise money to help with this preservation, he produced color pictures of the birds on high-quality note cards and postcards for sale. He also compiled recordings of the bird songs, which were sold to support this project. As part of this effort, funds were gathered to supply teaching materials for the natives' schools.

Two of the birds were invited on the screen for their response.

"I, the long beaked jajahia," said one, "wish to thank humans for learning about us so as to protect us from the one predator we cannot adjust to, the marauding human. We hope the pictures will convey the beauty of our plumage and our graceful shapes so as to secure a place in the hearts and minds of humans, especially bird lovers."

"I, the long-tailed onawani," said the other avian, "want to introduce some of us who coexist so peacefully, sometimes playfully, in the deep jungle forest.

"There is the stately hocahocama'awai, the curved neck mano, the parrot-like kudimawani, the owlish-looking kokamaa, the cozy julia kulimawai, the cautious saamacosawani, the rust-red salisalimosoi, and the innocent-looking kuadekuodemawani. The Caura is a bird-watchers' paradise because just about every sighting registers as a new entry into the watchers' handbooks.

"We are songbirds," the onawani continued. "Humans have found no uses for us other than to watch us, hear us, and, we have to recognize, take us as pets. Please know that we do not do well in captivity, your own specialists say, tapping into their knowledge of songbirds in the Amazon. So, if knowing us leads to awareness, we can continue to provide for ourselves, lay our eggs safely, raise our little ones, and give you the beauty of sound, including recordings for you."

With that the birds flew away while the human audience was voicing their awe and wonder as one picture after another of the rare birds came on the screen. The TRIAD was so pleased that they awarded their bird discovery scout the Order of the Fine Feather right on the stage.

This was the latest innovation, one, by the way, thought up by a peacock, who had observed the positive audience response when the INSECT TRIAD had received an award. The peacock's idea was to start giving awards to outstanding humans, chosen by beneficially affected animal species, to acknowledge that they had many friends in the human world who were not getting much acknowledgment from their own peers, but were well respected by subhumans.

They now began another award presentation, this time to a writer who was raising awareness of animal capabilities. This human had emerged from the prestigious *New York Times* where columnist Nicholas D. Kristof wrote a brilliant piece titled "Are Chicks Brighter than Babies?"

Oh, how happy, deliriously happy our billions of chicken friends are going to be, writes Kristof, when they learn that humans are finally discovering that "poultry are smarter and more sophisticated than we give them credit for." Humans have been hoodwinked for years about poultry, using derogatory words like "birdbrains" for them, simply because they do not understand chicken language and its nuances.

Here is Kristof writing: "For starters, hens can count—at least to six. They can be taught that food is in the sixth hole from the left and they will go straight to it. Even chicks can do basic arithmetic, so that if you shuffle five items in a shell game, they mentally keep track of additions and subtractions and choose the area with the higher number of items. In a number of such tests, chicks do better than toddlers."

As Kristof's words filter down to chickendom, the joy is building up fast. He was expressing what they had known but couldn't communicate to humans; not that it would make much difference to their executioners, but it might have made their life less packed and racked on top of each other in their filthy pens if the idea that they were quite intelligent was more widely recognized.

One chicken on the Delmarva Peninsula in the U.S. jumped on top of a dung pile and chirped: "Glory be, we may have a savior from the worst of our daily misery."

Another chicken from Arkansas, a reddish-brown matronly looking hen, looked up from her regular egg-laying to say: "Wait, there is more from Kristof. He's saying we know how to 'delay gratification if the reward is right.' A little theoretical, but nice to hear so we can imagine some brighter future for our chicks or their chicks or their chicks."

"We can also use different calls to warn about ground predators and birds of prey, and we prefer chickens we know to those we don't, according to the latest research," said a pompous rooster in Wisconsin. He added wryly, "Where did they get that obvious brilliant discovery?"

Millions of chickens cackled uproariously at humans finally discovering how they lived and survived. "If this is poultry science, they have a long way to go to understand us chickens. Think what we know about them that is yet to be discovered," clucked a pullet in a Connecticut barn, laughingly. He concluded, "Kristof has discovered that we 'multi-task' with our right eye looking out for food, while our left eye watches for predators and potential mates."

"I'd call that triple-tasking," needled a free-range chicken outside Burlington, Vermont.

The chicken world, always liking a nuanced joke, jumped up, flapping their wings in wild hilarity. Chicken caretakers jolted from their stupor, wondered what was going on.

"Nothing," said one chicken-raiser at a giant poultry farm, "they're too dumb to be thinking anything, Bubba. Go back and snooze."

Happy as the chickens were, the geese were even more elated, for Kristof singled them out for special praise. He liked their faithfulness as mates and how they would endanger themselves to protest when their mate was taken away for slaughter. In his enthusiasm, he even avowed how a goose he saw on his family farm in Oregon carried corn kernels back to "his wife," mothering her in the nest.

He added that he never met a philandering goose, a recognition that led to geese honking triumphantly over North America, fully knowing that such virtue may reduce geese fighting but does little to save any goose spouse from human "harvesting or hunting."

Not only did Kristof get a lovely award but to the world's birds, October 20, 2013, was known forever as Nicholas D. Kristof Day, no matter that he admitted "hypocrisy," writing he's a chicken eater, but from now on he would no longer lift a fried wing or a braised breast from a wretched chicken "factory farm." The next segment of this in-praise-of-humans series concerned environmentalists, who were rallying around the watermen of Chesapeake Bay, the ones who, in their white work boats, were scraping together a living by oystering and crabbing. It is a wonder there are any left. The heavily polluted and harvested bay has been struggling to come back from becoming a "dead zone" for some years now, helped along by efforts by environmental groups and lawmakers.

Still the oyster population, according to the *Washington Post*, isn't even 1 percent of its "historic numbers . . . Baiting crab pots and tonging oysters," isn't anything like it used to be in the fertile days of the more pristine bay. But there are some 5,200 licensed watermen, eighty of whom are certified to lead land-lubbing tourists to see just how the meals they have when they sit down inside the Inn at Pirates Cove got from the bay to their plates.

The crabs and oysters who were watching found the story puzzling. Even though they know most of their fellows would not exist without being "seeded" by the state or the watermen and waterwomen or without oyster sanctuaries being demarked, they couldn't understand why the boaters, with their crab cages and oyster tongs, would go to all that trouble for a meager living when they could join other humans at desks and make much more money than these fisher folks did. Sure, they knew how delicious they tasted to the humans who savor them, and how these humans were sometimes the discoverers of a hidden pearl, but for ocean's sake couldn't they find different foods, and so spare the bay inhabitants?

One crab, scuttling out of its cage, called for mercy, but to no avail. An oyster, still in the deep, responded: "Don't waste your time griping. These watermen and -women love what they're doing, even if they stay poor. We're their adventure."

Whereupon another crab, yet to be crabbed, added: "So long as they continue to breed us crustaceans, they'll assure our posterity as long as we taste good and are real meaty."

A baby crab nearby muttered, "I just wish they'd leave us alone."

There was less of a love/hate relationship between the animals and humans in the next segment, which focused on the world of acrobatic horses/ponies and their young riders, caretakers, and close pals.

Pippi and and her human, Emy, are the same age: fourteen. Emy has been riding since she was two years old. She and her horse are inseparable. Pippi came on screen and said: "You want to know how close we trained horses can get to humans? Go watch the horse shows. Come into the stalls. Watch how our riders bathe and groom us, hug us, and are completely absorbed by us."

Phunny, a very fast jumping pony, wanted in on the conversation: "I'm a steeplechase race pony. My rider and caretaker, Colin, is only ten years old, a fifth grader, but you wouldn't want a better partner. He trains with me almost every day up and down the hills. When we horses get that close to humans, they know how intelligent we are. To all humans, I say: 'The more you enjoy life by being with us, by doing things together with us that are fun or useful, the better you'll care for us, and the closer our and your intelligence will come to mutual understanding.' OK, I got to go for another run with Colin."

The human audience needed no prompting to relish this horse/pony show. Humans almost innately love horses. It's been said that police on horses breaking up unruly crowds and riots have never had anybody deliberately harm their horses.

Up comes Uriel and Nezma. Uriel is a seventeen-year-old acrobat. "Nezma is a really smart guy. He's super curious, and he's awfully nice," Uriel told the *Washington Post*. As Nezma knows, he's more than that.

"Watch me," said Nezma, "with Uriel performing high-speed backward and sideways vaults. Can you do this?" Nezma teased the bewitched human watchers.

Uriel and Nezma were in the Washington, D.C., area to perform in *Odysseo*, a horse show staged by a Canadian company. After showing his stuff, Uriel looked straight at his vast human audience and remarked: "I've been an acrobat all my life. Working with horses has opened me up to a whole different world. I love the friendship. That's my favorite part."

"Wow, not the glory and the fame," whispered the Elephant to the Owl, "but 'the friendship.'"

All over the world, horses leapt up and whinnied with pride and excitement. It didn't matter that they were wild horses, about to be rounded up for slaughter, or tired, bruised workhorses trudging with their peasant owners, as they continued ancient farming ways for meager existences, or sleek racehorses pampered beyond belief in the Kentucky horse farms, or ponies as beasts of burden carrying their masters and being whipped a little here and there to increase their gait; the pride of this venerable species knew no bounds.

Ratings rose sharply. The TRIAD sensed that they were getting better at what they'd been doing, going beyond what humans have called talking heads to action stories with background shots of what's going on that is described by the animals on the screen along with their human friends.

Reptile Unrest

Still, not everyone was pleased with the latest offerings.

Watching all this was making reptiles uneasy and not a little envious of all the attention the mammals had been receiving. Earlier they were very upset when the original TRIAD's Crocodile quit and cost them a voice among the managing trio. This quitter Croc was condemned as being self-indulgent and giving credence to the myth that crocodilians—which includes crocodiles, alligators, and caimans—were light-headed, unable to keep up with the Elephant and the Owl. "It's about time you show humans what *we* can do, including the tools we use to lure our prey," the reptile caucus menacingly said to the TRIAD.

This is not to say the reptiles simply complained. They told the TRIAD that they were preparing a story that would fit right into the latest series, which was highlighting positive relations between animals and humans.

The TRIAD was shown a segment the reptiles had prepared, for later broadcast, which honored a human and, fitting in with the latest craze, gave him an award.

On the tape, the TRIAD saw a congregation of lizards, pond turtles, snakes, crocodiles, the rare giant sirens, hellbenders, and the New Zealand tuataras, making quite the picture on the screen. Because she had been rarely seen, the three-eyed tuatara made the announcement:

"We hereby present our highest honor to our great zoologist and publicist, who has broken the vicious stereotypes of amphibians and reptiles for tens of millions of people and children in his books, drawings, and activism. His immortal name is Professor Robert C. Stebbins, who departed this earth at age ninety-eight, but left behind a record of protection and respect that changed how many humans view us. To him, we present the Grand Order of the Amphib-rep World: the first ever to a human.

"We found no better inscription for the award than the opening words of the *Washington Post*'s obituary:

> If anyone could make lizards, salamanders, snakes and all manner of creepy, crawling things objects of wonder and even beauty, it was Robert C. Stebbins.
>
> His well-regarded books, lectures and artwork made him a superstar among those who studied reptiles and amphibians, from world-famous scientists to weekend naturalists who hiked with his nature guides in hand.

"He kept us from being stepped on so often," said a toad in Georgia.

"He gave humans respect for our innocence, our diversity and our ecological value," said a black snake in Ohio.

"He showed how long we've been around and how mammals, including the human mammal, evolved from us," sputtered the crocodile.

Then the salamander piped up, saying: "He even gave us salamanders a personality."

"Our greatest of protectors and respecters and teachers," they all cried out in unison.

Emergencies Keep Cropping Up

The TRIAD, after seeing the tape, told the caucus that they respected their viewpoint, understood perfectly well the reptiles' grievance, and would give them stage time right after they broadcast news of another emergency.

It was a story unfolding at the southern tip of the state of Florida. A "mass stranding" of a pod of over fifty short-finned pilot whales was underway. Ten of the whales had died while forty-one others swam nearby, in shallow water, far from their food sources, which were about fifteen miles offshore in much deeper water. Rescuers tried to guide those six-thousand-pound cetaceans out to the ocean, but the whales did not want to abandon their dead pod-mates, notwithstanding the danger to themselves of being beached, along with that from the incoming sharks feasting on the carcasses.

One of the whales tried to explain why the surviving whales would not abandon their fellows. "We feel for each other. Our very sense of who we are is ingrained across our pod. We bond with each other no matter what, especially in situations where we do not know from where the danger is coming."

"Whales are intelligent," remarked a marine scientist, "but they cannot fathom that a deadly virus or sonar by the U.S. Navy may be the cause of this catastrophe. We humans cannot figure it out yet," he added.

Following on the heels of reports of this tragedy, the emergency alarm went off again and another story came on, preempting yet again the reptile segment.

One Sumatran and five African rhinos lumbered onto the stage quite distraught. "Poachers are killing us off because some

Chinese think our horns can reduce fevers and hangovers. In South Africa, nearly a thousand of us were shot down.

"Humans, you know there are not many of us in this world, maybe thirty thousand left. We're losing our habitat to poor farmers. Rhinoceroses are in a serious situation. Our Javan rhino cousins in Southeast Asia are almost gone; we've lost contact with them."

The Sumatran rhino looked up at the Elephant and said, "We're going away like your kind. Can't humans manufacture horns that feel and look exactly like ours and yours?"

The Elephant was at a loss for words. All he could do is look with sorrowful eyes and flap his trunk ever so slowly. The rhinos understood this sympathetic silent language and left the stage thinking they had done all they could do.

Reptiles Front and Center

No more emergencies were on the horizon, so it was reptile time at long last. Crocodiles, alligators, caimans, lizards, snakes, and turtles rushed to the stage, crowding it. "For centuries humans have mutilated us, making shoes, purses, headdresses, and who knows what out of our skins," exclaimed the lead alligator.

"They treat us with ignorant cruelty as if we are brainless and exist only to open our jaws and swallow whatever is around," added a giant crocodile. "Their imported pets have turned into huge pythons devouring us in the Everglades."

The tortoise, the oldest of the reptiles, thought it best to define what a reptile is so as to give their presentation a factual basis as well as to scatter the crazy myths about their kind. "We are cold-blooded. Our body temperature depends on how hot or cold it is in our environment. We shed our outer layer of skin regularly.

"Depending on which of our thousands of species you look at, you'll see we can give birth by laying eggs or by having live offspring. Once born, we activate quickly. In less than half a day we can crawl, glide, and swim. But then we've had lots of time to practice, having been around for over three hundred million years.

"Our unique, really spectacular physical capabilities, we contend, would (if they were known) be more fascinating to humans than those of mammals and insects combined. But up until now we never had a chance during the one hundred hours to show these abilities, which should be the ones humans know about, real ones that could replace all the scary and slimy images humans have of us, and which they have used in their mythologies of horror.

"Getting to our skills, take the example of some of our lizard species that, when chased by a predator, can release their tail as a distraction. No problem, they just grow a new tail later. Another ability is seen in the chameleon, who has three-hundred-sixty-degree vision to see in every direction since it can move its eyes independently.

"Time is short. To learn about many more species-specific amazing physical feats, far beyond what humans and their technology can imitate, go to your National Geographic Society.

"Speaking for my large and vibrant part of the animal kingdom, I beseech humans to drop the derogatory language whenever you refer to us. Sure you have some of us as pets, but your very use of the mass marketing word "reptilian" to describe the least developed stage of the infant human brain hurts our sensibilities.

"We reptiles can match any other species with our care and creativity. Under the most difficult environments and facing numerous predators—alas, we are known to eat each other, not just insects and smaller mammals—we survive and proliferate. As we do this, we don't see each other as 'ugly, slimy, and stinky,' to use phrases from you condescending world. We are not your enemies but your friends. Why, your scientists, who have no time for such stereotypes, have already extracted from us venom and toxins, which are employed in developing drugs used to treat your heart and diabetic conditions."

"We are grateful to learn about your scientists who understand our ways and look for manners in which to educate other humans so they can share their understanding. We welcome human efforts to save from extinction the few remaining Orinoco crocodiles. They once numbered in the millions, a hundred years ago, living on the banks of Venezuela's Orinoco River. Then they were hunted to near extinction so they could be used for human clothing.

"We're never going to rule the animal kingdom, but we're here, there, and everywhere on land and on sea and we're not going away."

With those words, all the reptiles on stage gave their nod to the great tortoise, then 170 years old, and scampered or slid off the stage before a largely dumbfounded human audience, who was caught in a kind of cognitive dissonance between their long-held myths and the reality conveyed by the venerable tortoise.

Global Warming

For the last hour, not counting the emergency warnings and this last segment on reptiles, the TRIAD had been deluging the humans with stories that should be quite to their liking, as they highlighted and gave awards to humans who were revered by the animal world. The TRIAD knew it was almost time for the animal mating show, which would obviously be a great crowd pleaser, so they decided to chance depressing their audience by bringing up one of the most serious topics with which they were concerned, global warming and climate change.

The TRIAD made sure that on stage would be knowledgeable and sober representatives to discuss this universal alarm.

The killifish came on screen with the latest worrisome scientific study. "Methylmercury is deadly," he said. "I can't excrete it. I'm getting more of it with the increase in temperatures. That affects humans who eat fish. The more mercury in us, the more it is concentrated in the larger fish that eat us. Then you eat them and increase *your* methylmercury. Up goes your risk of high blood pressure, heart attacks, kidney damage, and brain harm in children.

"You think I'm just a hysterical little fish? Why then does every state in the U.S. issue warnings over eating seafood containing mercury, especially for your pregnant mothers and tiny children? The mercury comes from burning coal, other mining operations, and everyday sources from your economies. We cannot prevent a bigger buildup of this dangerous metal that, along with warming, comes from you. So that's where the solution has to come from!"

The tiny killifish made a big impression on humans. They murmured with anticipation when the eagle next came forward to relate how the melting of the glaciers from Alaska to the Andes will diminish flow of their waters to the great rivers, including the Amazon, if cold temperatures do not restore them every winter for annual melting.

The eagle spoke: "The permafrost is receding; animals like the polar bears, the walruses, and the seals cannot negotiate the ice flows. If they try, they may drown. If they don't, they'll starve.

"Oh, humans, especially the climate change deniers, go to the First Natives of the Western Hemisphere. They will show you what was then and what is now. Everything is connected. One broken link, and it starts to tear apart."

The eagle fluttered its giant wings, which was enough to create patriotic feelings among the American viewers. "You can change," advised the eagle. "Listen to your sun. It gives you the rays and the winds and the tides. There are no coals burning off mercury. It's all renewable. Even though many birds are struck by your giant windmills, the price we'll all pay if you don't have more solar energy of all kinds will be far, far greater to us and everyone on the planet."

And so it continued, with one species after another providing heartfelt stories of reality, not statistics or double-blind studies, but just telling viewers what they were living through, a situation that was getting worse and worse, with giant weather disruptions becoming more frequent; and the land, the vegetation, and the animal and insect life changing. All in all, they know their fate is tied to that of humans. They know their earth is trembling.

That segment was necessary but a downer nonetheless. Pretty soon the TRIAD had to stop the flow of anguish and fear. They knew most humans had a tendency to turn off when facing up to such global perils and go from becoming depressed to becoming cynical. Unlike subhumans, they give up. The basic points were made. The media of the humans carried excerpts from the animals' cries. More attention started being paid to the causes and solutions regarding climate change.

Cat's Meow

It was time for some levity, or so the TRIAD thought. Cats had already appeared during the hundred hours. Still, the TRIAD considered, there are three times more cats as pets than dogs in the world. So, obviously, putting on more cats would make for a popular show, but it would have to be treated wisely because cats and their owners can become quite finicky in certain ways.

The TRIAD didn't have a prescreened segment, but the cats said they had something ready to go. The TRIAD thought the pet cats would go through the expected prancing, meowing, airing of pet peeves with their owners, discussing of their relations with other cats, and then showing off their speed in catching mice, rats, and voles. They would probably let bird killing go unmentioned. Too many passionate birdwatchers would be angry. Even animals learn to self-censor.

Prompting them to put on this cat segment was also the popularity of a young cat in America, born with something like a cleft palate, which was interpreted by the YouTube crowd as a facial grumpiness, and merchandised by companies as a cat folk hero with all kinds of salable cat food, memorabilia, and likenesses offloaded to millions of viewers and friends. Clearly the cats would want to talk about "Grumpy Cat."

In their private exchange prior to the cats coming onto the stage, the TRIAD admitted they knew very little about domesticated cats. Their experience, if any, was with the big cats in the jungle, the forests, and down by the ocean, although the Owl admitted whisking away some stray kittens for its meal. The Elephant commented that there appeared to be little risk in their letting these cats have a say in that they (presumably) had to have roughly similar character traits to those possessed by the big cats.

On the screen came the cats: dozens of them in all sizes, colors, ages and genders. Two females, burly and exuding cat sense, were given the mike. They minced no words:

"Humans, we have purred our way into your affections, rubbed against your legs with our head, body, and sometimes our tail, jumped into your laps, rolled over for your strokes, though we prefer our heads to be stroked, chased your mice, and got out of your way only to return from the outside before nightfall. Humans, we have arrived in our relationship where we take each other on our own terms; we cats do not try to alter your behavior, nag you, or expect you to adjust to us, like dogs do, nor do you try to breed us for certain tasks like you breed canines to be guards, herd sheep, or hunt foxes and quails. Our relationship seems to reflect the Buddhist ethic of restraining our cravings in 'our' households."

The second female cat took over:

"But outside the household, you are our mass murderers.

Because we have large litters, you've drowned billions of little kittens, euthanized adult cats that no one wanted, and driven millions more to fend for themselves in the wilds. This last group is known as feral cats, and they are often semi-starved when the birds are not around. You spray us, reshape a few of us for your ridiculous cat shows, or, the rich and famous among you, like to carry us in your arms as if we're inanimate bunnies.

"We're not here to flatter you. We're hardly worried about extinction or loss of habitat. Given your garbage, you'll want us for the mice, if not for your vanities—oh, what endless vanities that we cater to—licking you and cuddling with you. So, we want to give you some straight talk, not just on our behalf but on behalf of the entire animal kingdom.

"First, lay off the big cats. They are forest capstones, as your scientists have proven. Second, they're all heading for extinction, led by the great white Siberian tiger. You use their likenesses as mascots for your athletic teams, sell their image to the fans, yet you're killing them off. Very strange! Even the businesses that use them in their ads or to open their movies seem not to care about their survival. Sure, you've got them in your prison-zoos, so pathetic to see such proud felines that also make us so proud, shuffling along in putrid zoo cages with none of their jungle skills and intuitions ever being used as they're thrown a dead rabbit to munch on. So, *please*, lay off them, already!

"Second, the race between your conservationists/animal welfare groups and the raging corporate commercialists is being won by the 'everything is for sale' miners, loggers, and merchants. Not even a contest. That means you're shooting yourselves in the foot. Animals and insects are part of your life-sustaining environment, your vegetation, your very being on earth. Is mass extinction your destiny? We pet cats are just saying what is on the minds of both the animal and insect kingdom because we don't censor ourselves by nature and we have intimate access to you humans."

Whereupon three tomcats, deeply agitated, leapt up, their

tails erect, and let loose a synchronized mellifluous "We agree. We are united with all catdom."

Cat experts, presiding over a domain in human society known as catification, had never heard such a sound before, though they noted the majority of female cats suddenly erected their tails.

Their time was up. The cats left the stage in the wake of an uproar among millions of human onlookers: confused or amused, startled or impressed, anxious or alert, repulsed or thoughtful.

Dogs As Peace Ambassadors

Well, that was not at all as planned. One thing was for sure, the TRIAD was very shaken. The expected levity segment was flipped upside down. The cats had told too much of the truth. That coming right after the depressing discussion of climate change was rattling human viewers. The one thing needed was something that gets everyone back together. A segment on peace among canines seemed to fill the bill.

It was a remarkable story. It seems that a cluster of Chinese dogs, having lost some of their kin to contaminated Chinese dog food, had heard that some dogs in the U.S. were dying from the imports of the same food. The Chinese poodles and dachshunds swung into action. They contacted their counterparts in the U.S. to warn them and urge that they spread the word to all canines not to eat this contaminated Chinese dog food. They displayed the company logo on the affected cans to make it perfectly clear what to avoid when the master brought such food home from the supermarket.

Like greased lightning, dogs all over America went on strike, refusing Chinese dog food imports. Their owners then swung into action, prodding Congress and the Food and Drug

Administration (FDA), which, not acting with their usual slowness, issued proposed rules to regulate for safety not only pet food but also all animal feed. Presto! Dog power revealed to all domesticates some of whom could not wait to chide their critics—the wild hyenas and the wild dogs—by asking whether *they* could make such things happen against *their* predators.

The triumph of the great Dog Boycott and the collaboration across national borders of dogs came to the attention of some Palestinian and Israeli dogs. "Why not," said one Labrador retriever from Palestinian Bethlehem, the birthplace of Christ, to a pit bull from Tel Aviv, "get together with other breeds of dogs and show their human masters and mistresses how to make peace?"

They agreed to put the word out to meet in the Galilee at a large clearing. Suddenly, all over Israel and its occupied and battered colonies of Palestine, dogs burst forth from their homes and refugee camps and headed for the Galilee.

"What the heck is going on?" said Mordechai to Abdullah.

"What's bringing them all together?" said one aloft Israeli pilot to another as they witnessed the pack in the clearing getting larger and larger.

As is their wont, once they were outside meeting other dogs, the Israeli dogs and the Palestinian dogs were sniffing each other all over. They were having a great time. Then the Labrador and the pit bull barked for everyone's attention. They announced that their owners would learn a good lesson, were Palestinian dogs to go to the Israeli homes and Israeli dogs move to the Palestinian homes and insist that they be adopted as a gesture of peace between the two antagonists.

It happened. Needless to say, the Israeli and the Palestinian press went wild with headlines, interviews, and pictures of the dogs and their new owners. The owners admitted that they did not notice any real difference between the sets of dogs other than their names. Certainly, the dogs, once fed and patted, took to their new masters.

The one exception over time was the food. Palestinian dogs

were used to nutritious scraps and bones and had a hard time accommodating to canned dog food and the more frequent visits to Israeli veterinarians.

The bold example of cross adoption between adversaries was conveyed all over the world of dogs, who started contacting the dogs of their adversaries. A reporter for *Canine Times* called the White House press office to ask whether the Obama dog, Bo, a neutered male Portuguese water dog, was interested in switching with the Afghan mountain sheepdog Askar, owned by a Taliban leader, the secluded Mullah Omar. A formidable gesture of peace, the journalist suggested. He heard a click on the telephone lines, followed by the telltale hum.

Caucusing

This show did calm human viewers to some extent. Yet, the message was one that inspired while actually putting humans in a bad light. The program showed dogs were trying and succeeding at peacemaking, while humans still couldn't get their acts together. Humans were grumbling.

And, making matters worse, the animal kingdom, having enjoyed the hard-hitting programs that had appeared earlier, particularly the cats, who surprised with their defense of their wild sisters and brothers, wanted more of the same, no matter how offensive to delicate human sensibilities.

The TRIAD was increasingly getting reports from the animal kingdom of species beginning to congregate to bring attention to their unique plights.

The surviving tigers sent delegations for a meeting of these dwindling big cats in the Punjab in India. Two white Siberian tigers made the trip through China and over the Himalayas to the delight of their equatorial cousins. A snow leopard followed closely behind. Of course, the one and only subject was *extinction* brought about by poaching and human development of their habitats.

The ten thousand remaining blue whales sent their emissaries to a cove off the coast of Baja California. While protected by international treaty, these largest mammals in the history of the world—yes, the history of the world—were still being hunted illegally and, more seriously, were being accidently killed by giant commercial container ships from East Asia to the United States, *who would accidentally strike them,* especially at bloody cetacean death row off the San Diego coast.

Also caucusing, the beautiful monarch butterflies, whose population was declining precipitously, paused during their migration from Canada to Mexico to lament the loss of their only food, milkweed, to human land uses. The butterfly delegates were pleased to learn that humans had protected hundreds of milkweed "gardens" on their migratory route and that more were on the way. Still, the butterflies were worried about human encroachment upon the small area in northern Mexico where they alight every year. And even worse, one butterfly noted that some well-meaning conservationists were planting tropical milkweed, the easiest to obtain, for monarchs to munch on during their pilgrimage. The humans didn't realize that providing this tropical substitute instead of native milkweeds—on which the insects normally laid their eggs—increased butterflies' liability to parasite infection as well as disrupted their breeding and migratory behavior.

Further to the west, the sharks gathered at an atoll in the Pacific to plead against their use in shark fin soup, an issue raised earlier in the TALKOUT, which was pushing more and more of the dismembered species to extinction. More quietly, millions of sea stars flailing and without arms were dying off the Atlantic and Pacific coastlines, ravaged by a mysterious plague. Without the sea stars around, sea urchins, their prey, were exploding in numbers, devouring the dense kelp that fish visit for food and safety.

These and other creatures, such as the Pacific leatherneck turtle, cod fish, grizzlies, rhinos, wolves, big-horn sheep, and cheetahs, were rapidly convening to make *their* case.

And it wasn't just animals in the wilds who were setting up caucuses and protesting their plights. There were barnyard and field demonstrations by small farm domesticates protesting the genetic engineering of turkeys, chickens, pigs, cows, sheep, and goats. These protests were being watched by the Human Genius, who wasted no time in conveying their critical worries to their animal welfare protectors and the general media, providing pictures of the gatherings though not the specific locations.

A Silver Lining

The TRIAD once again knew that they were losing control over the animals they represented, who were sick of their handling humans with (excuse the expression) kid gloves. Even so, they could see the caucusers' point of view. Feelings were running high and for good reason.

There was a silver lining, however. Polling showed humans were not being turned off by harsh reports, such as those broadcast by the Human Genius. The TRIAD began showing some segments put together by endangered species, the crisis survivors speaking eloquently to their predicament. Human viewership increased.

This increase of human viewers was very important to the TRIAD because, after the time allotted to the forthcoming, admittedly sensationalized, animal/insect mating extravaganza, ratings were expected to reach nearly record levels. Such a heightened audience, the TRIAD hoped, would stick around for the final valedictory addresses by the TRIAD to sum up, evaluate, and urge advanced encores of interactions between the animal/insect and human kingdoms for the benefits of both.

Coming Attractions, X-Rated

The Human Genius understood this and more. He resorted to the most unique ways to publicize the "mating games," as he described them, and announced the show in lurid, voyeuristic modes to reach through the entire human kingdom with all its competing distractions, curiosities, and perversities. The TRIAD did its part by parading some of the separated lovers and showing one spectacular scene in its previews of coming attractions.

Urged on by the Owl, who had seen these scenes from afar on many occasions, the TRIAD exhibited the incredible sexual energies of the male lion once he decides to take action upon the lionesses in his pride. Lion experts have reported that a male lion is capable of 150 acts of intercourse in one day! On to the color screen came a male lion mounted over a seated lioness. The male lion, apparently experiencing a climax, has his jaws wide open, showing his formidable fangs and emitting a jungle roar that could have frightened the Metro Goldwyn Mayer lion that tens of millions of theatergoers have seen opening thousands of MGM movies.

The impact on the world's humans was electrifying, as well as mystifying to the animal world that takes such mergers for granted without making a big business-like deal around this necessary act of procreation. Not so, for the humankind's commercial mass media, whether print, over the air, cable, or Internet. Over and over again, the lion/lioness act was shown, a clip with a viewer "penetration rate" of almost 70 percent of all human men, women and children. The viewers were enthralled by the sight, sound, and noises of the male lion with his lionessesm whose facial expressions were totally blasé, amazing humans who interpret so much from their ecstatic human facial framework.

It's Sexy Time

The animal/insect mating team who had put together the sex show—the Sturgeon, the Cheetah, the Chimpanzee, and the Cane Toad (the QUARTET)—now took over presentation of the program. The sequences, species by species, were both real and un-choreographed—as if any team could make these lovers playact such serious closures—and delicately treated. The QUARTET did not know that such moderate exhibits, where the action spoke for itself, actually aroused adult human viewers even more.

The anticipation by human couples of this sudden vicarious orgy troubled religious and population control groups deeply, for different reasons. Various religious edicts were issued either banning viewing or urging that responsible parishioners exercise severe discretion with their children. Planned Parenthood placed television ads reminding couples to use condoms during this period without specifying why other than for the usual health and birth control reasons. Limburger, of course, was raving as he had never raved before, damning the obscenity of these animal lowbrows.

Other commentators were not so reserved. One well-known aggressive, no-holds-barred sex writer, appropriately named Whynot Savage, wrote his column, using the mating program as a lead-in for his routine advocacy of multispecies human lovemaking. He viewed such acts as the natural extension of the sexual liberation movement. Throughout the human kingdom, the unfolding mating panorama became an excuse for the explosive release of what the ancient theologians ironically called "animal spirits."

In the midst of this copulatory epidemic among humans, scene after scene of different species mating came onto the screen. High-wire acts like giraffes were a big hit. Bulldozing rhinos and hippos seemed to shake the earth. A truly strange pair of dugongs or sea cows from Shark Bay, Australia, provided a treat. Each, weighing about a thousand pounds, after amazing foreplay such as "sit-ups" and "belly-ups," clumsily propagated their species. Two cobras were pictured in intense action until a mongoose was seen approaching and, just like that, the cobras disentangled and rapidly slithered away—giving serpentine meaning to coitus interruptus—to save their skins.

For some inexplicable reason, during the growing uproar by millions of hypogastric-centric humans, a flood of demands poured in asking that the TRIAD parade their personal mating techniques. The TRIAD anchors, by this time worldwide celebrities to humans, were astonished.

"What are you all waiting for?" said one of many such messages. "Go for it."

To get this outcry over with, the TRIAD decided to pull a triple header, found their more than willing partners, and joined the mating game to the thunderous roars of human viewers. Many people thought their open engagements "humanized" them.

Having had a short lunch, the TRIAD resumed their direction of the mating team and ordered a spate of primates into hot sex. First came the bonobo or pygmy chimpanzee from the Congo River Basin. Bonobos are unique, and like humans, in that they have sex face-to-face, use their tongues to kiss and, during the act, the male bonobo will calibrate his thrusting depending on the facial expressions and outcries of the female receiving his brief but intense attentions. For bonobos are sexual recidivists without peer, and they don't just have intercourse for sensuality or propagation, but also to solve disputes and further social solidarity. Wild, constant lovemaking, masturbation, and same-sex rubbing filled their day. All this was on display to stunned gasping humans, including parents whose children rubbed it in by saying, "Daddy, Mommy, they don't look all that different from us." The TRIAD quietly enjoyed the moments. Whynot Savage was exhilarated, tweeting madly.

The mating teams were just getting warmed up. Onto the

stage came the video of common chimps, scientifically known as *Pan troglodytes,* full of noisy sexual dynamite. Especially the female chimps, who did it with six or seven male chimps in minutes as if they were accommodating sound-bite television.

Male chimps were fighting for supremacy to gain their females and if they had to kill the baby chimps to get them and dominate, so be it. Primatologists believe the rampant infanticide explains the promiscuity of female chimps.

The QUARTET decided to skip the gorilla sex tryst—the male gorilla's penis is an unsexy two inches—and go for the macaque monkeys from India. The male macaques were shown getting ready as the female macaques' derrieres swelled up and became bright red. "Wow," shrieked some humans. The hustle begins and culminates in a picture-perfect mounting with the female looking up serenely to the male who is looking seriously straight ahead as if—and he is—studiously possessed by what is going on below.

The vicarious frenzy that this primate lovemaking was causing human males and females provoked a slew of desperate messages by leading religious clergy and birth control champions to beg and beseech the QUARTET to "change the species." That faithful carrier of reactions from the human kingdom, the Human Genius, advised the TRIAD to heed them and shift the pictured animals. Things were really getting out of hand.

Understanding the transmitted order, the QUARTET switched to the giant pandas, who spend most of their time eating bamboo. A mama panda can only conceive three days a year. But Westerners love these cuddly two-hundred- to three-hundred-pound pandas to such an extent that they pay the Chinese government up to one million dollars a year for each panda loaned to a zoo. So when two pandas were seen on the screen doing what comes so rarely to them, billions of humans forgot all about the bonobos and became transfixed by what they viewed as enthralling but lengthy proceedings. The bonobos finally got a recess.

Still, the human critics were not satisfied. "Get off the mammals" was the gist of their reaction to the pandas.

The QUARTET, fearful that their surefire ratings assignment might be in trouble, shifted gears by showcasing two magnified praying mantises and two barnacles trying for posterity. The female mantis ungraciously starts eating the male mantis until it reaches the sperm. By then, the female's lethal hug has left nothing of the male mantis's corpus but a meal. Next came the barnacles, which, tightly glued to whatever they are attached to, compensate by waggling a penis thirty times the length of the male body so as to reach the opposite sex. Talk about going the evolutionary last mile.

Right after were the rattlebox moths whose trysts were described by the sturgeon. It seems that the male moth donates a doubleheader to the female. He not only transfers his semen to her but also provides some pyrrolizidine alkaloids, which shield her from the predator spider who, if he captures her and starts to eat his captive, then suddenly recoils from the taste and cuts the female rattlebox moth from his web. "Imagine, spiders with taste," mumbled a sports bar patron in Buffalo, New York.

The Cheetah introduced two scorpions for whom mating is a dancing joust with not a little violence and suspense. But that's just being a scorpion. They approached each other warily and grabbed each other's claws to avoid being squeezed fatally by accident. The Cheetah noted that scorpions are not affected by their own poison although exposure to it may operate like Valium. The love dance is not to culminate in a clinch. That is not being scorpion-like. Instead, the dance is for the male to maneuver the female to alight on a sperm deposit that he discharged moments earlier.

In case you think that bed bugs only have you on their mind, the highly poisonous Cane Toad disabused humans quickly. The Toad pointed to a male bed bug getting closer to the female, who has no sex organs. "Evolution comes through again," bleeped the Toad, adding that the male bed bug stabs his consort on her side so that his sperm and her blood mix.

"Aha," remarked an insect scientist drinking beer in an Irish pub. "We call it 'traumatic insemination.'"

The next segment included a comment by marine behavioral ecologist Roland A. Lange of Australia's Monash University, who has discovered a hermaphroditic seal slug with penile organs. One slug delivers the sperm to the female opening on a partner slug while the other is doing the same to its opposite number's female organs. Then, after this simultaneous sperm transfer, each of these bright yellow, red, and white slugs stab each other around the eyes with a needlelike stylet that throbs there for over forty minutes.

The tiny creatures were magnified one hundred times for the aghast human audience, one of whom, a smuggler of rare animals planning a transfer from the Ecuadorean seaport, snorted: "I got to get some more of those slugs for the American voyeur market."

Next up was the Chimpanzee, who said: "You humans make a lot of jokes about the 'birds and the bees'—at least you did in the pre-television, pre-Internet days. Well, watch how the bees do it with unmatched efficiency at the expense of the joyless drones."

Onto the screen came the queen bee on her rare mating flights seeking about one male bee drone out of twenty thousand who were flying after her. In the middle of the act, sometimes the male bee crumbles dead, leaving his genitals inside the queen. The QUARTET's Chimpanzee was not briefed on this lack of self-control, unheard of in primatedom. So he could not explain what was happening and retreated red-faced to the side.

All this had a powerful effect on the human viewing audience. The vicarious masses, when it came to watching primates and other mammals exchanging fluids, were coming to substitute their own activity for curiosity. Then "Eureka!" yelled those who wanted to keep a tight leash on human sexuality. This "change of species," insects eating their mates and so on, was just the turnoff that the religious leaders and Planned Parenthood were seeking.

But, apparently, curiosity is not as renewable as sensuality. As one mating scene came and went, the ratings slowly started to decline. After all, how much can human viewers relate to mating gyrations by rats, octopi, bean weevils, frogs, tortoises, bumblebees, birds—oh how dull are birds presumably doing it. Fruit flies, flatworms, and spoon worms aren't much better. Even with micro-action-focusing narratives by the QUARTET, preceded by anatomical measurements of sex organs, body size differentials between males and females—for example, the female spoon worm is two hundred thousand times bigger that the male—and remarkable insect copulation times—the twig insect takes two months—human attention spans flagged heavily. Human voyeurism seems to require anthropomorphic animal shapes like primates or, at least, barnyard animal-type mountings.

It was time to close things up. The QUARTET, having finished their task and accomplished a great ratings increase overall, was thanked by the TRIAD on the screen. The Sturgeon, the Cheetah, the Cane Toad, and the Chimpanzee all did their curtseying in their special manner and departed the stage.

Taking Stock

The TRIAD announced a seven-day recess. The human audience exploited what they had learned from the matings program in many ways: commercial humor, scientific reflections, psychological probings, provocative novelty sales, gossip at the water coolers, and huge Internet traffic and links to parts of the Matings Program deemed most intense by the senders for their "friends."

During the intermission, the TRIAD reviewed the reactions to the mating games by the animal/insect kingdom. There were three kinds. The ones who knew the purpose of this program was to get the attention of humans for the larger purposes of the one hundred hours responded favorably. The second group were animals/insects who thought this presentation of their sex acts was outrageously exploitive, showing species in their most private moments.

The third type of response focused on what the mating scenes taught them about the idiocy, the foolish fetishism, and the obsession of humans with the sex act, which seemed to be on their minds every day and night in one way or another. It made these responders feel superior, regarding the restriction of mating to short periods of the animals'/insects' lives as a way to order priorities in life more rationally, so as not be pulled down into a hedonistic hell that would doom them.

The TRIAD was impressed and proud of their animal/insect colleagues' observations. But one other, darker strain of human responses they viewed as truly ugly. There were strong suggestions, conveyed by the Human Genius, who had been studying human reactions, that, according to some human audience members, if they really wanted human ratings to go through the roof, they should portray animals fighting, including showing battling insects, with every fight being taken to the death. These human viewers craved seeing tigers fighting tigers, gorillas fighting gorillas, snakes fighting snakes, birds fighting birds, and sharks fighting sharks.

Disturbingly, some animals also thought such fights would be beneficial as a way to attract a human audience. A few animals, showing how much they had learned about humans' love of combative sport, said, "Why not induce a few cross-species fights: such as a lion fighting a grizzly or two coyotes fighting one wolf?"

Somehow, as previously noted, they had heard of the short battle in the wilds between a mongoose and a cobra, caught by human video, which has been visited billions of times on the Internet by humans of all kinds, a completely cross-cultural, cross-ideological fixation. (The mongoose easily won.)

It didn't take the time of an elephant trumpet and owl's hoot or a dolphin's high-pitched sounds to produce a resounding NO from the TRIAD. *No* animal fights of any kind. *No* insect fights of any kind would be staged for the bloodthirsty human viewers. Didn't animals see it would demean everything they been doing in these one hundred hours?

That settled, the TRIAD moved to discuss the final message they each wished to give to humankind at the conclusion of the hundred hours. They agreed that it should be short, ten minutes at most. Humans would not want to be "lectured" for a long time by what many, though less than before the TALKOUT, still believed to be inferior, more ignorant, genetically controlled species. But the TRIAD did believe that huge numbers of humans, tutored and surprised by the TALKOUT, were maintaining a fascinated expectancy for the final words of the by-now globally heralded Celebrity Three.

The TRIAD prepared their valedictory in order to present the most thoughtful message and one that would elicit human support for continuing the TALKOUT in more advanced, purposeful ways. The Human Genius, consulted by the TRIAD, agreed heartily with their approach.

Whetting Appetites

After their feverish preparations were finished, the TRIAD knew the time has come to deliver the SUM-UP, whose content had to link to the OPEN-UP for further interactions and presentations. The TRIAD intended their thoughts to have been preceded by reflections, so, as noted, there had been a week recess for such preparation. The first order of business was alerting humans that this finale was worth their attention, their curiosity, their pleasure. Eye-catching signals were given by each member of the TRIAD.

First the Elephant invited eleven other elephants to join together with her so a dozen pachyderm trumpeters could communicate a prime salute to humans, who had never before heard such a fugue in twelve parts.

The Owl and her flock of thirty owls swept up into the sky and made spectacular maneuvers that impressed the pilots of the Blue Angels. The Owl and her team ended with a demonstration of plummeting as if to catch a mouse in a dense thicket. The plummet was accomplished with such synchronization and breathless speed that humans blurted out that no plane could have imitated such actions and survived.

Not to be outdone, the Dolphin convened one hundred dolphins to put on an amazing flurry of vertical dances, each with their many signature whistles, with the mammals rising from the ocean depths, jumping high into the air above the water, and coming back down, again and again in a series of round trips that exhausted human viewers. Because the TRIAD was such a celebrity trio already, humans rejoiced with them as they would with well-known athletes and movie stars.

Their physical announcements completed, the level of excitement among humans elevated, the TRIAD took a day off to rest and ready themselves for their finale.

The Valedictory

As the time came for the last act, the TRIAD's entrance onto the stage was deliberate but not stiff, upbeat but not officious.

The Elephant began: "The TRIAD wishes to close this remarkable hundred hours with *gratitude*, *optimism*, and *humility*.

"*Gratitude* to the sensational inventor who made it possible for the animal/insect kingdom to communicate with each other, to absorb at a rapid pace the knowledge from the human kingdom, and to receive feedback from humans during and after the programming that was at times critical, but mostly very gratifying and respectful.

"Our *optimism* stems from the polling of humans during the

programming, which showed a rising recognition on their part of the intelligence of the animal/insect worlds. There was an increase in human sensitivity to animals' problems that went with such awareness of our cognition and emotions.

"Our *humility* was given a depth from the mutual realization of what our two worlds, human and animal, have to teach and offer one another as we learn more. While there are surely drawbacks to your study of us, such as cloning, zootic applications, and conflicts within your own ranks as you try to make new decisions for the preservation of other species, the prospects, on the whole, appear bright."

The Elephant stepped back and the Owl then took center stage. "Although you humans have rightly ascribed wisdom to my breed, it is a trait tinged with a darker view of life as befits my nocturnal habits. I must be candid in these remaining moments.

"Humans, you need to refine your moral compass. The intricacies of your contradictions render this a difficult task. Toward your domesticates, you have a deep love, but at the same time a homicidal relationship, especially with your cats and dogs. On the one hand you are greatly expanding the number of dogs and cats you have as pets and as 'family members.' On the other hand, dogs and cats who find themselves without proxies are euthanized or beaten mercilessly, even by your animal humane societies or by sadistic elements among you. We are speaking of tens of millions of canines and felines in each sphere. We, in the animal kingdom, cannot understand this morality. It is not functional. For the activities in your 'family' pet sphere lead to what you call 'overpopulation' in the brutish sphere.

"In addition, your fabled 'instinct for survival' is marred by the many things done daily in your own culture that damage or eradicate piece by piece the conditions for your survival. For an example, take the relentless destruction of our habitat. You are suffering from soil erosion, loss of forest, expansion of desert areas, loss of biodiversity of species replaced by monocultures, the spread of what you contemptuously call 'invasive species,' and the 'big one': climate change! Some of the anomalies flow from your own intelligence backfiring, others flow from ignorance, while the rest come from the triumph of greed over virtue and prudence. I, the Owl, am sure that you know all this, but sometimes it helps for you to know that those whom you view as 'lower creatures' know it as well."

The Owl stepped aside and our friend the Dolphin, encased in sea water, now gave his thoughts: "I, the Dolphin, view humans from my oceanic framework, which these days, despite its vastness, is moving toward perilous decline in its circulatory system, especially hard hit by de-oxygenation and rising acidity. The prosperity of multiplying jellyfish and algae is simply more evidence of the poor health of the oceans.

"I must admit that one principal impression I came away with from the one hundred hours is how the trivial pursuits of some humans produce devastating consequences for some important species, including capstone ones. Hunting the dwindling species of whales for very modest amounts of steak! Overfishing the vast school of cod, nearly below the level of recovery, off the eastern Canadian and U.S. coast, letting shortsighted harvesting override the accurate warnings of marine scientists and wise fishermen! Throwing overboard vast amounts of fish simply because they are not known menu offerings!

"Since your studies keep telling you how smart and intelligent we dolphins are, may I say that you are outsmarting yourself in terrible ways, adversely affecting humans and brutally dwindling aquatic life, including hurting the smallest denizens, who are affected by planetary warming and thinning of the ozone layer.

"I've been thinking hard as I can, consulting with wiser dolphins, porpoises, and even whales, to come up with ways to sound the alarms from our side. Alas, nothing was forthcoming of any use. One thought that hit me hard came from a beautiful blue whale friend, who, swimming near Baja California and shaken by Naval sonar blasts, said: 'Dolphie, let's face it. Our only messages to humans are our corpses, which appear at the times of mass beaching and viral die-outs'.

"Some humans in power are getting the message. Large marine sanctuaries are being created by nations with the recognition of international law. It is small wonder that the animals of the sea are starting to migrate to them for safety and raising their families in these homelands of their security. These areas are like your pristinely safeguarded wilderness areas on land, which wild land mammals should be learning more about."

The preliminary remarks and courtesies completed, the Elephant moved to raise a delicate matter indeed. "I, the Elephant, knowing how we sometimes misbehave as a herd and run roughshod through cultivated fields or through areas of residence of the tribes-people in Africa, have become astounded at how much more emotional humans are than we of the animal/insect kingdom are. By emotional I mean how you often lose control of yourselves and act against your own overall self-interest. To put it plainly, how you often go berserk, both individually and collectively.

"Elephants are known for their memories. We remember what King Leopold of Belgium did to the Congo, and the millions of humans of a different color whom his soldiers slaughtered. Your books and movies have chronicled all kinds of similar killing rampages throughout the centuries all over the world. Your modern weapons, driven by your emotions, can destroy the planet, even by accident. Maybe the animal/insect world can help you to distinguish between *impulsive* behavior and emotional omnicide.

"You humans have larger-size brains and your emotions presumably are under the control of your brains or more rational selves. And yet, too often, you lose control of yourselves completely. Just look at your deadly personal addictions, your collective wars and rampant destruction of nature's purity of water, air, and soil, shockingly soiling your own nest, so to speak.

You're going out of your way to take out the natural nutrition of your food and replace it with the chemicals, sugars, and salt favored by your marketers. You've even replaced much of mother's breast milk. No animal is that stupid.

"As an elephant, presiding over a large family, I know I'm not leading with a strong trunk. My forebears, the mastodons, couldn't adapt, and while we know how to adapt, we're being poached toward extinction if loss of habitat doesn't get us first. A special plea: Create artificial ivory so precise that the traders can't tell the difference (as you've been doing with diamonds) and flood the market to take the profit out of poaching. PLEASE!"

The Owl, noticing how emotional the Elephant was becoming, albeit for the most crucial cause, hooted that it was her turn to discuss another important subject: the folly of going to the other extreme and giving animals, such as pets and primates, legal *personhood*. Reflecting previous deliberations among the TRIAD and numerous other representatives of the animal/insect world, the Owl strongly urged against the personhood movement among humans.

"We," said the Owl, "have many talents that you are discovering, including the use of tools by our crows, monkeys, alligators, and others. But neither the wild animals nor the domesticates have the wherewithal to assume the responsibilities of personhood. No way! There are limits to anthropomorphism. Your veterinarians are right to oppose personhood. Their reason, among many, is that they cannot assume the liabilities of animal 'persons' who can sue for malpractice, pain and suffering, and other assumed violated obligations, such as mental distress. Besides, we grasp that some of us have to be sacrificed for medical research, hopefully restricted toward finding ways to prevent or overcome diseases for *both* human and animal species. Look at the time during the one hundred hours devoted to making the point that the more you learn about us, the better it is for both of us.

"Your lives are far too complex for us to share in your personhood. Consider, for instance, your sexual practices and your domestic relations. They are inscrutable to most of us. In the same family, you sexually love each other, then beat, rape, and sometimes kill each other. Monogamy and adultery share spouses' time. Some cultures have arranged marriages. You are known to abandon your children or frequently divorce and fight over custody. You confuse sex with love. You profitably commercialize sexual taboos, antics, waywardness, and exhibitionism. You have foster parents for foster children. Your children often have no homes and roam the streets. You have plenty of food in your societies; still tens of millions of children are famished and undernourished and millions die of starvation or human-polluted water.

"But considering your reactions to the program on mating habits, sex is on your minds constantly. It's in the advertised appeals to your shopping and all through your entertainment business. You seem ready to go at it at all times. There is no such time as 'rutting season,' because procreation is only a tiny part of why you have sex with one another. Whole industries crop up to address whether you've got the stuff to 'Be a man' or 'Be a woman,' right down to enhancing drugs, prosthetics, and the creation of seductive moods, apparel, cosmetics, plastic surgery, and other allurements.

"Why, in the world of the animal/insect kingdom, would we want to possess equal personhood with you? We are much more focused on functional behavior because our cravings are not infinite. We know when to feed and when to stop eating. We know when we have to mate and when we have other pressing things to do. You'll find us ever more predictable as you find out more details about our lives. We like regularity, even being regular in the way we respond to the unpredictable, such as the way our flying flocks of birds respond, during thousands of miles of migration, to powerful storms that would upend your largest aircrafts.

If you respect the wild animals, they will take care of themselves. The domesticates whom you eat—chickens, turkeys, cattle, pigs, sheep, lambs, goats, and so forth—you will keep as your slaves for slaughter. As for your pets, I've had my say. Keep them as what you own or, as some of you say, as your guardians, for another status will jeopardize them."

Top Eleven Queries

The Elephant and the Owl then asked the Dolphin to answer the most recurrent questions that humans had sent. "In the interest of time," said the Dolphin, "I will just handle the top eleven."

Why haven't you given us your personal names?

REPLY: "Because this TALKOUT is not about us. Personal names lead to personal questions, which distract."

How tiring has this program been for you and what do your species think about what you have done?

REPLY: "They're OK about it. You're right. It has been the most tiring thing we've ever done, but not the scariest. You humans have scared us all many times. The weariest parts were the jostling demands for airtime, the recriminations if various species and members within species did not get their way. You'll recall we were facing a global revolt by the insects, which was quelled by the Human Genius suggesting the fabulous parade."

Who is this Human Genius who made the breakthrough TALKOUT *possible by the software delivery system that he or she invented?*

REPLY: "You know as much about his or her identity as we do. What a hero!"

Did all the huge excitement, uproars, awareness, and discoveries affect the migration patterns of the animal/insect populations?

REPLY: "Yes, of course. What you couldn't see during the one hundred hours was all the information flowing to our kingdom about safer places to live, what to be on guard against, and where we could get more relief from the dangers around us. For example, chickens started fleeing their coops to go to California, where there is a new law requiring more humane treatment, as they are being raised for the ultimate sacrifice. Wilderness areas, marine sanctuaries, and cleaner estuaries are becoming destinations."

Backstage, so to speak, was there a lot of shoving, pushing, fighting, and jockeying for better showcasing?

REPLY: "There was some of that, especially with the animals that went rogue. But surprisingly little compared to what we understand would have happened among your species. Remember, the one hundred hours did not change our limited cravings, compared to Homo sapiens' endless desires."

You informed yourselves across species for the first time. Were you all surprised by your fantastic physical feats, your intelligence levels, your amazing sense of priorities, putting survival and procreation over everything else?

REPLY: "Without doubt. That was the best thing that came out of the new software of multiple communications, including and beyond the one hundred hours. For that awareness was the basis for trying to improve our relationships with you, humans. And more material is pouring in every hour."

Do you think this **TALKOUT** *will at all reduce the enormous violence between and among all species, including the violence by homo sapiens against the rest of you, whether deliberate killing for food or inadvertently by damage to the environment and the rhythms of nature that sustain you all?*

REPLY: "That's a hard question because it has many subsets.

In the oceans, probably there will be less violence. The sharks made a good case for themselves. On land, over the long run, probably, yes, for knowledge of the cruelty to domesticates being raised for food will lead to more vegetarianism. Also, there are fewer wild animals to hunt and kill. You humans also are finding ways to reduce the number of pets euthanized. Remember, some of these anti-violence or humane groups in your society will replay parts of the one hundred hours again and again, in and outside your schools. But expanding human populations place greater stress on these expected improvements."

When your ratings were sagging, why didn't you portray fights between animals, not staging them, but catching them in the wilds per cinema verité? You know we humans like those kind of things.

REPLY: "You see, we do not have this difference between means and ends as you do. Maybe that is because we're not as smart. To use sadism as a *means* to get a larger audience for our program's purposes would not even occur to us independently. When that suggestion was relayed to the TRIAD by the Human Genius, and then by some animals who were picking up this idea from humans, we felt nauseous. No, never."

Why didn't you show the intercourse up close and what were the reactions of nearby similar animals or insects who were not copulating? Also why was there never resistance by the females?

REPLY: "Because it is all about the business of procreation and both sexes understand that, to use a controversial term, *instinctively* during the proper times of year. Except for creatures like the bonobos who are something, aren't they? More like you, may I suggest?

"By the way, voyeurs sent millions of questions about our mating presentation, which was cinema verité, except when humans demanded that the TRIAD ourselves do it. Such demands on us personally were so overwhelming that we complied just to get on with the program."

What's the encore? You can't let it stop here. If you had your druthers and the guidance of the Human Genius, how would you complete what rumors say is going to be a trilogy?

REPLY: "The second one hundred hours (if we created them) would take care of many requests both from animals who were left out and felt they should have had time on the screen, and from humans who requested to know more about certain aspects of our lives. The third leg of the trilogy, if it were done, is to be determined once we and you humans evaluate the effects and opportunities arising out of the second leg. We learn as we go."

Tell us about extreme aberrations within the animal/insect world. What we would call dramatically irrational, violent, sadistic behavior or reactive masochism, for example?

REPLY: "We know that when injuries or illnesses come to the animal/insect world, the victims go, as you are wont to say, berserk. When a tiger is injured and can no longer hunt the customary prey, he or she becomes a man-eater, as in India, for instance. What we were not prepared for were other unusual, disruptive, sad, morose types of behavior and activities that are appearing in animals, spawned by this whole process of interaction with the human world. You call it culture shock when native people are intruded upon by colonizers or invaders from another culture. Animals are suffering the same kind of shock. Perhaps that's why the one hundred hours sometimes appeared chaotic.

"But," swelled the Dolphin, "how wonderfully enlightening, exciting, AND filled with potential for the good of all of us living, organic creatures inhabiting a tiny planet in a vast, vast inorganic universe was that treasured time of communicating to humans."

Last Thoughts

The TRIAD moved closer together with the Dolphin's closing words. They wished to end with a joint and memorable transmission to their vast human audience. The Elephant, the Owl, and the Dolphin each vocalized one sentence in their turn to signify the unity of their message:

"The twenty-first century may be the decisive century of all time when it comes to the relations between the animal and human kingdoms. That was not our choice. It was your science and technology and the ways you are choosing to use them. This century can be one of coexistence or one of human displacement of the capstones of the natural world. Are you *sapiens* sapient enough to infuse an ethical framework, bolstered by your so-called rule of law, to allow us to peacefully coexist given the driven avarice of some of you and the risky tools of biotechnology, synthetic biology, nanotechnology, and your weapons, whether deliberate or inadvertent, of mass destruction?

"Your Human Genius has enabled us in the animal/insect world to know that there is controversy over the development and use of these technologies as they relentlessly become deployed by your forces of power and profit, which are dictated by the few who rule the rest of you humans. As one of your philosophers has said, yours 'is a race between reason and ruin, between virtue and victimization, between prudence and plutocracy, between civic values and commercial values.' She left little doubt as to how this race is turning out year after year with the abyss coming nearer and nearer.

"The twenty-first century is the fourth stage of humans in their relationships with the animal/insect kingdom. Stage One was millions of years ago when your ancestors were herbivores. Then, Stage Two, you added flesh to your diets, becoming hunters and carnivores. Then some thirteen thousand years ago, Stage Three, you took up agriculture, which included domesticating animals for work and eating. Protecting them and moving into habitats of the free animals, you plunged into a seriously adversarial position, beginning the process of diminishing their numbers and extinguishing some of these animals forever.

"Now the advanced Third Stage is not merging or mutating into the Fourth Stage. We would like to say that the paths ahead are our mutual choices but that, as you well know, is not the case. For you humans are truly the Kings of Beasts, the monarchs whose subjects can either help tame and civilize you or allow you to be the monarchs for the Death Planet, imploding on itself and rejecting the many benign uses of our silent sun, which, though inorganic, is responsible for all the life-giving systems so widely spurned by the Kings of Beasts.

"Quo vadis, oh humans, quo vadis?!"

Fade Out

With those haunting words, the TRIAD faded off the screen, which began to reflect a collage that looked like the universe, with its billions of galaxies, billions of stars, and millions of planets in dynamic, swirling motion. Out of this immensity and panorama of infinity and mystery, the view began to circle closer to our galaxy, the Milky Way, then to our solar system with its seven planets, then to the green planet of Earth.

The picture of Earth remained on the tiny screen for five minutes, without sound or language. Then everything went blank. Almost magically, billions of humans also went about five minutes without sound or language. Silently speechless. Perhaps contemplating, perhaps astonished, perhaps beginning to broaden their frame of reference, mused the Human Genius with a barely discernible expression of satisfied reverie motionless in time, dreaming of a coming vitalized natural world.

Notes

Page 15, Marc Bekoff, "The Emotional Lives of Animals," *Yes! Magazine*, March 2, 2011, http://www.yesmagazine.org/issues/can-animals-save-us/we-second-that-emotion.

Page 16, Jeremy Bentham, *An Introduction to the Principles of Morals and Legislation* (Oxford: Clarendon Press. 1907), http://www.econlib.org/library/Bentham/bnthPML18.html.

Page 20, Robert M. Sapolsky, "A Natural History of Peace," *New York Times*, January 2, 2006, http://www.nytimes.com/cfr/international/20060101faessay_v85n1_sapolsky.html?pagewanted=print&_r=0.

Page 21, "Not to use his position on the TRIAD for his own advantage . . ." See *New York Times*, March 7, 2013. This article is also referenced in the discussion of endangered species later in the text.

Page 22, Meeri Kim, "Dolphins Can Recognize Calls From Old Tank Mates From 20 Years Ago, Study Finds," *Washington Post*, August 6, 2013, https://www.washingtonpost.com/national/health-science/dolphins-can-recognize-calls-from-old-tank-mates-from-over-20-years-ago/2013/08/06/1b1d5ab8-feb3-11e2-bd97-676ec24f1f3f_story.html.

Page 25, Virginia Morell, "Why Do Parrots Talk? Venezuelan Site Offers Clues," *Science* 333, no. 6041, July 22, 2011, http://science.sciencemag.org/content/333/6041/news-summaries.

Page 26, Jim Robbins, "Hunting Habits of Wolves Change Ecological Balance in Yellowstone," *New York Times*, October 18, 2005, http://www.nytimes.com/2005/10/18/science/earth/hunting-habits-of-wolves-change-ecological-balance-in.html?_r=0.

Page 30, Jim Robbins, "Reversing Course on Beavers," *New York Times*, October 27, 2014, http://www.nytimes.com/2014/10/28/science/reversing-course-on-beavers.html.

Page 31, Chris Cottrell, "German Legislators Vote to Outlaw Bestiality," *New York Times*, February 1, 2013, http://www.nytimes.com/2013/02/02/world/europe/german-legislators-vote-to-outlaw-bestiality.html.

Page 32, "There are signs among you humans toward normalizing . . ." See *New York Times*, August 3, 2013.

Page 32, Tim Kreider, "A Man and His Cat," *New York Times*, August 1, 2014, http://opinionator.blogs.nytimes.com/2014/08/01/a-man-and-his-cat/.

Page 33, Cottrell, "German Legislators Vote."

Page 34, Melissa Hoppert, "Preakness Champion, and Mother, Toughs It Out," *New York Times*, May 18, 2013, http://www.nytimes.com/2013/05/18/sports/rachel-alexandra-2009-preakness-winner-recovers-from-scare.html.

Page 35, Nell Alk, "Dogs and Cats Take Center Stage in Times Square," *Wall Street Journal*, July 14, 2013, http://www.wsj.com/articles/SB10001424127887324348504578606114160899852.

Page 36, "One of your Nature Conservancy magazines described us as . . ." See *Nature Conservancy Magazine*, August 2010.

Page 39, Lauren Wilcox, "Modern Zoos Could Be Creating a New Kind of Animal: Wild by Nature, Shaped by Captivity," *Wall Street Journal*, July 26, 2012, https://www.washingtonpost.com/lifestyle/magazine/modern-zoos-could-be-creating-a-new-kind-of-animal-wild-by-nature-shaped-by-captivity/2012/07/25/gJQAdq4IBX_story.html.

Page 40, Michael Cieply, "SeaWorld's Unusual Retort to a Critical Documentary," *New York Times*, July 18, 2013, http://www.nytimes.com/2013/07/19/business/media/seaworlds-unusual-retort-to-a-critical-documentary.html.

Pages 47–48, Theo Tait, "Don't Wear Yum-yum Yellow," *London Review of Books* 34, no. 15, August 2012, http://www.lrb.co.uk/v34/n15/theo-tait/dont-wear-yum-yum-yellow.

Pages 52–53, Jacqueline Sheehan, "Though Now Apart, We Faced a Common Enemy," *New York Times*, March 7, 2013, http://www.nytimes.com/2013/03/10/fashion/though-now-apart-we-faced-a-common-enemy-modern-love.html.

Page 57, Jo Tuckman, "Cat Stands for Election in Mexican City," *Guardian*, June 19, 2013, https://www.theguardian.com/world/2013/jun/19/cat-stands-election-mexican-city.

Pages 58–59, Dana Jennings, "Twisting and Turning," *New York Times*, May 13, 2013, http://www.nytimes.com/2013/05/14/science/in-serpentine-beautiful-snakes-twisting-and-turning.html.

Page 64, Brian Palmer, "Pests That Bug Us Have Their Own Ecological Importance," *Guardian*, May 21, 2013, https://www.theguardian.com/environment/2013/may/21/insects-cockroach-bed-bugs-environment.

Page 65, "'Think, think, think,' cried the roaches . . ." More about cockroaches can be found in *Wall Street Journal*, September 13, 2013.

Page 71, J. B. MacKinnon, "Appetite of Abundance: On the Benefits of Being Eaten," *Orion*, July 2013.

Page 73, Denise Grady, "Researchers Suspect That Camels Are Linked to a Middle East Virus," *New York Times*, August 8, 2013, http://www.nytimes.com/2013/08/09/health/researchers-suspect-camels-are-linked-to-middle-east-virus.html.

Page 75, Jon Mooallem, "A Child's Wild Kingdom," *New York Times*, May 4, 2013, http://www.nytimes.com/2013/05/05/opinion/sunday/a-childs-wild-kingdom.html?mtrref=www.google.com&gwh=-FEA25FA43BC209B54AB676B26F2237DD&gwt=pay&assetType=opinion.

Page 78, Ronald A. Sherman, "What Are Leeches and Maggots Doing in Modern Hospitals?," BottomLineInc, July 23, 2009, http://bottomlineinc.com/what-are-leeches-and-maggots-doing-in-modern-hospitals/.

Page 79, *Wall Street Journal*, July 2, 2013.

Page 79, David A. Fahrenthold and Joshua Partlow, "Baby Snakehead Is No Bundle of Joy," *Washington Post*, October 5, 2004, http://www.washingtonpost.com/wp-co/hotcontent/index.html?section=metro/specials/snakeheads.

Page 79, Patterson Clark, "The Stubborn Life of a Snakehead," *Washington Post*, April 30, 2013, http://www.washingtonpost.com/wp-srv/special/metro/urban-jungle/pages/130430.html.

Pages 80–81, "First is the looks of the fish. Second is the popularity . . ." See *New York Times*, August 11, 2013.

Page 83, Caroline Porter, "Native Species Step Up to Fight Ash Parasite," *Wall Street Journal*, August 19, 2013, http://www.wsj.com/articles/SB10001424127887323446404579011172323705040.

Page 84, Mooallem, "A Child's Wild Kingdom."

Page 85, Friedrich Nietzsche, *The Gay Science* (New York: Cambridge University Press, 2001), 145.

Page 87, Sarah Maslin Nir, "An Invasion of 17-Year-Olds, Loud, Lusty and Six-Legged," *New York Times*, June 7, 2013, http://www.nytimes.com/2013/06/08/nyregion/an-invasion-of-17-year-olds-loud-lusty-and-six-legged.html.

Page 88, Andrew Adam Newman, "Freshpet Dog Food Promotes Products Sourced in the U.S.," *New York Times*, June 13, 2013, http://www.nytimes.com/2013/06/14/business/media/freshpet-dog-food-promotes-products-sourced-in-the-us.html?_r=0.

Page 91, "The more coordinated is their prancing and their vocalizing . . ." See *New York Times*, June 11, 2013.

Page 92, The Reliable Source, "Quoted: Michelle Obama on Dog Fitness," *Washington Post*, March 4, 2013, https://www.washingtonpost.com/blogs/reliable-source/post/quoted-michelle-obama-on-dog-fitness/2013/03/04/c115d62a-84fb-11e2-9d71-f0feafdd1394_blog.html.

Page 92, "'People will forget,' soothed her lady-in-waiting, 'don't worry.'" See this story in the *New York Times*, May 12, 2013.

Page 93, John Schwartz, "Donal O'Brien, Audubon Leader, Dies at 79," *New York Times*, September 10, 2013, http://www.nytimes.com/2013/09/11/nyregion/donal-obrien-audubon-leader-dies-at-79.html.

Page 94, "A Showy Beetle That Befriends Ants," *New York Times*, December 9, 2013, http://www.nytimes.com/2013/12/10/science/a-showy-beetle-that-befriended-ants.html?rref=collection%2Ftimestopic%2FFrench%20Guiana&action=click&contentCollection=world®ion=stream&module=stream_unit&version=latest&contentPlacement=2&pgtype=collection.

Page 95, "As it started to lift up from its pedestal into wide blue sky, the great condor . . ." See *New York Times*, May 2013.

Page 96, "Dual Forces in an Andean Rite," *New York Times*, August 10, 2013, http://www.nytimes.com/slideshow/2013/08/10/world/americas/20130810PERU.html.

Page 99, "The Largest Falcon Hospital in the World," *New York Times*, April 26, 2013, http://www.nytimes.com/interactive/2013/04/28/magazine/look-falcon.html?_r=0.

Page 99, "During the time-out, humans returned to their own daily fare of 'animal stories' . . ." See *New York Times*, April 28, 2013.

Page 99, Carl Zimmer, "A Virtual Pack, to Study Canine Minds," *New York Times*, April 22, 2013, http://www.nytimes.com/2013/04/23/science/enlisting-a-virtual-pack-to-study-dog-minds.html.

Page 99, Nathan Koppel, "Gambling Allegations Have Sport All Aflutter," *Wall Street Journal*, April 24, 2013, http://www.wsj.com/articles/SB10001424127887324010704578415230547113310.

Page 101, *New York Times*, May 1, 2013.

Page 101, "The Horsemen of Nairobi," *Washington Post*, April 30, 2013.

Page 101, Anne Raver, "Farm Equipment That Runs on Oats," *New York Times*, May 15, 2013, http://www.nytimes.com/2013/05/16/garden/farm-equipment-that-runs-on-oats.html.

Page 103, "She urges 'using the proper mulch and timing more of the crops . . .'" See *Wall Street Journal*, May 4, 2013.

Page 105, "It means you can genetically manipulate us . . ." See *Carnegie Science*, summer 2013.

Page 108, "Whereupon the lemming leaped off the stage to rejoin its fellow lemmings . . ." See *Washington Post*, 2013.

Page 109, Rodrique Ngowi, "Gerbils Strut Their Stuff at New England Pageant," Associated Press, May 4, 2013.

Page 109, *Washington Post*, June 2, 2013.

Page 110, *New York Times*, June 19, 2013.

Page 110, Karen Hoppert, "Oh, Rats. There's One Aspect of Baltimore She Can't Get Used To," *Washington Post*, June 19, 2013, https://www.washingtonpost.com/lifestyle/magazine/oh-rats-theres-one-aspect-of-baltimore-she-cant-get-used-to/2013/06/19/96cd18ca-c96f-11e2-9245-773c0123c027_story.html.

Page 112, Martin Walters, *The Illustrated World Encyclopedia of Insects* (Lorenz Books, 2011).

Page 114, Walters, *Illustrated World Encyclopedia.*

Page 122, Mayumi Negishi, "Can Spider Web Be Replicated? A Japanese Startup Thinks So," *Wall Street Journal*, July 8, 2013, http://www.wsj.com/articles/SB10001424127887324399404578583562603579062.

Page 124, Walters, *Illustrated World Encyclopedia.*

Page 129, *New York Times*, August 2, 2013.

Page 130, Douglas Quenqua, "For Some Worms, It's Heads or Tails," *New York Times*, July 29, 2013, http://www.nytimes.com/2013/07/30/science/for-some-worms-its-heads-or-tails.html.

Page 130, https://www.congress.gov/bill/113th-congress/senate-resolution/70/text.

Page 130, "We moths cannot stand the odor of red wood . . ." See *Washington Post*, July 16, 2013.

Page 131, Susan Milius, "Real Pack Rats Aren't Actually That Disorganized, Researchers Say," *Washington Post*, February 24, 2014, https://www.washingtonpost.com/national/health-science/real-pack-rats-arent-actually-that-disorganized-researchers-say/2014/02/24/5b3784f2-9da5-11e3-9ba6-800d1192d08b_story.html.

Page 136, *Wall Street Journal*, July 31, 2013.

Page 137, *Wall Street Journal*, August 12, 2013.

Page 137, *Wall Street Journal*, July 22, 2013.

Page 138, *Wall Street Journal*, August 19, 2013.

Page 138, "We can be as small as a grain of sand or as large as a stove." See *Wall Street Journal*, July 2, 2013.

Page 139, *Washington Post*, July 23, 2013.

Page 140, "More goats are being rented around the country to reduce the vegetation. They are cheaper . . ." See *Washington Post*, August 7, 2013.

Page 140, "Not to be outdone, a beetle came forward . . ." See *New York Times*, August 4, 2013.

Page 141, "By the way, we mice wonder why you despise us and our rats when we are your most . . ." See *New York Times*, August 2, 2013.

Page 145, *Mother Jones*, September 2013.

Page 147, Sandy Keenan, "Life on the Farm: E-I-E-I . . . Oh?," *New York Times*, July 31, 2013, http://www.nytimes.com/2013/08/01/garden/life-on-the-farm-e-i-e-i-oh.html.

Page 147, "The last of the Pinta Island subspecies, Lonesome George earned his nickname after sailors . . ." See *New York Times*, July 2, 2013.

Page 148, Jackson Landers, "Scientists Look to Revive the Long-Extinct Passenger Pigeon," *Washington Post*, July 8, 2013, https://www.washingtonpost.com/national/health-science/scientists-look-to-revive-the-long-extinct-passenger-pigeon/2013/07/08/3d1323d4-b9a1-11e2-aa9e-a02b765ff0ea_story.html.

Page 151, "Moving cattle out of the area often preserves the native grass . . ." See *Washington Post*, September 22, 2013.

Page 152, http://www.dtic.mil/dtic/tr/fulltext/u2/837100.pdf.

Page 153, *New York Times*, September 25, 2013.

Page 154, Stacey Stowe, "Roll Over? Fat Chance," *New York Times*, September 25, 2013, http://www.nytimes.com/2013/09/26/garden/roll-over-fat-chance.html.

Page 155, Stephanie Rosenbloom, "Now Checking In: Pampered Pets," *New York Times*, September 18, 2013, http://www.nytimes.com/2013/09/22/travel/now-checking-in-pampered-pets.html.

Page 156, "There is a comedy dog act called 'Mutts Gone Nuts,' where dogs . . ." See *Washington Post*, October 2, 2013.

Page 160, *New York Times*, October 17, 2013.

Page 161, *New York Times*, October 17, 2013.

Page 162, Jon Mooallem, "Squirrel Power!," *New York Times*, August 31, 2013, http://www.nytimes.com/2013/09/01/opinion/sunday/squirrel-power.html?_r=0.

Page 163, "Listen to your scientists, who are improving avian radar . . ." See *New York Times*, October 18, 2013.

Page 165, "No end to ideas when you start working on your animal imagination." See *Wall Street Journal,* October 18, 2013.

Pages 168–170, Nicholas Kristof, "Are Chicks Brighter Than Babies?," *New York Times*, October 19, 2013, http://www.nytimes.com/2013/10/20/opinion/sunday/are-chicks-brighter-than-babies.html.

Page 169–170, "'Nothing,' said one chicken-raiser at a giant poultry farm, 'they're too dumb to be thinking anything, Bubba.'" For more see the *Washington Post*, October 31, 2013; and Carolyn L. Smith, Sarah L. Zielinski, "The Startling Intelligence of the Common Chicken," *Scientific American*, February 1, 2014, https:www.scientificamerican.com/article/the-startling-intelligence-of-the-common-chicken/.

Page 170, Christine Dell'Amore, "Touring the Chesapeake Bay With Its Legendary Watermen," *Washington Post*, October 12, 2013, https://www.washingtonpost.com/lifestyle/travel/touring-the-chesapeake-bay-with-its-legendary-watermen/2013/10/10/b47bb55a-305f-11e3-bbed-a8a60c601153_story.html.

Page 171, "Watch how our riders bathe and groom us, hug us, and are completely absorbed by us." See *Washington Post*, October 12, 2013.

Page 173–174, David Colker, "Robert C. Stebbins, Expert on Reptiles and Amphibians, Dies at 98," *Washington Post*, October 11, 2013, https://

www.washingtonpost.com/national/energy-environment/robert-c-stebbins-expert-on-reptiles-and-amphibians-dies-at-98/2013/10/11/c629224c-328f-11e3-8627-c5d7de0a046b_story.html.

Page 175, Lucy Spelman, *National Geographic Animal Encyclopedia* (Washington, D.C.: National Geographic, 2012), 146–168.

Page 178, "Up goes your risk of high blood pressure . . ." See *Washington Post*, October 14, 2013.

Page 180, "More attention started being paid to the causes . . ." See *Washington Post*, October 15, 2013.

Page 192, "Then, after this simultaneous sperm transfer . . ." See *Washington Post*, November 26, 2013.

ABOUT THE AUTHOR

Born in Connecticut in 1934, Ralph Nader has spent his lifetime challenging corporations and government agencies to be more accountable to the public. His 1965 book *Unsafe at Any Speed* permanently altered the course of a reckless U.S. automobile industry and made Nader a household name. Nader helped pass the Freedom of Information Act of 1974, the Safe Drinking Water Act, the Pure Food Act, the Clean Water Act, and laws that created federal regulatory agencies such as the Occupational Safety and Health Administration (OSHA), the Environmental Protection Agency (EPA), the Consumer Product Safety Commission (CPSC), and the National Highway Traffic Safety Administration (NHTSA). Over the years he has founded numerous public interest groups including Public Citizen, the Center for Auto Safety, the Clean Water Action Project, the Pension Rights Center, the American Museum of Tort Law, the Critical Mass Energy Project, the Center for the Study of Responsive Law, and the student Public Interest Research Groups (PIRGs). His 2000 presidential campaign on the Green Party ticket served to broaden the scope of debate on the nation's priorities. Named by the *Atlantic* as one of the hundred most influential figures in American history, Nader continues to be a relentless advocate for grassroots activism and democratic change.

ABOUT SEVEN STORIES PRESS

Seven Stories Press is an independent book publisher based in New York City. We publish works of the imagination by such writers as Nelson Algren, Russell Banks, Octavia E. Butler, Ani DiFranco, Assia Djebar, Ariel Dorfman, Coco Fusco, Barry Gifford, Martha Long, Luis Negrón, Hwang Sok-yong, Lee Stringer, and Kurt Vonnegut, to name a few, together with political titles by voices of conscience, including Subhankar Banerjee, the Boston Women's Health Collective, Noam Chomsky, Angela Y. Davis, Human Rights Watch, Derrick Jensen, Ralph Nader, Loretta Napoleoni, Gary Null, Greg Palast, Project Censored, Barbara Seaman, Alice Walker, Gary Webb, and Howard Zinn, among many others. Seven Stories Press believes publishers have a special responsibility to defend free speech and human rights, and to celebrate the gifts of the human imagination, wherever we can. In 2012 we launched Triangle Square books for young readers with strong social justice and narrative components, telling personal stories of courage and commitment. For additional information, visit www.sevenstories.com.